D0722322

The Lone Traveller

Susan Kelly read French and English at London University. She then worked as a freelance computer consultant before becoming a full-time writer. She lives in West London with her solicitor husband and cat.

a&b

Susan Kelly

The Lone Traveller

First published in 2000 by
Allison & Busby Limited
114 New Cavendish Street
London W1M 7FD
http://www.allisonandbusby.ltd.uk

Reprinted 2000

A catalogue record for this book is available
from the British Library

ISBN 0 7490 0462 2

Printed and bound in Great Britain by Biddles Ltd,
www.biddles.co.uk

Down to Gehenna or up to the Throne,
He travels the fastest who travels alone.

'The Winners', Rudyard Kipling

For Francis Clarke
Antony and Cleopatra
2.ii.133

Author's Note

I've tried to stick to the topography of Hungerford, Kintbury and Newbury, but I have invented the stone circle on Hungerford Common, known as the Hungerford Horseshoe, and the summer fair held there at the solstice. Fox Close where the Abbots, mother and daughter, live, is also fictitious.

Prologue

This was a place of sacrifice, two millennia ago.

Not, in fact, a stone circle but a horseshoe, four sarsen uprights remaining, the stone imported from west of here, from Marlborough country, by long toil. The lintels are gone, chipped away over the centuries to build huts for humans not for gods. No longer any discernible shape, even from the air. A rambler coming on them unalert might see a few oddly-shaped rocks distributed randomly on Hungerford Common and lose their meaning in his indifference.

Not today, though, since the sunny downland is scattered with caravans and camper vans, giving significance to the place. It's Friday, June the nineteenth, and the summer solstice is hard upon them. Two distinct groups here: real gypsy caravans holding real Romanies, with their horses and chastened dogs, their unfathomable tongue; new-age travellers with their bells and beads, their crystals and giro cheques. Undistinguished and equally despised by the law-abiding taxpayers of Hungerford, they should be allies but affect not to notice each other.

The new-agers are here to emulate, for no particular reason, long-dead ceremonies that they don't understand. Also, more practically, to sell vegetarian burgers from their greasy kitchen and perhaps a few soft drugs. The Romanies are here as part of a complicated system of travelling that's been passed down for generations but badly eroded by unco-operative councils and unsympathetic policemen.

More immediately and commercially, they're here for the midsummer fair: not a funfair with dodgems and whirligigs but a traditional English fair with crafts and country skills on display – carving, whittling and basket weaving; shire horses, music, laughter; beer and cider; hot dogs and ice cream vans; bowling

9

for a pig and a display of soaring falconry. Most stallholders will come by the day with their home-made amber necklaces and hand-embroidered blouses, their asymmetrical pots.

Strictly speaking, no camping or caravaning is allowed on Hungerford Common, but the fair has been held here for more than two centuries and for five days each June the elected Overseers of the Port Down are tolerant and unlock the barrier at the Inkpen Gate for the horses to pass through.

Apart from the two groups and belonging to neither is a lone caravan, Romany in appearance, its broad-shouldered horse grazing fitfully on the drought-browned grass, a fire burning safely inside a ring of stones with a tin of water coming to the boil. The new-agers nod greetings to its owner which he wordlessly returns. The Romanies won't go near him or acknowledge his existence, except for one middle-aged man, built like a farrier, who glances in his direction and spits into his own fire, a sizzling of saliva, then turns away, making the sign against the evil eye.

Twenty-five years ago a human sacrifice took place here. The lone traveller is retribution, or possibly justice. Nothing is ever forgotten.

Two millennia, twenty-five years: the intervals grow shorter, since another life will be sacrificed on these downs before the solstice dawns. In the end, more than one.

In Fox Close, a horseshoe of council bungalows on the edge of Hungerford – although they're mostly owner-occupied now – Jordan Abbot asks her mother if she can go to the common and play before supper, meaning can she go and look at the gypsies.

They'd come into town this afternoon, while Jordan was being fetched from school, and she'd watched in fascination as a tiny woman in full gypsy regalia led a huge teenage boy by the hand, trekking from door to door, offering pegs and wooden toys for sale – carved geese, cows, even a bear. She'd smiled at the boy and he'd grinned back, eager if shy, and offered her an oaken puppy until her mother called to her sharply to come away.

No, she can't, Josie Abbot says. Why not? Because . . . because they're dirty, because they're foreign, because they're not like us, because they kidnap little girls and sell them. Because they steal children.

She can't say this, not in the nineties. Because I said so. Because tea will be ready in half an hour. Because it might rain.

Because you're only six years old and blonde and beautiful and if I lose you too then I shall die.

'I wish I was a gypsy,' the little girl announces, 'and lived in a caravan and sold peculiar wooden toys and didn't have to go to school.'

Josie smiles, remembering when she too had such fantasies. They never quite die either. Even in adulthood there comes the occasional longing to be off with the raggle-taggle gypsies, oh!

'And that funny boy could be my brother,' Jordan adds. 'His name's Lashlo. He told me. I asked him. Isn't that a peculiar name?' Peculiar is a word she has recently learnt and she likes to use it whenever she can.

'I expect it's a gypsy name,' Josie says and explains dutifully that the boy isn't 'funny'. 'He's mentally handicapped, darling. That means that though he's got such a big strong body, in his head he's just a little boy.'

'Good!' Jordan says. 'The little boy can play with me and the big boy can beat up the other big peculiar boys who try to pull my hair.'

* * *

In the graveyard of St Mary's church at nearby Kintbury a recent headstone stands in one of the last vacant corners. It's

11

white and plain, no pictures of trumpeting angels, no ornate writing. Frederick Summers, it says, 1975-1997, beloved husband and son. And, at the bottom, 'One Man Loved the Pilgrim Soul in You.' Not religious, although it sounds it and fooled the vicar until it was too late, since he is a modern vicar and has a degree in Sociology rather than Greats.

The man who chose it doesn't believe in a God or gods, certainly not ones demanding sacrifice, nor in a soul. Not any more.

A miniature rose grows on the plot, one white flower in bud. No weeds. Someone comes regularly.

And in Newbury that evening, Detective Superintendent Gregory Summers, the loving father who can quote Yeats, is living one of his worst nightmares, and he has many.

1. Friday, 19th June

At least he'd done the siege course at Hendon two years ago, had some idea what to do, although nothing could prepare you for the reality of being held at gunpoint by a man who is probably reconciled to dying and has no doubts about taking company along for the journey.

He was in a bed and breakfast on the outskirts of town, a place that relied not on tourists but on the steady supply of homeless families sent by the council. Clean, though, comfortable enough. Greg had seen many worse places, stayed in worse places. The room – a bay-windowed, high-ceilinged oblong at the front of the building – held three narrow beds, a fridge, a rudimentary cooker, a washbasin, a wardrobe and chest of drawers, a table and two unmatched chairs. On that table were the remains of a takeaway meal.

Something sweet and sour.

It must have been a pleasant room once, Greg thought, when this was a family house. Now plaster coping – a flower and leaf pattern – was crumbling in the corners. Walls were propped up with Anaglypta. There were pictures, one a lurid Sacred Heart, the organ in question full and red and fit to burst. Floor space was at a premium, like a handkerchief dance floor amid nightclub tables.

He'd had plenty of time to examine his surroundings in the five hours he'd been stuck here. For the first two he'd been terrified, convinced that the thief had come in the night when he was least prepared for him. Then fear had given way to calm, then boredom. His pounding heart and sweaty hands were now merely lethargy and a nagging hunger.

The B&B stood on a busy arterial road. The rush hour was long over; even so, it was noticeable that not a vehicle had passed them in hours. Outside, nothing revved, or hooted, or noisily changed gear; no bursts of rap music rocked the still summer air through open car windows before speeding on. It was light at nine o'clock, since the solstice was two days away. He knew if he could look out of the window he would see dozens of policemen and women, grave and quiet, crossing their fingers for one of their own, hoping for the best since the worst was inconceivable.

Superintendent Gregory Summers sat on one of the beds and tried to think. His school teachers had been inclined to say that he spent too much time thinking, as, later, had some of his superior officers while he worked his way up the ranks; but how could anyone think too much?

If the gypsy boy sitting on the upright chair opposite him, the one with the loaded shotgun, had thought harder then he wouldn't have shot the woman lying on the floor between them, tidily prone, the blood and blasted guts hidden beneath her, although a stain was creeping across the carpet. Her head was cramped to one side, giving Greg a glimpse of a bony, sallow, not unhandsome face with black hair falling in an undisciplined lock over the one dark eye that he could see, now fixed on nothingness.

The boy looked twenty at most but the children were his, two of them, both girls, asleep on the bed in the corner in a cosy heap. The elder must be about ten, he calculated, making Huwie Lee at least twenty-eight, probably older. A middle-aged woman, a fat, red-Irish biddy, the owner of the small hotel, wept silently on the third bed and crossed herself at intervals, her dough face kneaded into a tragedy mask.

Middle-aged? She must be about his own age, which was forty-seven.

Greg wasn't a big man and he wasn't a brave one either. He wasn't going to rush his adversary, risking the lives of everyone in the room. What a siege needed was patience, a gradual de-

14

escalation of adrenaline and fear, time to let the man with the gun appreciate the hopelessness of his situation, the need for sense to prevail.

He shifted his weight slightly, his skinny left buttock starting to ache, and the gun was immediately aimed at his face.

'Bum going to sleep,' he said pleasantly, 'that's all. I'm hungry. Didn't get any supper. How about you?' He glanced automatically at the remains of the takeaway but the foil baskets were empty, licked clean.

I am a human being, like you. I have the same hopes and fears you have. I eat, I crap, I get cramp and wind, catch flu in winter just when it's most inconvenient. I shop and read the newspaper and slump in front of the TV at night until it's time for bed. You don't, you really don't want to shoot me. I am innocent.

'Huwie,' he said, when the man didn't answer his question, 'how are you expecting this to end?'

'You talk too much –'

He broke off as the elder girl stirred on the bed, uncurling herself like a dancer, blinked. As she pushed back the blanket Greg saw that she wore only her vest and pants, both white cotton, although 'white' was an optimism. She disengaged herself from her sister with care, not waking her, and went over to Greg, rubbing the sleep from her eyes, assessing the stranger without fear.

'Hello, sweetheart,' he said, 'what's your name?'

'Romy.'

'My name's Gregory.'

She looked at him speculatively, her eyes alight with a shrewd intelligence, then decided she liked what she saw. 'Have you got any little girls?' she asked.

'Yes,' he said, 'two.'

He knew that Huwie Lee was listening to their conversation, whatever he might pretend to the contrary, and he wanted to be a family man with small children depending on their daddy's safe homecoming.

'What are their names?' she asked.

'Anne and Louise,' he said, at random. Safe, sensible names, the sort of names he might have given his daughters if he'd had any, although his ex-wife would have wanted to call them Melissa and Miranda.

'How old are they?'

'Anne is about your age. Louise is two years younger.'

'Like Bonnie?' She glanced over at the bed where her younger sister slumbered on.

'Yes, that's right,' he said with a smile.

'Is Anne like me?'

'Not very. She's got blonde hair and green eyes, like her mother.' Romy was as dark as the gypsy of the cliché. To his surprise, she climbed confidently on his knee and laid her head on his shoulder. How many children of her age, he wondered, would show such trust in an era when mothers warned relentlessly of the charming stranger, the man in the park with the bag of sweets? He wanted to be worthy of her trust. He put his arms round her thin body. It was boyish, flat, no hint yet of puberty beneath the grubby vest.

'Are you still tired, Romy?' he asked, caressing her clean fine hair.

'No. I'm hungry . . . Dado, I'm hungry.' She showed no fear of him.

'Shut up, Romy. Do,' Lee said in an agitated voice. He sat, hunched and thin on his wooden chair, his shotgun at the ready between his knees, the green and purple nylon bag in which he'd smuggled the gun through the streets and into the house abandoned at his feet. 'You know there isn't anything to eat.' His voice was tired, and his eyes. His body language swore defeat, but defeated men are dangerous.

Greg cradled the child in his arms, feeling a pleasure in a human touch that he hadn't felt in a long time, affection

16

without self-interest or desire. She was very light. He noticed the line of old bruises up her left leg and similar yellowing marks on her arms. He touched one as gently as he could but she flinched and he murmured an apology.

'He has such a temper,' she said without rancour. She put her thumb in her mouth. 'Daya hasn't moved for hours.' Greg deduced that she was talking about her mother. He glanced at Lee who looked away. 'I think she's dead,' Romy continued, matter-of-factly. She went quietly back to sleep, leaning against his shoulder.

Lee made a hopeless gesture with the shotgun. 'She's a nice kid,' he said inadequately. 'Bright as a button.'

'You must be proud of her.'

'Yeah.'

They were all exhausted. Now might be the psychological moment to bring this ordeal to an end, if Greg could find the right thing to say. His throat felt dry and he found that he knew no words, only senseless syllables. He'd read the books, he'd done the role-playing, but that was rehearsal: this was the first night and there was no one in the prompt box. If he fluffed a line, there might be no second night for any of them.

'Huwie, how are you expecting this to end?' he asked again.

The young man sat up, alert. 'No tricks!'

'Huwie, you know your wife's dead, don't you?'

'Of course I do. I'm not fucking stupid. I shot her, didn't I?'

'So, how do you expect this to end? Do you love Romy?'

'Yes.'

Without emphatic protestation, it convinced him. 'Do you want to risk hurting her, or Bonnie?'

'No,' he said uncertainly. 'I've got no choice, have I?'

'Did you mean to shoot your wife?'

'No . . . I came to get her and the kids back, or just the kids. Romany kids can't live in houses, it kills their spirit. Or she'd have let them be taken into care, knowing her. I brought the shotgun so's there'd be no argument but she hadn't the sense she was born with. She struggled with me, the gun went off in her chest. Stupid cow.' His voice trembled and he turned to address the inert body on the floor as if he believed she could hear him, his voice almost affectionate. 'Bloody stupid cow, aren't you, Reyna?'

He turned back to Greg and there were unshed tears, making his black eyes huge. 'It doesn't matter what I do now, does it? Nothing can make any difference. They're going to lock me up for years and years. I live for the open road. I'd die in one of those places so I might as well die here, quickly and cleanly, and my girls with me. Better than some children's home.'

'It does make a difference,' Greg insisted. 'If you shot Reyna by accident, then it isn't murder, only manslaughter. You'll be out in a few years. You might even get off if the jury accepts that it was an accident. But if you let any harm come to the children, or the landlady, or me, then there'll be no hope for you.' He met the younger man's eyes, his own looking steadily, signalling truth to his adversary without compunction. The police were the world's best liars, apart from his ex-wife.

'Shut it!' Lee flared up, turning the shotgun in Greg's direction once more, although Romy lay like a breastplate before him. Greg could see both barrels loaded: one for him, one for the woman; then plenty of time to reload for the girls and, finally, himself.

Greg waited a moment until he'd calmed down then began again. 'They won't wait much longer, Huwie. It's still daylight but only just. They won't want this to drag on into the night. They're under pressure. The press are out there. They're waiting for something to happen. They'll have called the specialists in. They'll be on the rooftops opposite. They're trained marksmen, Huwie, not like you.'

'I'm a bloody good shot. You better believe it, *muscro*.'

At that distance, Greg knew, he couldn't miss. 'Good enough at potting rabbits, maybe, but they're professionals.

They'll shoot to kill if they decide to storm the place. If the children die too, and me, what consolation will that be to you? . . . Huwie, are you listening?'

'Shut it, I said.' But it was half-hearted now. He was in a deep hole and the hole was rapidly filling with sewage. He longed for a responsible adult to give him an arm and haul him out and Greg knew just the man.

'Put the gun down, Huwie, and we'll walk out of here – Romy and Bonnie and you. Me and Mrs McArthur. You don't want to die, Huwie, not really, none of us does, certainly not like this. I'll speak up for you, Huwie, at the trial. Manslaughter with diminished responsibility.'

'It was her fault.' The young man began to sob in earnest. 'It would have been all right if she hadn't taken the kids away from me. We don't do things like that, not us Romanies, not go running to the *diddycoy* Social. They're my daughters, aren't they?'

'Of course they are,' Greg said, 'and you'll be able to see them. Put the gun down, Huwie. On the floor, between us, and push it towards me with your feet. It'll be all right. I promise.'

Romy murmured in her sleep, not English words, or none that he knew, and put her arms more tightly round his neck. He held his breath for a moment. There was complete silence. Lee laid the gun down on the floor in front of him. 'If you've lied to me, *muscro* . . .'

'No lies.'

The boy pushed the gun away with his foot. Greg got up slowly. It was still nearer to Lee than it was to him and there was the danger of a last-minute change of heart. The vital thing was not to startle him and he prayed silently that the woman would continue to keep quiet and still and panic nobody, least of all himself. He laid the sleeping Romy down beside her sister on the bed. He picked up the gun, broke it, took out the ammunition and put it in his pocket. The landlady crossed herself again and began to pray aloud. 'Hail, Holy Queen, mother of mercy, hail our life, our sweetness and our hope.'

Greg let out a long breath. He felt faint with relief. Above the woman's prattle he said, 'Hold your hands out, Huwie.'

'To thee do we send up our sighs, mourning and weeping in this valley of tears.'

The young man stretched his hands out obediently before him, his head bent in a classic gesture of submission to the man who had mastered him. Greg took a pair of handcuffs from his pocket where he'd hastily stuffed them on leaving the station five hours earlier, convinced that it was an unnecessary precaution and let that be a lesson to him. He fastened them round Lee's wrists. They were the new sort, the ones with the short and rigid bar between the bracelets, locking the hands close as if in prayer.

'Turn then, most gracious advocate, thine eyes of mercy towards us.'

Shut up, woman. For God's sake, just shut up or I'll wish the boy had *shot you.* 'Huwie Lee, I'm arresting you for murder. You're not obliged to say anything, but it may harm your defence if you fail to mention when questioned –'

Lee's head jerked up, his eyes accusing. 'You said manslaughter!'

'It will be, Huwie. The Crown Prosecution Service will accept a manslaughter plea, but I have to arrest you for murder now.' He completed the incomprehensible caution and added more helpfully, 'Keep quiet and don't say a word until we get you to the station and find you a lawyer.' He turned to the landlady who was still gabbling to the Virgin Mary, wanting to give her something practical to occupy her before he was obliged to hit her. 'Will you waken the girls, please? Can you bring them? Better wrap them up in blankets.'

The man began to sob uninhibitedly, calling the dead woman's name in a croak. Greg crossed to the window. He opened it carefully – you couldn't be sure that one marksman wouldn't turn out to be trigger-happy – and looked out. In an instant the crowd was completely silent, a hundred faces raised eagerly to him for benediction.

'Okay,' he called. 'We're coming out. Panic over.'

Wakened, Romy ran to her father and wrapped her arms round his waist, her head pressed into his stomach. His fettered hands had to loop over her head to return her embrace.

'It'll be all right, Dado,' she said. 'It'll be all right.'

Greg was desperate for a piss.

Camera flash went off from all directions as he came out of the front door, shepherding Lee before him. Two constables immediately took charge of the young man and bundled him into the back of a van. Greg handed the shotgun to another PC who whisked it away into the evidence chain. A tough-looking woman in civvies rounded up the children and drove them off in a white saloon car. He thought her hair was purple but that might be a trick of the fading light.

To the landlady he said, 'I shall need you at the station to make a statement,' and she nodded wearily, prayered out.

'Greg, you okay?' Chief Inspector Stratton had appeared silently at his side, a walkie-talkie in his hand, his nondescript face all concern. Harry Stratton, forty, family man, straight as a Roman road. A competent DCI but he wouldn't go any further. 'Christ!' he went on, 'd'you have any idea what a do like this costs? The Chief'll have kittens when he gets back from his golfing holiday in Portugal.'

Greg nodded, agreeing with all of it. 'I'm fine. You can stand the Tactical Firearms Team down.' Stratton spoke into his crackling handset for a few minutes then Greg added, 'Keep an ambulance back for the dead woman.'

'There is a body then?'

'His wife. Older than him by the look of it. My guess would be she'd looked out for him all his life. He shot her

21

by accident in the middle of an argument and panicked because she wasn't there to tell him what to do about it.'

'Vive le psychobabble,' Stratton said with a grin. 'Are the kids okay, that's the main thing?'

'They're fine.'

'You're a hero.' He glanced round at the crowds, restrained behind a metal barrier. 'The local TV news people are after you, Superman.'

'Sod them.'

'Better get it over with if you ever want peace again. Go on, give a dignified interview, get your fifteen seconds of fame –'

'Fifteen minutes.'

'You'll be lucky.'

'Harry, has anyone told Angie?'

'No, I thought about it but there was no answer on the phone and no sign of life when I sent a girl round to your place. Isn't Friday late night closing at the supermarket?'

'Yes, nine o'clock.'

'There you are then. Hope she wasn't expecting you to pick her up.'

'There's a company minibus. She'll get on that if she doesn't see my car waiting. She's used to last-minute changes of plan.' He sighed and ran his fingers through his thick hair. 'I'm glad she wasn't there. I don't want her to know. She has enough worries.'

'She's tough,' Harry said. 'Tougher than you think. Tougher than you are.'

Greg recoiled as a microphone was thrust under his nose at that moment, a hairy grey gonk. Someone had made it through the barrier. Three people, in fact: sound, camera and what he'd heard referred to ironically as the talent. 'Superintendent Summers? Adam Chaucer from Newbury Newsround. Have you a word for our viewers?'

He said woodenly, 'The Thames Valley police is relieved

that this incident has been brought to a conclusion without further loss of life.'

'You've arrested a man?'

'A man, Huwie Lee, is helping us with our enquiries.'

'Quite the hero, Mr Summers.' Greg looked at him sharply but the young man apparently meant it, his voice respectful, his handsome face bland.

'I was doing my job to the best of my ability.'

He turned away from the cameras. He'd seen himself on TV: a thin man of 5'10", with dark hair greying round the edges but not receding yet, thank God; dark eyes, regular but undistinguished features, neat office-type clothes and well-polished shoes. He looked like Everyman and it took him half a minute to recognise himself as if he didn't see that face in the shaving mirror every morning.

He shouted to the nearest police car to take him to the station. He wanted to make his statement and deal with his prisoner, then get home before his daughter-in-law saw the evening news.

A few hours earlier Josie Abbot had tucked Jordan up in bed and left the hall light on to shine a thin, reassuring line under her door till morning came. 'Goodnight, sleep tight.'

'Mum? Can I go up to the common tomorrow? Can I go to the fair? Pretty please.'

'We'll go together. All right?'

'All right! G'night. God bless.'

Josie tiptoed out, pulling the door to behind her, and went into the sitting room where the TV played, just audible so as not to disturb a sleeping child. She watched Coronation Street. She watched a sitcom. She couldn't afford to go out and didn't want to. Where would she go? What life was there for a widow of thirty-five with a young child and no money?

The bungalow was small: two bedrooms and a sitting room, with a galley kitchen, poky bathroom and tiny garden. The furniture she'd brought from their house in Inkpen had been nearly new then but was now getting shabby and couldn't be replaced. She'd given up work to raise Jordan, assuming that Pete's earnings would keep them in comfort if not in luxury. Now she had her widowed mother's pension and income support.

You made plans and they came to nothing. Had anything in her life ever gone according to plan? It was, as her daughter often said when denied some treat for lack of funds, so unfair.

Just before eleven, Josie looked in on the child as she always did before going to bed herself. It was a warm night and, although the window was open a few inches, Jordan had kicked away her Snoopy duvet and lay on her right side, hugging the Charlie Brown pillow in her small, pale arms.

2. Friday, Later

Angelica Summers was making peppermint tea as Greg came into the kitchen. He could smell it. She didn't bother to ask if he wanted one, knowing the answer. He opened the fridge and helped himself to a beer, pulled out the ring and stood drinking from the can. His wife would have chided him and told him to use a glass but Angie wasn't like that. She wasn't petty like other women.

'You're late,' she said, but not as an accusation.

'Bloody paperwork.' He kissed her chastely on the cheek. 'Thought I might as well catch up on it as you were working till nine, then forgot the time. Why I wasn't there to pick you up. Sorry.'

'Doesn't matter. I got a lift from the deputy manager. Thought you might have gone to the pub with Harry Stratton.'

'Who, me?'

They both laughed. Once, maybe. He drank only beer these days, wine on special occasions. He didn't keep spirits in the house.

She was of medium height, perhaps 5'5", and had grown thin this last year, since Fred's death, although he made sure that she ate sensibly. She was blond, but dishwater rather than moonlight, her hair pinned out of the way – in accordance with Savemore supermarket's staff hygiene regulations – which enabled him to detect that she'd been on the deli counter that day. Loose, it fell just below her shoulder; like this it left her ears looking vulnerable, a pair of cheap enamel earrings – gaudy teddy bears – stabbed through the holes. She had a large mouth with prominent teeth. Fred had teased that she could eat an apple from the far side.

She was twenty-three, a quarter of a century younger than Greg.

His son Frederick had brought her home three years ago. He'd loved her name at once: Angelica, with its promise of sweet candy, its hint of heavenly hosts. Frederick and Angelica – like something out of Jane Austen; Fred and Angie – that nice ordinary couple next door.

Fred – his full name too pretentious for either of them, his mother Diane's choice – had refused an offer of a university place at eighteen, not wanting to saddle himself with student debt, and won a trainee managership with a northern chain of supermarkets called Savemore, up and coming. Three years ago they'd started spreading south and Fred had been coincidentally appointed assistant manager of the Newbury branch, fresh and red on a trading estate three miles out of town in the middle of a massive carpark.

Father and son were almost strangers since Fred had lived with his mother since the divorce when he was two, but they were friends. They liked each other. They weren't much alike. Fred was made on an altogether larger scale, over six feet tall and built for his passion of rugby football. He had his mother's pale brown hair that the inimical might call mousy, her hazel eyes, the deceptively open features that had allowed her to lie to him so comprehensively during their brief marriage.

Gregory had wanted desperately to offer his son a home in the four-bedroomed house in Kintbury where he rattled about, but feared to cramp the boy's style; Fred had longed to live with his stranger-father but not wanted to intrude on his long-nurtured solitude. It had taken several pints of beer in the pub, followed by whisky chasers at home to overcome their natural English reserve and settle things to their common delight.

Which was when Fred had first mentioned Angie.

'Angelica Lampton.' He teased the name out like a silken thread. 'Isn't that music? And I'm not talking Andrew Lloyd Webber here.'

'Very pretty. Who is she?'

'And you know what's even more musical? Angelica Summers.'

'Oh,' he'd said, shocked that it could be that time in his son's life already. 'Congratulations.'

'Steady on, Dad. I haven't asked her yet.'

'But girls usually say yes, don't they?'

Fred had looked amused. 'What an old chauvinist you are. When did you last have a girlfriend, as a matter of interest? When did you last have a full service, or even get your oil changed?'

'Oh, I can't remember. Years ago.'

There had been women, of course, for a few weeks or months – dinners, cinemas, walks on the downs, love making that was pleasurable if not ecstatic. Followed by partings that were oddly lacking in emotion, more like a drifting than a severance. Then there had been the two- or three-night stands with women officers from other forces on training weekends, married women usually, no strings, no bullshit. Don't call me and I won't call you. No one woman who'd ever mattered, and none at all recently.

'What does she do?' he'd asked.

'She works at the supermarket, same as me, on the tills mostly, or the deli counter. She'll transfer here with me, if all goes according to plan.'

He'd been disappointed, had hoped for something better for his only son than a shop assistant.

'I know we're only twenty,' Fred went on, 'and people don't want to settle now until they're thirty or more, don't want to make the commitment in case something better turns up, but there isn't anything better, Dad. Angie and I want to be together until death do us part.'

And they were.

As she lowered her green eyes over her mug, poking at the tea bag with a stainless steel spoon, he saw the smear of eye-shadow above each one, melting during the day into a fine crease, rust coloured. He wondered how it would taste if he licked her eyelids.

They'd moved in with him straight after the wedding. He'd vacated the master bedroom with its en suite bathroom to them and installed himself in the second bedroom at the back, out of earshot of the young lovers.

He'd searched his conscience and found that he wanted to be a grandfather, soon, that it wouldn't make him feel old and decrepit but part of the continuity of time and history, offering some point to his work-soaked life. Angie was an intelligent girl but, coming from a fatherless household, had left school at sixteen to pay her way. She seemed to have no ambition and he hoped that meant a family before long.

She wasn't conventionally attractive, yet the men they'd passed that first evening as the three of them walked by the canal had looked twice, even the poor energy-sapped creatures from the health hydro. She didn't play up to the men, didn't notice them, had eyes only for Fred. He'd understood by then why his ambitious son had settled for a shop assistant.

He'd thought she looked older than twenty. He'd at first taken her to be a few years his son's senior, whereas they'd been born less than a month apart. Girls grew up sooner than boys – one of those true truisms.

He'd have been glad to be her father but she was used to doing without one and he had to settle for being her friend. In their puppyish quarrels Fred would complain, 'You always take *her* side.'

It was unusual in the nineties for young people to live with their parents once married, and after a year Fred had started to talk about buying a flat of their own, getting on the first rung of the housing ladder, as he put it, being nearer the shop, their friends, the fleshpots of Newbury.

'But all this will be yours one day,' he'd said, laughing.

'Come on, Dad,' Fred said, 'you'll get hitched again your-self one day.'

Angie had supported her father-in-law and said there was no hurry and that they were fine where they were.

At least she'd called him Greg from the first, not Dad. That would have been too much to bear.

'Shall we watch a bit of the news?' She'd lost her short, northern vowels after three years in the Thames Valley, a chameleon. She hoiked the tea bag out of the mug and binned it. He crumpled his beer can in his hand and dropped it in after. The bin needed emptying.

'Oh, it's so depressing,' he said. 'Politics, all that crap.'

'Some of us like to take an intelligent interest in the world outside, Greg.'

'Not tonight, love.'

'Well, I won't force you if Jeremy Paxman brings you out in hives.'

They stood staring out of the kitchen window which was curtainless and unshaded, not overlooked. The lawns and flowerbeds sat in darkness. It was a big garden and needed more time than he could give it. He thought the bindweed looked pretty with its pure white bells.

He and Diane had bought the house shortly after their marriage and it had been more than he could afford, plunging him into debt to satisfy her desires, consumer rather than carnal. Inflation and promotion had seen to that and he now had the deeds, stuffed in a drawer in his desk. He'd felt so grown up back then, twenty-three, called 'Sarge', newly-married, with a massive mortgage. He'd felt more grown-up then than he did now.

These days, Diane lived in a mansion outside Maidenhead, with a flat in the Barbican for her nights at the opera. Things were what had mattered to Diane and things were what her second husband had been able to give her in a way that no honest copper could. She called herself Diana since the early eighties, thought it had more class. Poor cow.

Angelica was still wearing her overall: green and white check, wholesome and crisp. She'd taken off her pantyhose and her legs were pale and sturdy with white-gold hairs, her feet bare on the terracotta tiles. He knew she wore nothing beneath the overall and he stood behind her now, slithering the polycotton up her thighs, baring the tight and untanned buttocks. He felt her clench them, hollowing two dimples in the flesh, and kneaded those dimples with his thumbs in a way he knew she liked. Then he slid his hand between her legs and began to finger her. She was wet but tight. He continued for a few minutes, feeling her open ever wider to his hand as his fingers probed inside her, until he knew she was ready for him. Then he unzipped and took out his erection – quite service-able, he thought, for a middle-aged man who'd had a hard day.

'Summers is icumen in?' she said. It was their special joke.

'May I?'

'Of course.'

She leant forward over the draining board as he pushed into the narrow space between her thighs, her head turned sideways so that she could see him, just. For a second it reminded him of the dead gypsy woman's face at that same odd angle and he looked steadily into the night, almost disen-gaged, before closing his eyes to allow his other senses free rein. The smell of peppermint was foremost. Sweet and sour.

He'd never asked how he compared to his son as a lover, how experience vied with eagerness. He never would.

He kept up the slow, steady rhythm that she liked, that soothed him too after the strain of the last few hours when any sudden movement might have been his last. He reached forward, pulling the pins clumsily from her hair and letting them fall in the sink, ruffling the straight, fine, buttery fila-ments with his fingers. She was quiet, her ever deepening breathing the only sign that she was aware of his presence behind and inside her until, at the end, she let out one wild sharp cry like an animal released from a trap. He stood there after he too had finished, unmoving, until his limp penis finally slumped out of her and he tucked it quickly away because it looked daft hanging there with the inevitable dewdrop on the end. Nothing needed to be said either of pleasure or closeness.

Instead he said, 'Thought for a minute there you'd gone to sleep on me.'

'No.' She straightened up, tossing her freed hair to settle it to her liking. She groped in the sink for her damp pins and put them in the breast pocket of her overall which bore the logo – crossed white swords on a green background, oddly bellicose – of Savemore supermarkets. On her left hand were the wedding and engagement rings Fred had given her. She wore them still – he supposed as an armour against the world.

Her peppermint tea was cold but she didn't bother to microwave it, just drank it in one gulp. She sat on one of the stools at the breakfast bar, not troubling to pull her skirt down. He could see the glisten of his drying semen on her thigh and in her pubic hair. 'My feet are cold,' she complained. He knelt and took them one by one and rubbed them in his hands, kissing the grubby soles, the cramped toes. He blew softly on the white hairs of her calves, against the nap, goose-bumping them.

'I would give anything to be able to marry you,' he said.

She shrugged. 'I've been married and so have you. We're no different from, say, a gay couple.'

He was shocked. He tried hard not to be homophobic but the fact was that he'd grown up in an era when it was illegal and despicable and he wasn't comfortable with the comparison.

Rugby was such a passion for Fred that he'd arranged his shifts around it and so had Angie, shouting with vigour at

31

him and waving her club scarf as he ran and passed and scrummed. Greg went whenever he could although he wasn't a sporting man – that came from Diane's side of the family, those ruddy, thick-necked brothers of hers. She'd thought him less of a man because he didn't give a damn who won the cup and had never grasped the complex rules of cricket.

Fred made Newbury first eleven within a year of coming to live there, but in the second year his game seemed to drop off. He trained hard, joining a gym, going jogging, but he tired easily and was losing weight and, when he hadn't scored a try in six matches, the captain talked about standing him down and the Summers household fell glum like storms on the day of the family picnic.

'Those are nasty bruises,' Greg had remarked one warm Saturday evening in the pub. 'Too much horseplay in the bath after the match?'

'Don't know how I got those,' Fred had replied, examining the browning thumbprints up his arm with a frown of surprise. 'Old Ange been beating me up again. God, I'm knackered! Must be getting old.' He drained his glass. 'Your round, I think, Squire.'

'You want to get some arnica on those.' It was what his mother would have said.

Romy's injuries had reminded Greg of his son's damaged skin, of the ensuing weeks when the bruises didn't heal, as the little girl's would.

The doctor didn't try to offer hope. This type of leukaemia struck fast and fatally, apparently randomly. Both Greg and Angelica tested for their bone marrow type, the only chance of even a temporary reprieve, but neither was a good enough match. Diane, strangely, was even less of a possibility. They were reliant upon the kindness of strangers and it was not forthcoming. Fred didn't quite believe it. None of them did. He was twenty-two, for God's sake. What sort of a sick world

32

was this that destroyed the life of a kindly, harmless lad before it had half begun?

Greg had seen horrors: he'd been one of the first on the scene at Hungerford that day when Michael Ryan snapped; he'd seen the violated bodies of children and the tortured remnants of unlucky prostitutes, but he'd never known true anger until that summer when his son died.

His only child. The end of the line.

He sensed that Diane blamed him and understood her: he blamed himself. She came to the funeral and the interment but wouldn't come back to the house afterwards. Her manner towards Angelica was cold, as of a mother who'd lost her only son to an unworthy chit.

'Frederick married too young,' she said, tight-lipped, as if this had sapped his strength.

She looked good, Greg thought without lust. She was forty-four and looked thirty-eight, elegant, relentlessly slenderised. He thought she didn't yet have to dye her hair, although when she did it would be done with great artistry and expense. She'd risen in the world after divorcing him, as she'd wanted, married one of the men she'd deceived him with on the long nights when he was making the Thames Valley a safer place to live in.

Her second marriage seemed happy, which told him that the fault had lain with him.

Fred had been an accident, Diane frightened of childbirth and, especially, of losing her figure. It hadn't stopped her claiming him as a possession in the divorce. None of which meant that she didn't love him. She had had no other child.

'It was such a waste,' she said, her voice rising needlessly loud, making him suspect that hysteria was one ill-chosen word away. 'A supermarket, for God's sake! He had a good mind. He should have gone to Oxford and then Daniel would have found him a place with his firm.' As if this would have saved him, although then he wouldn't have met Angelica Lampton.

Her second husband was a banker in the City of London and a stalwart of the local tennis club. Greg felt no resentment towards him: Daniel Greenwood had done him a favour and, in making an honest woman of her, saved him a fortune in alimony payments. They shook hands at the graveside and Dan sympathised without need of words.

'What will you put on the gravestone?' Diane asked as she was leaving.

'Something simple. "Beloved husband and son".'

'Son and husband, perhaps.'

'No. A man is a husband before he's a son.'

She stared at him, her hazel eyes with their uncreased green shadow full of contempt. 'Don't be obtuse, Gregory. How can he be?'

'Well, not literally, obviously, Diane – Diana.' He corrected himself quickly as she opened her mouth to do it for him. She'd always been literal, one of the things that had come between them, a chasm of mutual incomprehension. 'I meant that it's the most important thing about him.'

'Not as far as I'm concerned.'

'Do you like her?' he'd asked Angie, when she'd driven off in a flurry of Mercedes tyres on gravel. She shrugged. 'You can't like her.'

'Diana's heartbroken, Greg, and she's not capable of articulating it, and that only makes it hurt more.' She glanced at him sideways under her pale lashes – no mascara to streak with tears. 'You must have loved her once.'

Puzzled, he said, 'I suppose I must have done.'

A number of people did come back to the house, including as many of Greg's colleagues as were not on duty that afternoon. The police looked after their own, they were your family. They ate sausage rolls and drank sweet sherry and, later, tea. Several of them had sneaked bottles of decent drink in, real drink, scotch and brandy. By the time the last of them had left with their final murmured words of consolation to a man who could never be consoled, he felt drunk and unutterably tired.

He'd sat weeping in Fred's favourite armchair. She'd come and taken him by the hand and led him up to the second bedroom, his bedroom, and taken him to bed, but he'd been too drunk. She'd stayed with him all night, her naked body pressed against his and he'd said, 'I love you,' over and over again until he fell asleep in mid sentence. He'd felt no guilt, no shame, not then. It was as if Fred had left her to him as a sacred trust and he was only embarrassed that he couldn't consummate that trust tonight.

He'd awoken in a thirsty daybreak to find her tonguing him into life, then straddling him. He'd groped through excruciating hangover towards unaccustomed sexual ecstasy, the explosion in his brain a mixture of orgasm and sour whisky. He'd reached up and kissed her, knowing how bad his mouth must taste from the outside, but needing it more than any other joining.

He'd held her afterwards for what seemed like hours. 'It's been a long time,' he'd said finally.

'Yeah. Why d'you go without, Greg, a good-looking bloke like you?'

'I was saving myself,' he said, perfectly serious, 'keeping myself pure for you.' That had been a year ago and his love had proved a real thing, and a thing of revelation.

He loved her but he couldn't marry her. It was in the Book of Common Prayer: A Table of Kindred and Affinity. A man may not marry his mother, daughter, father's mother, mother's mother and so on, through son's wife, via mother's sister to sister's daughter. Some strange couplings they'd envisaged enough to forbid, these sick men of biblical times: what sane man wanted to marry his grandmother?

Leviticus, that woolly liberal, prescribed the death penalty for them both.

Another reason to believe no longer in that murderous God. Or did they understand in their wisdom – those ancients – that May-September marriages seldom worked? And English law upheld these prohibitions, although half of them were not blood kin, since husband and wife are one flesh and to love his son's wife was to love his daughter.

It would take a private act of parliament, costly and time-consuming. He knew, too, that the gutter press picked up such 'human interest' stories with eagerness. It would be like taking off your clothes in the middle of Piccadilly Circus, shouting, 'Look at me, dirty old bugger that I am, who wants to marry his dead son's wife and was probably fucking her before the poor sap died.'

There would be hate mail from practising Christians. Practising to torment the sexually incontinent in the flames of hell.

'Have you eaten?' she asked.

'Yes,' he lied. Sometime that evening, hunger had passed.

'Only there's a shepherd's pie got to be eaten up today. It just needs microwaving.' He was used to meat that had to be consumed that day, sold off cheap to staff at closing time. He ate bruised fruit.

'We're not poor,' he told her over and over, but her days in a single-parent household had made her frugal.

'Right,' he said and took the dish out of the fridge and put it in the microwave. Suddenly, he was ravenous.

He glimpsed her sometimes with her pals from work, other girls, boisterous and rowdy with the easy vulgarity of the young. She didn't stand out among them. Was it he who kept her so silent on her pedestal? At home she was a serene matron, a widow, flitting noiselessly about the house. It was a conspiracy, he thought, the two of them stepping on eggshells around each other. She was ordinary, he had to remind himself of that, the girl next door, loved for her ordinariness, like most women. She worried about a spot on her nose, like other girls. She was grouchy before her period. She left hairs in the sink.

Sometimes people referred to her as his daughter. He'd blown up one day at the woman at the village shop who'd politely asked after her health, 'She's not my bloody daughter!' and stormed out without his newspaper. The next morning he'd gone in with a grovelling apology. She'd pulled her cardigan more tightly round herself and looked contempt at him and now he bought his paper in town.

He wanted her to make something of herself but her plans, big or small, came to nothing. 'I might go to Leeds this weekend,' she would say, to see her mother, then she put it off. 'I might do an evening class. I might train for something, a lawyer, a teacher, a nurse.' He agreed that this was a good idea. She had a good brain, was wasted in a shop. Nothing was ever done and he thought that at twenty-three she had her life before her, while knowing that the years would pass at scary speed.

She had money. There was a tiny widow's pension from Savemore's pension scheme, a death-in-service lump sum of twenty thousand pounds in the bank. She could take three years to go to university as a mature student and plan another life.

'I meant to be a mother,' she would say, 'quite soon. But now . . .' and he agreed that it wouldn't happen now. He was too old to go through that again, too busy. Policemen made lousy fathers and rotten husbands.

* * *

She never went to Fred's grave. Not because she didn't love him enough but because she loved him too much. He went once a week to tidy away litter, to weed, to water the rose bush,

37

Tomorrow was Saturday. He would go tomorrow while she was at work.

He wondered what his colleagues knew or conjectured. It had to look odd, her still living with him a year after her husband's death. Or perhaps they thought nothing of it. Perhaps they never thought about him.

3. Saturday, 20th June

'Do you want me to pick you up from work tonight?' he asked her the next morning at breakfast.

'Not today. We're having a bit of a do for Irene whose last day it is. She's getting married next Saturday. Didn't I say?'

'If you did I forgot. Sorry. I didn't think girls did that any more, leave work when they got married.'

'She's seven months gone.'

'Ah.'

'So it won't be long or raucous, I don't suppose.'

'No gorillagrams?'

'Doubt it, though a male stripper would be nice.'

'They didn't have those when I was young,' he grumbled, 'nor female ones outside of Soho.' Now you couldn't go safely into the pub on a Friday lunchtime without some woman coming in, incorrectly dressed as a WPC, with the uniform skirt up around her arse.

Anything you say will be taken down.

Knickers!

They're coming off!

'Will you take a taxi home?' he asked.

'There's the last train at 11.40. I'll have plenty of time to catch that.'

'Please. I'll pay.' Everyone had their little meannesses and taxis were hers. That and bruised fruit.

'All right,' she said finally, getting up and sweeping the debris of her breakfast into the sink. 'You can pick me up. At the White Bear, at ten past eleven. Don't be late or I'll walk back.' She'd never learned to drive. Fred was a bit macho and didn't see the need. It wasn't as if he'd have allowed her to drive him anywhere. 'I didn't think you were going in today,' she said, noticing his office suit, clean white shirt, his tasteful striped tie.

'For a few hours.'

'Not a new case?'

'No, no. Some loose ends to tie up. Tedious paperwork.' Absolutely no gunmen holding him hostage at all.

'Thought I might go to the fair tomorrow as I'm not working.'

'Only the brave deserve the fair.'

'Did anyone ever tell you you're a wit?'

'Not really.'

'I wonder why.' She picked up her bag and swilled down the last of her coffee standing. The young had cast-iron digestions. 'I'm off next weekend,' she said. 'It'd be nice if you could keep it free. We could go somewhere. Oxford, maybe. London. The theatre . . . Greg? Are you listening?'

'I'll take you anywhere you want, sweet Angelica.' He patted his suit pocket, looking for a packet of Chesterfields and a gold-plated lighter that weren't there. He'd given up smoking over a year ago when cancer had become more than a word to him, but he sometimes forgot, especially when he was nervous about lying to her, convinced that she read his thoughts, could see right through him.

She looked at him oddly over the top of her coffee mug and he tried hard to look reliable and reassuring.

* * *

He'd put Lee on suicide watch overnight. He seemed the type. He knew what the public thought about deaths in custody – that the cops had helped him along and, in the case of a murder suspect, good job too. In fact it was the worst thing that could happen in any station, short of an officer dead in the line of duty, a real heartsink, with internal investigators swarming over you like body lice.

The custody sergeant reported that his charge had been quiet as a mouse and had slept like a baby.

'He wasn't as good as gold, by any chance?' Greg asked.

The sergeant replied without noticeable irony, 'Yes, sir. He was.'

By nine Greg was installed in an interview room with Harry Stratton, Huwie Lee and a duty solicitor who looked bored. Lee gave his age as 'thirty or thirty-one', and his address unsurprisingly as 'no fixed abode'. He had admitted readily that he'd shot his wife. The question was what the charge was to be, manslaughter or murder.

Or could he convince two cynical policemen that the whole thing had been a tragic accident?

Greg was being kind, not playing good cop but genuinely sorry for the lad, since there'd been a period of perhaps ten seconds twenty years ago when he'd probably have shot Diane if he'd had the means. What a good job English policemen weren't armed, not tempted by what American cops called the Smith and Wesson divorce.

'Did you have some breakfast, Huwie?' he asked. The boy shook his head. 'Not hungry?' Another shake. 'Cup of tea?'

'No thanks.'

When the tape was running and he'd introduced those present he said, 'I want you to tell me it from the top, Huwie, starting with how your wife left you and took the girls.'

'I felt so angry –'

'Not your feelings at the moment, Huwie. Plain facts. How, when, why, that sort of thing. Let's start with where?'

'We'd been camped outside of Marlborough for a while, a week or so back. There was a fair there too.'

'What makes you decide when and where to move on?' he asked, not because he thought it was germane to his investigation but because he was genuinely curious.

He shrugged. 'We go when Rufus says, and where, but we've always done good business at the Hungerford fair.'

'Rufus?'

'He's our leader.'

41

A gypsy king? It sounded exotic but probably meant that he owned more bald car tyres than the others. 'Rufus what?'

'Rufus Lee.'

This was getting complicated. 'He's what then? Your uncle? Cousin?'

'Distant cousin, I suppose. Lee is one of the Romany names. Half the travellers you meet are called Lee.'

'Gypsy Rose Lee,' Stratton put in.

'He's Reyna's father, though,' Huwie said. 'My father-in-law.'

'Oh!' He sounded like someone Greg needed to talk to.

'He wouldn't have let me marry Reyna if I hadn't been related.'

'No?'

'No. We like man and wife to be related, even if you have to go back generations to find it. Rufus and Orlenda set a lot of store by that.'

Like Andy and Fergie, Greg thought, Charles and poor Diana. Who did these people think they were?

'Mr Lee has been informed of . . . Mr Lee's arrest,' the solicitor said, 'and of his daughter's tragic accident, of course.' He examined his fingernails, apparently satisfied with their condition, as Harry muttered, 'Accident, be fucked,' not loudly enough for the tape recorder.

Gregory teased it out, thread by thread. Huwie Lee had a temper, was famous for it. Reyna had known it when she married him so how could she complain about it after? He meant nothing by it. He loved his wife, his daughters. Anger shone brightly but briefly, like a lightning flash, and he was always deeply penitent.

So why that day in Marlborough had been any different, he didn't know. Only Reyna knew and she wasn't telling. They'd had words that morning and, yes, maybe he'd given her a bit of a tap, no more. No, he couldn't remember what the argument had been about. About nothing. Women fussed about

42

things a bloke never thought twice about and they weren't respectful the way they used to be. No, he was certain sure he hadn't laid a finger on either of the girls. Ever. It was not the Romany way to hit children; it was the *gorgio* way.

He'd come back from a jaunt into town with the other men – do a bit of business, a bit of trade – to find her gone with his girls, his van picked clean of their ultra-feminine presence. The other women said they'd tried to stop her, as perhaps they had, but she wouldn't listen.

It had taken him a week to find her. Summers had learned after half an hour on the telephone that morning that she'd gone to the domestic violence unit in Marlborough and asked for help but refused to press charges of assault. It was possible nowadays for the police to proceed against violent husbands without the wife's co-operation, but they had no evidence of a history of maltreatment and felt it wouldn't stand up in court. They'd passed her on to Newbury to put a bit of distance between her and her abuser. It was routine; the fact that the abuser was a nomad and heading that way came outside the scope of that routine.

Huwie had wanted to talk to her, reason with her, gain her forgiveness, see his girls.

'With a loaded shotgun?' Harry Stratton said. 'Do you usually go asking pardon with a deadly weapon? Listen, pal, if you ever offend me, don't bother coming round to apologise.'

They put him up before the magistrates that morning, got him remanded in custody. With a dead wife and no fixed abode, he was staying in prison until he came to trial. In the end Greg had charged him with murder, ignoring the wounded-puppy eyes that called him a lying bastard. He thought the CPS would accept a guilty plea to manslaughter to save time and trouble, but you couldn't reason away that loaded gun.

He was taken to the prison at Reading to await trial.

'Let's go and talk to Rufus Lee,' Greg said to Stratton on the steps of the court, 'before the fair gets going after lunch, search our Lee's caravan. See if we can come up with evidence of premeditation.'

He kept seeing Reyna Lee's face, its sharp profile, its one dead eye.

'How's young Angie these days?' Stratton asked as he drove them to the gypsy camp.

'Good, thanks. She's well.'

'Any sign of a new man in her life yet?'

'What!'

Stratton's voice was apologetic, startled by his boss's fierce reaction. 'Well, it's bound to happen one day, sir. She's young and attractive and nature doesn't make pretty girls to live like nuns, you know. It won't mean she's forgotten poor Fred, or stopped loving him, just that she's done her grieving and is ready to move on to the next stage of her life.'

'Now who's psychobabbling?' Greg asked grimly.

'Don't take it too hard when it comes, mate, that's all. Be supportive. Don't let her think she's hurting you and feel guilty. In the event it probably won't be worse than for any other bloke with a young daughter. Listen, my fourteen-year-old's started dating and that's what I call bloody scary, even if the boy doesn't look old enough to be out on his own.'

'Little Ruth?' Greg said, surprised.

'Little? She has to buy her clothes in the adult department now. And when you hear half of what goes on out there, you don't want to let them out the door. The perverts that are about these days, poofs and weirdoes and child molesters. It's worse being a copper, we know what's out there under the manicured lawns. It gets me down.'

He sounded depressed and Greg said cheerfully, 'Good job she's got her boyfriend to protect her then.'

'Be ready for it, that's all I'm saying.'

But that was something Greg could never be ready for.

'What is it about these people that pisses me off so much?' Stratton asked as he parked their car about twenty yards from the outermost caravan. He straightened his tie as if it might protect him from contamination.

'The fact that you're a policeman.' Greg unleashed his seat-belt. 'It's your problem and not theirs.'

'Oh, well. We could all loaf about in bloody gaudy caravans, not paying our taxes and stealing chickens.'

Greg began to laugh. 'Stealing chickens?' He picked up the car phone. 'What's the number for Interpol again?'

'Heard of zero tolerance?'

'Yes, and I heard we'd need ten times the manpower to implement it.'

He stood looking round for a moment while Harry ostentatiously locked the car and double-checked the doors. There were eight gypsy caravans in a loose ring, their livestock tethered in the middle, horses mostly but one donkey and even a goat. Twenty yards away, on the other side of a flare of hawthorn hedges, stood three camper vans, their windows opaque with closed gingham curtains, their bodywork swirling with painted flowers, birds and runic signs. One was a mobile chip van with 'Ozy's Wholefood Veggie Burgers' painted haphazardly over the shuttered hatch. Above the cabin of another were male and female signs, the retiring cross on top of one circle, the rampant arrow lunging up at it from the other.

The yin and the yang, Greg thought, the lingam and the yoni, cause of half the trouble in the world.

One solitary gypsy caravan stood on its own, in a place where it had a good view of the others, as if keeping guard over them. But guardianship worked in two ways – to protect or to imprison.

In the distance brightly-dressed men and women were unloading trestle tables from Volvo estates and laying out their wares – pottery, knitwear, paintings, jewellery, all the arts of the professional crafter – with practised speed, consulting their watches at intervals. The fair began officially at noon and it was well after eleven. As Greg watched, an ice cream van pulled gently off the road onto the grass and paused to contemplate his best spot. The Hungerford Town Band was setting up, one of the musicians oom-pah-pahing with summer glee. An ambitious cow had strayed over from the Port Down and lowed at them as they passed with its own oom-pah-pah.

It was shaping up to be another of those long, hot summers that had divided the English populace in recent years – splitting them into those, mostly young, who welcomed the apparent climactic upheaval and went to open-air cafés and organised street parties and the others, mostly old, who grumbled that the garden needed rain. Greg suspected Harry was one of the latter whereas he, in his secret heart, was one of the former.

'No better than graffiti,' Stratton said, grimacing at the hippie vans.

'They're their vans, I assume. They can do what they like with them.'

'I'm sure some of this lot were at the Newbury by-pass protest, probably chucking stones at innocent coppers. All-purpose troublemakers.'

'Impossible to tell, but they don't look like idealists to me.'

He could give them a hard time, check for MOT certificates, road fund licences, bald tyres, food hygiene, also drugs, but why should he? They hadn't done him any harm and weren't involved in any current investigation. Uniform could do that if they had the time and thought it worth their while, if they wanted to get their arrest numbers up this month.

Superintendent Summers had more important things to deal with.

Rufus Lee was a huge man, perhaps 6'5", with the over-developed shoulders and upper arms of a weight-lifter. Or an old-fashioned blacksmith. Smithying was a traditional gypsy trade, Greg remembered, and the ones that weren't called Lee were called Smith. The name Rufus had misled him to expect a redhead but Lee was, like his compatriots, a swarthy man with straight black hair which he wore slicked down and eyes so dark that it was hard to see where iris ended and pupil began, disconcerting when the dilation or narrowing of the eye could tell so many tales.

His skin was a reddish brown, thickened and coarsened by years of attempting to protect itself from the sun. His beard grew fairer than his hair, with the odd streak of grey in it. He must be in his mid-fifties, Greg thought, but showed no sign of losing the bodily power of his prime.

He brought out the macho in Harry Stratton, who straightened his back to make himself taller while growing simultaneously several inches broader across the shoulder. Lee reacted by standing in an aggressive posture with his hands on his hips, his pelvis tilted slightly forward, making his mongrel dog growl uneasily. Greg had known tough guys complain that other men picked fights with them but hadn't believed it till now. He felt like a referee.

Rufus accepted their explanation of the charges and remand of his son-in-law with a brief nod. It was impossible to detect in his face or his eyes any reaction to his daughter's brutal death, any strong feelings towards the man responsible. 'If Reyna had a problem with Huwie,' he said, 'she only had to come to me about it. There was no call to go running off to the police and social services. We deal with our own malefactors.'

Nice word that, Greg thought, malefactors. 'How would you have dealt with it?' he asked.

'He thumps my daughter. I thump him.'

And anyone thumped by Rufus would stay thumped. Greg had no problem with that amount of rough justice. As a deterrent, it ought to have worked well enough, so what had gone wrong? 'What about the children?' he asked. 'What about when Huwie started hitting them?'

'I don't believe it. That I do not believe. He adored those girls.' But the worst domestic beaters, Greg knew, were the ones who protested the most love in between punches, as if violence were the best or only way of expressing it. 'We don't hit our children,' Rufus went on, as his son-in-law had. 'It's not the Romany way.'

Glancing round, Greg noticed a man watching them from the steps of the solitary caravan, another gypsy, not young – Rufus's age – shorter than Lee, perhaps 5'11", thinner, pale for his race, beardless. He didn't appear nervous of the police, nor even curious, but looked steadily in their direction. Greg sensed that Rufus was mindful of him and was deliberately ignoring him.

'Listen,' Stratton said, seeing him too and aware of the interest they were arousing among the new-agers and the trestlers. Odd how people knew a policeman on sight, even in a nice suit and clean saloon car. 'I don't suppose we could go into the van, could we? Have a bit of privacy?'

Lee was clearly reluctant to open his home to them, but finally led the way up the few wooden steps and pushed open the door into the narrow living quarters, folding his bulk through the entrance. The dog ran whining with him but was knocked sideways off and went to sulk under the front wheels. 'Not in the van, *mochardi*!' the gypsy snapped.

A very small woman with the look of Reyna Lee about her got to her feet at their entrance, letting fall something she was sewing, perhaps a doll's dress. This must be Rufus's wife and Greg couldn't help wondering, given the good eighteen inches difference in height, how they could talk together, let alone kiss and couple. She was dressed startlingly in what he thought of as traditional gypsy garb with flowing, multi-coloured skirts and scarves and a turban wound round her

48

head. It was the more unexpected because Rufus, along with the other gypsies they'd seen, looked perfectly normal in heavy cotton trousers with braces, a check shirt and red neckerchief, muddy walking boots – old-fashioned perhaps but nothing out of the ordinary.

A large young man also rose, bending his head to fit it under the ceiling, as Rufus did. He was in his mid to late teens with an open face and a ready smile but something missing behind the eyes.

'My wife,' Lee said, 'and my son, Lashlo. He's simple-minded.'

Political correctness clearly hadn't penetrated the Romany camp. Nor yet feminism. Lee gave a curt nod of his head to dismiss them both and said slowly and clearly to his son, 'Start putting out the ironmongery for the fair, Lashlo.' The boy nodded eagerly and they left the van, closing the door behind them.

'Have you other children?' Stratton asked and Rufus replied with his first sign of emotion, 'Not any more.'

Greg looked round with interest. There was a pleasing compactness about it. Everything served at least two purposes, so that a seat by day was a bed by night and had storage space beneath it at all times. It reminded him of a happy week he and Fred had spent on a barge on the Oxford canal when his son was fifteen. 'May I?' He sat without waiting for a reply. 'Have you a shotgun yourself, Mr Lee, as a matter of interest?'

'Of course.'

There were certain classes of people who took guns for granted, farmers mostly, putting their sheer deadliness out of mind. He'd once prosecuted an absent-minded landowner who was inclined to leave a loaded shotgun lying around where any five-year-old could pick it up. The man had been speechless with disbelief.

'Don't suppose you've got a licence for it?' he said.

'As it happens, I have. I got fed up with your people harassing me about it.' He sighed. 'Do you really want to see it?'

'No, I'll take your word for it.' He wasn't going to nit-pick with a bereaved father.

Lee said, 'So when can my wife come and pick up the girls, my granddaughters?'

The question took Greg by surprise. 'Eh?'

'With Reyna gone and Huwie banged up we're their closest kin. Obviously they must come to us.'

'They've been taken into care. A place of safety order was obtained for them last night.'

Fury flashed across Rufus Lee's face and was instantly stifled. For that fraction of a second it had been terrifying and Greg shifted uncomfortably in his seat. 'They're Romany kids,' Lee said with a cold calm that was more alarming than the brief anger. 'They belong with their own kind.' Then, slowly and deliberately, 'We will not let you steal our children.'

'It's not a police matter, frankly. I'll give you the address and phone number of social services and you can deal direct with them.'

But don't hold out too much hope, he added silently as he wrote the information down. The purple-haired woman he'd seen outside the B&B last night would be glad of any excuse to get those girls into a proper house with regular baths and, above all, school every morning.

'We'd like to take a look at Huwie's van,' he concluded. 'I've got a search warrant.' He pulled it from his inside pocket and held it out but Lee waved it away and Greg said courteously, 'Will you show us which one?'

'Lashlo's moved in there now,' Rufus said. 'No point in leaving it empty.'

The boy had retired to his sister's sometime home and looked up as they came in, his honest face happy to see his new friends again. He was delving into two large crates filled with black iron doodahs – teapot stands, coal shovels, novelty doorstops.

'You make that stuff?' Greg asked and Lee made a dismissive noise that sounded like 'Tchah!' which Greg took as a negative. Lee bought the stuff in bulk and sold it at twice the price to people demob happy at the fair. There was no law against it.

'My wife tells fortunes,' Rufus volunteered.

'Gypsy Rose Lee?' Harry put in.

'Her name's Orlenda.'

That explained her weird outfit, Greg thought thankfully. It was nothing sinister but her working uniform, like Angelica's overall or the scratchy blue serge, big shiny buttons and comical helmet he'd worn for eight years on the beat, what seemed like half a lifetime ago, perhaps because it was.

He looked around. How, he wondered, could two adults and two growing children have lived in this tiny space?

'We spend as much time as possible outdoors,' Rufus said, reading his mind. 'In summer we sleep under the stars.'

'Hello, Lashlo,' Greg said. 'I'm Gregory.'

'Hello, Greg'ry.'

'Do you mind if we take a look round your van?'

The boy shook his head, proud to show off his new acquisition. He picked up one of the full packing cases and carried it without difficulty out of the van although it must have weighed a hundredweight. The narrowness of the doorway was the only thing that gave him pause and, after a good deal of thought had furrowed his brow, he squeezed the box out at last with a gasp and a puff.

'How old is your son?' Greg asked, when he'd gone.

'Seventeen.'

'And his mental age?'

Rufus shrugged. 'Maybe six.'

'I needn't keep you any longer,' Greg said. 'I'm sure you've got lots to do.'

Lee wasn't falling for that one. 'Lashlo will see to it.' He sat down on the bed where he could hold his head up at last and watched as the two policeman began their methodical scrutiny.

What had they hoped to find? Some carefully constructed plan Huwie Lee had made to track down and murder his wife? These people didn't think that way. They lived in the moment.

There were two sorts of people in the world, Greg thought, as he concluded the fruitless search – the ones who wanted to be gypsies and run away from it all and the ones who didn't. He hadn't made up his mind yet which group he belonged to.

As they left Huwie's caravan, Greg nodded towards the other Romany van set apart from the rest, the home of the pale man. Turning to Rufus he asked, 'Is he a relation of Huwie's?'

'He is not!'

'He's one of your own, though, not one of the hippies?'

Lee spat on the ground. 'He's no kin of ours and he's not welcome here. He's *mochardi* – unclean. I told you, we deal with our own malefactors and if we'd been left to deal with that one twenty-five years ago, then that would have been a damn good thing.'

'Name?' Greg asked.

He was reluctant, then a sneer spread across his face and he said, 'John Smith,' and added, 'He's a *bavolengro*.'

'Sorry?'

'Ghost is the nearest I can come to it in English but it's more than a ghost. It's an evil spirit that brings ill fortune wherever it goes.'

'Clearly he's done something,' Stratton said as they headed back towards their car. 'Broken some obscure gypsy law, worshipped the wrong god. Should we talk to him?'

'About what?'

'John Smith: how original. We could probably arrest him for that.'

'Twenty-five years ago,' Greg said thoughtfully.

'You were stationed here then, weren't you, sir?'

'Raw-faced PC in uniform.' A single man without a care in the world, still inclined to be pimply which he blamed for his failure to get girls to go to bed with him. 'No,' he said, 'it's too long ago. Still, that's what we have archives for.'

Written, computerised and, above all, human.

One of the new-age travellers was standing by their car, leaning on the bonnet, a man the right side of thirty; tall, thin, his long brown hair badly split at the ends. He was wearing a yellow caftan above pale blue jeans, ragged at the knee, his hairy chest on display like an ape's rainbow behind. His feet were bare and not clean, the nails curving long and ragged.

Stratton bristled. 'Can I help you, *sir*?'

'I was about to ask you guys the same question.' He had a mid-Atlantic accent, like a radio disc jockey's, which set Greg's teeth on edge.

'We're fine, thanks,' he said easily. 'And you are?'

'I am what?'

'I was wondering what your name was.'

'Ozymandius.'

'Unusual.'

'Isn't it?' He backed away, making a peace sign at them, two fingers facing them. Stratton was visibly wrestling with the urge to make the reverse sign back but contented himself with taking out his handkerchief and fussily dusting the young man's handprints off his paintwork.

'Ozymandius' turned away to the five young women clustered round the camper vans and said something which made them laugh sycophantically. They were a varied lot: two beautiful if unkempt, one fair and one dark, in jeans and crop tops that left their tanned midriffs bare; one earnest in spectacles and a crew cut with dungarees; one fat and limp-haired in an Indian dress; one averagely fanciable if nothing better was on offer.

'Which of those is his bird, d'you think?' Harry asked.

'Oh, all of them, I expect,' Greg said. 'Ozymandius's harem.' He was like the Pasha of old Baghdad, only thinner. The fat girl looked bad-tempered and Greg wondered if she was getting her fair share.

'What sort of name is that?' Harry snapped.

'A take-the-piss-out-of-the-stupid-pigs name.'

'Back to Mill Lane?'

'Yep. I'm finished for the day. Things to do.'

Like tending his son's grave.

* * *

She wasn't wearing her overall, of course, when he collected her from the pub at eleven. She'd taken a change of clothes into work with her, party clothes or what her undressy generation saw as such: blue jeans and a tight black top with a silver thread running through it, making her glimmer in the dark. Her hair hung loose about her shoulders. She'd added an extra layer of make-up since this morning.

He thought she looked beautiful.

He was punctual but she was waiting for him in the carpark and folded herself into the passenger seat, her raincoat on her lap although there'd been no sign of rain for days. She was a cautious girl. He leant across to kiss her cheek and she accepted the tribute coldly, making him feel like Humbert Humbert. She smelt slightly of gin.

'Why didn't you tell me about that siege, Gregory?'

She called him by his full name only when she was annoyed with him, or at solemn moments. He put the car into gear and released the clutch. 'I didn't want to worry you.'

'What sort of a fool did I feel when Irene asked if that was

54

my dad on the local news last night and I hadn't a clue what she was talking about? That was why you wouldn't let me watch the telly, wasn't it?'

'Among other reasons,' he said, remembering their sweet coupling at the sink and feeling the first pricklings of arousal. Saturday night, not yet late, no work tomorrow. An early night and a long lie-in.

'Were you in any danger?' she asked.

'Not really,' he lied.

'You were a hostage to a man with a shotgun who'd already killed once and you weren't in any danger?'

'He was a frightened child, my love.'

Frustration poured out of her. 'Why do you need to . . . to protect me all the time, Gregory?'

He didn't answer the question since she knew why: he thought she'd suffered enough grief in her short life. Instead he said, 'Forgive me.'

'I forgive you.' She didn't bear grudges, another thing that distinguished her from other women.

'I hope you told her I'm not your dad.'

She shrugged. 'I didn't bother. She said you were quite tasty, by the way, but I expect that's the glamour of you being on the telly.'

'Let me get this straight. This is the girl who's seven months up the duff?'

'Uh huh.'

'And getting married next Saturday?'

'Uh huh.'

'Lovely. How I envy her eager groom. Good do?'

'There was a stripper.' Her face opened into a grin as a streetlight illuminated her features, but it was mischief that lit up her eyes.

'Did he go all the way?' he asked demurely.

'He stripped down to a posing pouch and cavorted about a bit like that while we stuffed fivers into it –'

'Oh, you can stuff a fiver into some wanker's privates, but I have to eat bruised fruit?' She laughed. 'You gangs of girls frighten the life out of me. I'd rather deal with a herd of football hooligans any day.'

'Yes, it was so much nicer when you were young, before the first world war, and we girlies were modest and feminine and prim, and did as we were told by big strong men –'

'All right, all right. Was that all you got for your money?'

'Not quite. He whipped the pouch down for a second before the lights went off. Nothing to write home about.'

'What were you planning on saying? "Dear Mum, saw a strange man's willy tonight"?'

'That's an old-fashioned word, a child's word.'

'Willy?' She nodded. 'I'll give you old-fashioned – peego, John Thomas, organ of generation, *membrum virilis*.'

She giggled. 'Sweet, funny man. What if your name was John Thomas?'

'Then you were screwed. I should arrest him for indecent exposure.'

'Except that we were consenting adults and you've got more important things to do.'

As if to support this assertion the car phone rang. He cursed mildly and pulled over to the side of the road to answer it. 'Summers.' He listened and said, 'Why did she leave it so late to report it? I see. I'm on my way to Kintbury now then I'll go straight to the house in Hungerford. Give me the address. All right. I know it. Meet you there in twenty minutes.' He hung up.

Early night. Long lie-in. Yeah, right.

He said, 'I'll run you home then I have to go out.'

'So I gathered.'

He didn't usually tell her about his work but for some reason – perhaps her complaint that he was over-protective – he said, 'Kid gone missing from a house in Hungerford. Six years old.' She made a small noise of concern or distress. 'I

56

expect it'll be nothing but it seems the mother put her to bed at the usual time then didn't realise she was gone till she went to check on her last thing. She'd apparently dressed and climbed out the window.'

'Six?'

'Six.'

4. Saturday Night

He liked Hungerford, although eleven years ago a lone youth with a Kalashnikov AK47 semi-automatic assault rifle had destroyed the peace of that town. Its people had not been the same since. Trust had died that day, and innocence. Even so, with its canal and rivers, its antique shops, the open downland surrounding it, this was England as she should be, the England Gregory Summers liked, the civilised England of his youth.

He'd spent his working life in Newbury and there was little to recommend it from a policeman's point of view. The problem was the M4. A criminal could be in London in an hour, Wales in not much more, or in Birmingham or Devon via the M5 in two hours. Heathrow Airport was a thirty-minute ride away or you could strike south on good 'A' roads to Portsmouth and Southampton. If you wanted to design a place to give a crook the maximum chance of escape, you'd design Newbury.

A child-abductor could be anywhere by now, but that didn't bear thinking about. Start with the assumption that the kid had wandered off on her own and would eventually find her way back.

He drove up the High Street and turned right into a clutch of post-war houses, cheaper than the Georgian ones in the centre of town, smaller, meaner. It was hard to park in the cramped close. A panda car stood with its lights silently flickering. He recognised two other cars as unmarked ones from his own station.

He rang the doorbell at number five and was promptly answered by a woman sergeant in plain clothes: Barbara Carey, someone he was glad to work with. She was twenty-eight, experienced, and could hold her own in the rough-

and-tumble of police life. She was attractive and amusing, independent and tough. He'd never seen her with the same man twice and she gave it as her free and uninvited opinion that men were good only for one thing and most of them not much good at that.

'Fill me in,' he muttered as he stood inside the front door, his hands in his jacket pockets. The other doors leading off the windowless hall were closed and he felt as if he was in a cupboard. Or possibly a coffin.

'Jordan Abbot, aged six, only child of single mother, Josie. Put to bed around seven-thirty, as usual. Mum looked in on her as always when she was going to bed herself, just before eleven, found her gone and the window wide open –'

'Had she left it unfastened when she put the girl to bed?'

'Yes, slightly ajar. It's a warm night.'

'So someone could have come in for her? I see that the close backs onto open land.'

'Let's not jump to conclusions. They're dusting the window for prints now, inside and out.'

'Did the kid get dressed?'

'A pair of denim dungarees and a white cheesecloth shirt are missing, and her favourite trainers.'

'Which suggests that she wasn't abducted against her will. It's hard to dress a struggling child.'

'He could have knocked her out first.'

'Risky. The mother might have come in at any time. So, at the moment it looks like someone she knew and went with willingly.'

'Or she went on her own.'

'Footprints?'

'It hasn't rained for days. The ground's packed hard.' She went on with her story. 'Josie dialled emergency at once. With Hungerford station being part time, the call came through to us at Newbury and one of our patrol cars was here within ten minutes. The boys took a look round the garden and surrounding area, found nothing, decided it was something to get alarmed about and shouted for CID.'

'And you rang me, which brings us up to date. Thank you, Barbara.'

'Hope you weren't partying, sir.'

'Not me. I don't party.'

'We're getting a serious search together but I thought you'd like a word with Josie. She's in the sitting room.'

'What do you make of her?'

'She's calmer than I'd like, almost resigned.'

He looked at her steadily. She had an instinct he trusted. 'What are you saying, that she's behind it herself?'

'Not yet, although she wouldn't be the first.'

'Has the house been searched?'

Again she said, 'Not yet.'

He lowered his voice. 'But if it was her she'd have surely got rid of the body before calling us out.'

'People panic. We're not always rational in such circumstances.' He thought that Barbara Carey was always rational. She turned towards one of the closed doors, a cheap, plain, wooden affair, a little scuffed.

'Through here.'

* * *

About thirty-five, he thought, first impressions feeding in faster than his brain could process them. Not bad-looking: short, dark, cuddly, sitting straight-backed on a shabby two-seater sofa, next to an unplugged log-effect electric fire, dry-eyed. Drab clothes: grey slacks and a washed-out black cotton sweater with a crew neck, too big for her, maybe a man's, canvas slip-on shoes, holes in her ears but no earrings to grace them.

A picture of self-neglect, of a woman who'd given up the fight.

Barbara introduced them and left them alone, nodding to the woman constable who'd been keeping Mrs Abbot company to follow her. He sat opposite her in an armchair, leaning forward across three feet of plain brown carpet to invite confidence. 'A few questions if I may, Mrs Abbot.'

'Josie.'

'Josie.' He listened intently while she went over the facts he'd got from Barbara, searching for a discrepancy but finding none. She didn't object to repeating it. She looked mostly at the floor but met his eye often enough for him to see a well-concealed anguish. When she'd reached the end of her story, he said, 'Jordan's father, have you been in touch with him?'

She stiffened. 'How? By Ouija board?'

'I'm so sorry.' You took it for granted these days that single mothers were divorced or never married, as if there were no young widows about.

'Eighteen months ago.' She looked round the cramped room as if she hated it. 'Peter was a plumber, self-employed, doing okay. He was killed in a car accident one December night, just before Christmas, on the way home from an emergency call-out. By a drunk driver who got a year's imprisonment for robbing my husband of his life and Jordan of a father, and who served seven months in an open prison.' Greg murmured something, it didn't matter what so long as the noise was right. 'He's been walking the streets again now for a year, going to work like before, making love to his wife, playing with his children. His name is Frank Meldrew and he lives in Froxfield and he thinks he was hard done-by to do time at all, because it was "just one of those things".'

'I'm so sorry,' he said again. 'Such sentences are derisory, an insult.'

'Pete hadn't got much in the way of life insurance, pensions. You don't, do you? Not at thirty-five. You don't think about it. The bank foreclosed on the mortgage six months later and the council rehoused us here.'

61

'You've made it nice,' he said and she stared at him, unbelieving.

She said, 'I knew I wouldn't be allowed to keep her.'

He pondered this. 'I don't understand.'

'We'd tried for years, you see, tried and tried without any luck. Jordan was born by IVF. We had it done privately because the NHS waiting list was too long. That was where our savings went, what should have been the insurance premiums and the pension contributions, not that I begrudge it. But it's like I wasn't meant to have her and so she's been taken away again.'

He stared at her in appalled fascination, understanding a guilty logic. Most people were born in random and haphazard ways, when their parents had had too much to drink and got careless, or had run out of condoms, but Jordan had been planned and hoped for, down the years, probably through many false alarms and failed treatments. How, if she wasn't meant to be?

'We'll find her,' he said.

'Have you got children, Mr Summers?'

'No.'

'Wife?'

'No.'

She made an attempt at a smile. 'Confirmed bachelor?'

'No,' he said, 'not in any sense of that phrase.'

She told him how they'd walked up to the common that afternoon, to the fair, the two of them, hand in hand, both in summer dresses with flowers on them, sandals on bare feet. 'She was fascinated by the gypsies,' Josie said, 'the real ones, I mean, with the painted, horse-drawn caravans, not the scroungers with the diesel vans.'

They steal little girls and sell them.

'Did she talk to any of the fair people?'

'Several. She bought some cheap, childish things and had a go on a shire horse and bowled for a pig which we stand no chance of winning, thank goodness. We had some pancakes with maple syrup at tea time. She had her face painted to look like a rabbit –'

'I'm sorry?'

'No, I can tell you haven't got children. They did her a black nose and whiskers, a pair of floppy ears here.' She ran her hands down the outside of her cheeks. 'She's an outgoing child, not shy, able to talk to anyone.'

Which was good in some ways and dangerous in others.

'The boy especially. There's a boy, a young man, late teens but with the mind of a child. He seemed fascinated by her, followed us for a bit, kept stroking her hair and saying "Pretty, pretty". I suppose with them being so swarthy, a blond girl . . . I stayed close but he seemed harmless enough.'

They're not like us.

'I think he is,' Greg said. 'Harmless.'

'Oh, and a man gave her a carved whistle he'd made. Funny, I didn't think gypsies ever gave you anything. I offered to pay him for it but he laughed and wouldn't hear of it, said he'd once had a little girl like that, every bit as beautiful. She played with it all evening until it was . . . it was driving me mad and I *yelled* at her to stop.'

She felt down the side of the sofa. 'I hid it, hoping she'd forget. Yes, here it is.' She handed him a wooden whistle, the sort of child's toy he hadn't seen for years in a world where children played with computers and mountain bikes and *Star Wars* figurines. He turned it over in his hands. It was exquisite in its simplicity. He blew a breath into it where childish lips had puffed so recently. He expected shrillness but got a deep – almost mournful – note. Without thinking he slipped it into his pocket and she said nothing to stop him, perhaps glad to see the back of it.

'Would you know him again?' he asked.

'He was apart from the others.' John Smith, he thought. 'Yes,' she continued, 'I can point out his caravan.'

'He was selling these whistles, from a stall?'

63

'Oh, no. He was sitting on the steps of his van as we went past, whittling another one. Jordan went right up to him and asked him what he was doing and he played us a tune, like a jig, then gave it to her.'

Odd that Smith wasn't doing business like the others. So why was he there?

'But several of them spoke to me,' Josie went on, 'said how pretty she was, how she would bring luck.' For the first time her voice faltered and he watched as she dug her short nails into the palm of her hand to rein in tears, a useful trick and one he'd employed himself. She jumped up and fetched a framed photograph from the sideboard and handed it to him. 'Although come to think of it they didn't specify what sort of luck.'

'She is pretty,' he said with the respect that plainness owes to beauty. An arresting blond child in a sky-blue jumper that matched her eyes. A big face, pink cheeks, full lips in a real smile, not the smile nervous children make for the camera. Jordan had a Biblical ring about it, like a gift from God. Presumably people like the Abbots wouldn't christen a child Dorothea or Theodosia. Too fancy.

He turned it over and read the sticker on the back. 'Piers Hamilton. Photographer.' An address in Hungerford High Street.

'Her grandparents live in New Zealand – Peter's parents, that is, mine are dead. They went on and on about not having an up-to-date picture of her, so I had it done for them three months ago, just after her birthday, and I bought a copy for myself. She's their only grandchild.'

'Can I keep it for the moment?' As she hesitated, he said, 'I'll treat it like the crown jewels, but it will reproduce well in the paper or on the TV.'

'Of course.'

'Although it probably won't come to that. Lots of kids go missing and most of them turn up safe and well within a few hours.'

Mostly the older ones, though, the twelve-, thirteen-years-olds, not the six-year-olds. He put the photo in his pocket next to the whistle.

She said, 'But she didn't look like that tonight. Tonight she looked like a rabbit.'

'Still?'

'I wanted her to wash it off at bedtime, of course, but she wouldn't. She's an obedient child in general but when she's made her mind up about something . . . I was afraid it would get on the bedclothes but she wanted to be a flopsy-bunny when she woke up and, in the end, I hadn't the heart to deny her such a small thing.'

He asked, 'Had there been any sort of row?'

'Row? No!'

'It could be the most trivial thing. Kids have a different set of values to us and something we don't think twice about festers in them.'

'For a man without children,' she said, 'you know a lot about them.'

He and Barbara sat in his car for privacy to consult, to exchange first impressions, but they were both reluctant to begin. He told her, 'I'll ring Angie, let her know it'll probably be an all-nighter.'

'In case she thinks you're out with another bird?'

He looked at her thoughtfully, a smart young woman in a grey trouser suit and black leather lace-up boots that could deliver a crippling kick. Her dark hair was short and neat, her familiar face bare of make-up, a face that was pretty off-duty but only businesslike now. She was the cleverest person he knew but her eyes on him that night were benign as well as shrewd and he was tired of the lie of omission.

'I know it looks sordid,' he said with dignity, 'but it isn't.'

'Live and let live,' she said. 'Does anyone really care about that sort of thing these days?'

'I suppose people have different sensibilities (and to many it would be disgusting, depraved, beyond the pale.) I certainly don't want it the subject of general discussion in the canteen.'

'They won't hear it from me. Just don't give me any grief if I shack up with an 18-year-old bodybuilder, an 80-year-old monk or a bull dyke.'

'Or all three?'

'Or all three.'

'It's a deal.'

He punched in his home number and heard the machine answer after two rings. He waited for the tone, thinking how long the message was, how pompous his voice sounded. Finally, 'You in bed? I'm set for the night, I'm afraid, unless we get a stroke of luck. See you tomorrow.' Then he added with a touch of defiance, 'I love you, Angel.'

He put the telephone down. Barbara said, 'There isn't enough love in the world, Greg, don't get all gloomy and Scandinavian about it.'

'No. Mind you, you're probably allowed to marry your daughter-in-law in Sweden.'

'You're probably allowed to marry your *daughter* in Sweden. You were on your own a long time, weren't you?'

'I'm a loner,' he said.

It was true, although the tabloid newspapers seemed to think that loner was synonymous with murderous psychopath. 'He was a loner,' the neighbours said after a tragedy, 'kept himself to himself,' as if that absolved them from responsibility. People who hadn't known him had called Michael Ryan a loner, when what he had been was lonely.

They fell silent, watching the comings and goings of their colleagues at the bungalow. They couldn't put it off any longer. She said, 'Is the kid dead?'

'What do you think?'

'I think she is. I think she died soon after leaving her bed.'

'Have you got an address for the grandparents in New Zealand?'

'No. You don't think – ?'

'Worth looking into. They've lost their son. Maybe they want their only grandchild as a memento.' Anything so long as he could convince himself she was alive.

Babs said, 'She's still prime suspect – Josie – as far as I'm concerned.'

'Because she's not hysterical? Grief takes people in different ways. She's had one great sorrow in her life, when her husband died, and something like that either destroys you or makes you strong.'

'Still. Single mother, not enough money, no social life, no bloke wanting to saddle himself with another bloke's kid. It doesn't take much to make you snap and a child that young is dead before you know what you're doing.'

'A jaundiced view from a sad spinster,' he said. 'I pity you, Carey. That girl means everything to her. God knows, she went to enough trouble to get her.' He explained about the IVF.

'I see,' Barbara said. 'Even so. Jordan took all her money – the pension and life insurance her husband should have had – and left her in the poverty we see. Not dire poverty, not abject, but dismal, lonely. Besides, it's become so frighteningly . . . commonplace.'

He knew what she meant. It seemed to happen more and more often in the nineties. People killed their own kids, their lovers, then claimed a plausible scenario of how some masked intruder had done it, some road-enraged car driver, some drug-crazed joy-rider, some tramp. Their motives were unfathomable, inexplicable, trivial.

But only a parent knew how crazy children could drive you, how something insignificant could blow your fuse.

They saw too much crime on TV, he thought, real and imagined. They knew how to manipulate the media, thought they knew how to manipulate the police, although they

67

quickly found themselves mistaken in that. The newspapers gave the impression that violent crime was an everyday occurrence, lulling them into the idea that their story would be believed because it was the sort of outrage that happened all the time.

'Do we pull out all the stops tonight?' she asked.

'She's six years old,' he said. 'We search tonight.' He opened the car door. 'We search now.'

5. Sunday Morning

Word spread in a small town, seeping through the walls to the house next door. By the time Greg and Barbara gathered their forces in the High Street some time around one a.m. a group of fifty had mustered, mostly men but with half a dozen women. They had torches, warm clothing, stout shoes, purposeful faces. There was a lot of ground to cover and these people knew that ground better than his men and Greg wasn't going to reject their amateur help.

Barbara was incongruously cradling a white teddy bear in her arms, Jordan's favourite, the one she took to bed with her. The dogs had used it to get the child's scent. Josie had wanted to come but had been persuaded to stay behind, to be at home if a penitent Jordan turned up.

Several uniformed officers from Newbury station, coming off the evening shift at ten, catching an exchange of messages over the police airwaves, had turned out to help, on a Saturday night too. Greg wanted to hug them.

Someone entrusted with a key opened the Baroque Town Hall for them to use as a base. Barbara installed herself at a desk with a telephone in the community information centre. A middle-aged man introduced himself as one of the local newsagents and shyly produced a handful of maps of the area. 'I thought they might come in useful.'

'A practical man,' Barbara said. 'I think I'm in love.'

He blushed scarlet and ran away into the safety of the crowd.

Greg introduced himself and Barbara and explained the purpose of their gathering in case anyone was in doubt. They were looking for a girl child about three and a half feet tall, bonny, blond, with a face painted like a rabbit, wearing denim dungarees and a white muslin shirt with trainers. He told them that Barbara would stay put in the hall to receive reports and co-ordinate their efforts.

Search-areas were apportioned and they moved off in groups of two or three, with a police officer or dog-handler where possible, no one alone, except for one man who seemed to have been overlooked. He was thirtyish, tall, good-looking, wisp-thin, with well-kept fair hair that he had to brush from his eyes every two minutes. He wore too-smart jeans and a coat that looked like cashmere. A man with no friends, apparently.

As he turned uncertainly away towards Park Street, Greg borrowed Barbara's mobile phone, took his heavy-duty torch from the boot of his car and raced to catch him up. 'You look as if you could do with a partner.'

'Oh, thanks.'

'I'm Gregory.'

'Piers,' the young man said readily. He had a pleasant voice, educated, civilised, mellow.

Not a common name. 'Not Piers Hamilton?'

He stopped and his eyes flickered over Greg with more interest. 'Do I know you?'

He explained about the photograph. 'So you know Jordan.'

'There aren't many people in Hungerford who don't,' the younger man said, walking on, 'but, yes, she's a terrific kid, asking loads of questions all the time, like she's really inter-ested, sensible questions. I enjoyed working with her, espe-cially since she's so photogenic. You wouldn't believe some of the kids I have to photograph – faces only a mother could love.'

'Was her mother there for the sitting?'

'Oh, yes, all the time. Nice woman. But . . . sad, somehow.'

Greg understood him to mean sad-unhappy, not sad-pathetic as Angie and her friends used the word, to his middle-aged irritation. So Josie had been dispirited before tonight, perhaps depressed.

'She tried to flirt with me,' Piers added, 'but terribly inept, and barking up the wrong tree, poor love.'

'You live in the town?' Greg asked.

'Above my studio at the top of the High Street.'

'Alone?'

'Yes.'

'Who told you about Jordan going missing then?'

'I was still awake, developing some pictures, bit of a night owl. I heard the commotion in the street, saw a crowd forming outside the town hall, so I went out to see what was going on, not wanting to miss any excitement. As soon as I heard what it was about I got my coat and torch and joined in.'

He didn't take exception to these questions as if, Greg thought, he'd been expecting them, prepared for them. 'Got any kids yourself?' he asked.

'No, I'm, er.' He coughed. 'I thought you understood. I'm what they used to call "not the marrying kind".' He gave Greg a cheeky grin, looking suddenly very young. 'Why d'you think none of the other blokes wanted to come out alone with me in the dark?'

'Oh!'

They followed Park Street, the road Greg had driven in on earlier, passing the silent police station that kept office hours. They paused to examine the side road that led down to the railway track. There was plenty to look at, behind and under: the station car park, now deserted, the last train long gone; a small industrial estate; the Railway Tavern, emptied for the night; an agricultural supply depot, the St John's Ambulance office and the recycling bank with its array of colourful tubs, newspapers overflowing onto the ground and a scattering of broken glass.

'I hope I don't end up here,' Piers remarked. 'With the rest of the rubbish.'

They called out the child's name periodically. Greg wished he'd asked Josie if she had a pet name – Jordy or Jody, or something unguessable.

71

'Do we cross the track?' Piers asked when they'd satisfied themselves that no child was hidden here.

'That leads to the canal,' Greg said, 'and other people have gone that way. Let's do the rest of Park Street and head up to the common.'

There were driveways on both sides of the road, blocks of flats to check behind, a new development up the hillside around a disused chapel. Greg tapped on the door of every garage in each rear driveway, calling softly, 'Jordan? It's all right, pet. Don't be afraid.'

Piers, who was at least known to the child, identified himself each time and called, 'You aren't in any trouble, Jordan. No one is angry with you.'

Getting no reply, they finally passed through the Down Gate and onto the common. Greg checked his luminous watch and saw that it was almost three. No one could say they hadn't been thorough.

They could hear other searchers calling to each other to their right, on the Port Down, flashes of torchlight, the barking of dogs, so bore left, covering the area between the road and the railway, heading towards Dun Mill lock. The gypsy camp was dark and silent, its occupants long abed, and with no sign of life at the camper vans. A copse yielded no movement except a few small rodents and they skirted the stone horseshoe, glancing behind each monolith. They stumbled across a ditch, like a ha-ha, and ran parallel with the track, examining the thick hedges that lined the fence.

The temptation was to hurry things, to cut corners, but method was the only sure way, otherwise you ended up having to do it again, or missing something vital, especially in the dark. Their torch beams played along the ground, crossing now and then like mating glow worms, sometimes lingering on what turned out to be debris. A solitary plimsoll excited them for a moment but was too large to be hers, its sole hanging loose, discarded on the spot in disgust by some

72

jogger. Rabbits, not expecting to be disturbed at this time of night, stood transfixed for a few seconds with erect ears before scuttling away from the moving lights.

Time passed quickly and the first glimmers of morning were appearing in the east ahead of them when, 'Been in Hungerford long?' Greg asked, after a substantial silence.

'About two years. Shall I tell you now that I've got a criminal record? Save tears and recrimination later.'

'What for?' Greg asked, shaken.

'Belting nosy coppers over the head with a torch in dark places.'

Greg laughed, finding that he liked the man. 'Not when their torch is bigger and heavier than yours, surely?'

'Indecency in a public lavatory. Sorry, that should be *gross* indecency.'

'Oh, that.' He was prepared not to interfere with homosexuals provided that they didn't interfere with him, but he couldn't understand why they wanted to have sex with complete strangers in the cramped and smelly setting of a public convenience. At the same time he didn't see the point of wasting police time and resources in stopping them, especially in *entrapping* them.

'Did it cure you?' he asked.

Piers raised his eyebrows. 'Of being gay?'

'Of cottaging.'

'No, but it made me more careful.' Hamilton grinned and said in a high falsetto, 'I'll show you my torch if you'll show me yours.' Before Greg could begin to think of a reply to this, his mobile rang. 'Ooh, saved by the bell,' Piers said.

Greg fumbled for it, praying that it was one of Barbara's boyfriends, a chronic insomniac, knowing that it wasn't.

Their quickest route was to join the canal at the lock and run back along the towpath towards Hungerford Bridge. Greg reached this conclusion after two abortive attempts to find a

73

way across or under the railway line that resulted in a barbed-wire tear to the sleeve of his shirt and a gashed finger. They moved as fast as they could on the dew-damp grass, slithering from time to time. Piers ran without apparent effort, faster than Greg who was quickly breathless. The photographer seemed to know his way around better than his companion did.

'Don't tell me,' Greg gasped. 'You come jogging here.'

'Sometimes.'

The waterway ran straight and in the dirty dawn light Greg could see Barbara well before he reached the place. Her body language told him she was not a happy sergeant. She'd been proved right but he knew she would much rather not have been. She had uniformed men with her and was taping off the crime scene. The towpath was narrow here, squeezed between fence and water, and those present jockeyed for position.

'I'm not sure I want to see this,' Piers said, stopping.

Greg said impatiently, 'Then return to the lock and go back along the road.' At least the man wasn't one of nature's gawpers.

'No, I'm tired out. I'll stick with you.' It was at dawn that a night without sleep began to tell on you.

The sun struggled above the horizon after the year's shortest night as they reached the bank where the body of Jordan Abbot lay, fully clothed, on her back, one leg bent beneath her, her head at an odd angle, her hands crossed neatly over her stomach with nibbled nails. No one would ever imagine that she was merely sleeping, although her eyes were closed.

A copper beech shaded her from the elements as, lower down, did a dog rose, white with yellow hearts.

Her face looked tragic and also comic: the nose black, more like a dog's than a rabbit's, the nostrils contrasting garishly pink. Greg thought it must feel cold and wet to the touch. Three dark whiskers preened out on each side and brown and white ears made a frame for her pretty face. The make up was hardly smudged, made to last. It wouldn't have soiled Josie's sheets.

One of the Alsatians growled at Greg and he said unconvincingly, 'Good boy.' Barbara nodded to the handler and he led the animal away. Greg sucked at his sore finger, although it was no longer bleeding: the metallic taste of the dried blood gave him comfort.

The three youths who'd found her stood woebegone on the towpath, uniform in ripped blue jeans with white tee shirts and oversized tartan shirts worn loose, white trainers that seemed too big for their feet, with tongues like shin pads. They looked about seventeen but Greg knew they could be any age from twelve upwards. He was used to seeing adolescents towering over him and had ceased to be made nervous by it so long as they weren't armed. They had the close-cropped hair that seemed to be fashionable again at the moment and which did not necessarily make them skinheads. He'd have eyed them suspiciously if they'd been loitering on a street corner but now they were trying hard not to cry.

Strange word, youth, when used as a noun. It contained wrong-doing in its definition. No one ever said, 'He's a nice youth.'

'You haven't touched her?' he said.

They shook their heads dolefully and the largest of them turned away to be sick at the thought. Piers looked as if he'd like to join him and Greg nodded curtly to him to be on his way. He squeezed past Barbara without seeing her, averting his eyes from the small body on the bank, and disappeared at a fast, loping pace towards the bridge.

Babs looked after him for a moment then turned to Greg and raised her eyebrows quizzically. 'Who's your new friend?'

He shrugged. The biggest youth came back, wiping his hand across his acrid mouth, a blob of yellow glistening on his collar. 'It's them dirty, fucking gippos,' he said. 'They're behind this.'

A murmur of agreement came from his companions. Greg rubbed the sore spot between his eyes where he should wear glasses. 'Have you any evidence for that, son?'

'Stands to reason, don't it?' the smallest boy said. 'They arrive two, three days ago, then this happens.'

'Yeah,' the others growled. 'Yeah.'

They're foreigners, outsiders. They steal children. But what had Rufus Lee said? We will not let you steal our children.

'Sergeant Carey will take your statements,' Greg said, 'if you'd like to follow her back to the town.' He added to Barbara, 'I'll wait here for the pathologist and the photographers.'

She nodded wordlessly, rounded up the hairless lads and led them away. She would also have the miserable responsibility of breaking the news to Josie.

'What was that?' Greg exclaimed.

Barbara turned back. 'What?'

'I thought I heard a noise, like a gun blast, some way off.'

They both listened but heard nothing. 'Must have been my imagination,' he said.

'Oh, Sol,' Ozymandius intoned, as the sun's first rays fell on the stone horseshoe, 'strong father of us all, protect us.'

'Oh, Sol, protect us,' the girls repeated.

'Oh Gaia, sweet mother of us all, nurture us.'

'Oh Gaia, nurture us.'

They wore colourful robes, except for the man whose robe was white with runic symbols embroidered on it in black. He turned his face up to the sun, his eyes closed, and began to sway and babble in some strange language while the women danced in a circle round him. A ghetto blaster began to churn out music at maximum volume, whale songs perhaps, or the belly rumblings of the Earth, nothing melodic.

76

'Bring down your strength upon us,' Ozymandius commanded in his pseudo-American voice. 'Imbue us with your potency.' He began to grind his hips in a repellent way and the girls cast off their robes, leaving themselves naked, although some of them looked more comfortable with it than others.

'We worship you with our bodies –' The noise of a gun being cocked not many inches from his ear popped his eyes open and he said in a broad Dorset accent, 'Bloody hell! You can't point that thing at me.'

'Do you know what time it is?' Rufus asked in a reasonable voice.

'It's sunrise,' the new-ager said, 'at solstice. When the forces of nature are at their most powerful and we –'

'Bloody load of bollocks! You don't fool me, son. All you're interested in is tupping these silly ewes.' The girls had hastily snatched up their robes and stood with them pressed protectively against their breasts, looking embarrassed. 'Fertility rites? Or am I wrong?'

'Well, naturally –'

'I don't want to interfere with your fun, sonny, but I can't stand that bloody racket at the crack of dawn and nor can my wife and she's had enough to put up with these past few days.' He wheeled round and fired one blast through the rusty side of the nearest camper van as every bird and animal for miles around fell silent. 'So pack it in. Clear?' They nodded dumbly and Rufus turned and walked away without a backward glance, a man accustomed to being obeyed.

'He can't talk to you like that, Clive,' one of the pretty girls, the dark one, said when he was safely out of earshot. 'It's a free country.'

'He's spoilt the mood,' Clive-Ozymandius said petulantly, clicking off the ghetto blaster. 'I'm going back to bed.' To the pretty brunette he said, 'Coming, Cathy?' and walked off towards his van – not the damaged one – taking her acquiescence for granted. After a moment she scuttled to catch him up, leaving the other four looking sullenly after them.

'She's been dead anything from four to six hours,' the pathologist said, removing the thermometer. 'Seven at the outside.' He moved one arm gently as if he feared hurting her. 'Rigor is just setting in.'

It was shortly after four a.m. Her empty bed had been discovered at eleven. The chances were that it had been too late by the time Greg's car phone had rung.

'Cause of death?' he asked.

'Her neck's been broken, as you can see. I shall be able to tell you after the postmortem if that was the cause of death.' He peered at the pale skin more carefully where it emerged from the white cheesecloth shirt, now stained with grass. 'Some indication of manual strangulation first, bruising on the windpipe, not really developed yet. A child this young – a man could break her neck by mistake while restraining her.'

'Only a man?'

'Strong woman. It'd've been quick, no pain, probably no realisation of what was happening.'

Gregory walked a few paces along the towpath and back again. It had to be asked. 'Has she been . . .' He steeled himself. 'Interfered with?'

Dispassionately, the doctor answered him. 'No sign that her clothes were removed except for that.' He indicated where one strap of her dungarees was unbuttoned, the button torn away, leaving some stalks of white thread, the strap flapping loose. 'But, again, best wait for my report.' He stood up, a tall elegant man, no more than forty, in a white overall and rubber boots. 'All right. You can take the body away.'

'Did she die here?' Greg asked. 'Or was the body dumped here after?'

'Hard to say where there's no blood spilt. Those grass stains weren't made here though.' He touched Greg briefly on the arm. 'See you at the PM?'

'I suppose it'll have to be me.' He wasn't squeamish but he didn't want to witness this far worse violation of her body than her peculiarly peaceful death had wrought. In autopsy all rights and dignity were gone, but it was his job as senior investigating officer and he would do it. He said, 'I'll be right behind you but it may take a while to get the formal identification done. The mother's likely to be in a state. Possibly in need of sedation.'

The doctor nodded understanding. 'Is there no one else who can do it?'

'A shortage of close relations, I'm afraid.'

The doctor said with distaste, 'I should get that muck off her face first, then. It's a travesty now.'

Greg spoke to a scene-of-crime officer who was waiting patiently for instructions. 'I want that missing button found,' he said, 'and if you can't find it here then I want it found wherever it is, if you have to search the whole of Berkshire. Understood?'

'Understood.'

6. The Longest Day

The world was awakening to normal life by the time Greg returned from the autopsy shortly before ten, normal for a Sunday anyway, although Sundays were no longer so easy to distinguish from working days as they once had been. As he entered the police station in Mill Lane, somewhere on the other side of the Kennet church bells were summoning the faithful to prayer.

Jordan Abbot had died quickly as her neck snapped, a simple fracture. There had been no sexual interference, vaginal, anal or oral. This would be a huge relief, Greg knew, to Josie, but such interference might have yielded valuable body fluids to secure a quick arrest and a conviction.

But he was glad the pretty child had not been violated before she died.

A couple of bruises were developing on her upper arms where someone must have held her, perhaps shaken her. One tooth had worked loose, as baby teeth easily did. A firm hand over her mouth to silence her? There were no old injuries, no evidence of previous battering that would have pointed a cruel finger at Josie Abbot.

But the fact that she hadn't been raped might suggest a female perpetrator, and every abuser had to snap for the *first* time.

Eleven o'clock wasn't late, especially for a Saturday night and it was hard to believe that anyone could have led a small girl by the hand – let alone carried an unconscious child – through the streets of Hungerford without being seen. A car? In the boot or hidden under a blanket on the back seat? Josie had no car. He had all the men his station could spare doing house-to-house enquiries in the town that morning under the diligent supervision of Sergeant Barbara Carey.

'Find out if there's a boyfriend,' he'd told her before she set out. 'She's been widowed a while, well over a year.' A year had been the usual acceptable period of mourning for a dead husband when he was young. Now it seemed to be a much shorter time, or no time at all.

Barbara, inevitably, had thought of that. 'I asked last night if there was anyone I could fetch for her, a sister, a man friend. She said not. Then I asked to use the bathroom while I was waiting for you and looked in the cupboard and the laundry basket. No shaving gear, no men's underpants or dirty socks. If there is a boyfriend he doesn't stay over regularly and why would a casual lover murder her child?'

'Paedophiles often prey on lone mothers with young children.'

'Well, if there was a boyfriend, I'm sure one of her neighbours won't hesitate to tell me. See you later.'

The six a.m. shift had long come on duty and Greg went to have a word with Sergeant Dickie Barnes, who was coming up to retirement and had been at Newbury police station for more than thirty years. As a young PC, Greg had been terrified of him; either time had mellowed him or he'd never been terrifying in the first place, except to an unworldly eighteen-year-old straight out of school after failing two of his three A levels.

He'd managed a 'C' in English and teacher training college hadn't appealed. He'd been tall enough for the police force and nothing else had beckoned. Thus were careers determined, lives mapped out.

He spent half an hour logged on to the Police National Computer in his office, since he was no luddite and welcomed all the help he could get. Both encounters made him greedy for more information and he left word with the front desk that if anyone wanted him he would be in Hungerford for a while, then on the common with the gypsies.

81

'I knew you'd find an excuse to come and see me,' Piers Hamilton said, a mischievous glint in his brown eyes as he looked Greg up and down on his doorstep, taking in his crumpled clothes and tired eyes. He was wearing a pair of well-pressed indigo jeans with a black leather belt, but was bare from the waist up, not long out of bed, his hair still tousled, shoeless. His chest was as smooth and hairless as a baby's and he smelt of a subtle perfume or shower gel, not after-shave, presumably, since he wore a five o'clock stubble as if he meant it.

Almost thirty years as a policeman had taught Greg to keep an electric razor in the office and he ran his hand over his smooth chin with satisfaction. 'A few questions, sir, if I may.'

'Ah, but two of your lovely constables have been here already this morning, simply dragging me out of bed. You don't fool me, Gregory.'

'May I come in?'

'Of course. I was having a shower but I'm finished now.'

Hamilton led the way upstairs to his flat, through a stripped oak door into what seemed to be a bedsitting room, his damp feet leaving a trail on the varnished floorboards. He moved with ease and grace as if he liked his body, enjoyed living in it. He had high arches, Greg noticed, and wouldn't have been excused National Service on the grounds of flat feet, only of sexual predilection. There must be ugly, pudgy gay men in the world, surely. Men with spots and beer bellies. Men with bad breath.

There were two types of bachelor accommodation, the chaotically untidy and the anally-retentively neat. Greg preferred the former and so, it seemed, did Piers. There were piles of books on the floor, mostly large photographic volumes, interspersed with half-empty coffee mugs and crumby plates, last night's clothes strewn around where they'd fallen, no sign of any pyjamas. 'I'd have thought the flat was bigger,' he remarked.

'There is a bedroom but I use it as a darkroom.' He gestured at the unmade double bed. 'Sit down, if you're not afraid of catching anything. Your PCs wouldn't. I love a man in uniform.'

Greg squatted on the edge, at the pillows end. The sheets were cream polycotton which was somehow disappointing, as if he'd been hoping for black satin. He wasn't sure why Hamilton's outrageous flirting didn't disturb him, perhaps because it *was* so outrageous, too blatant to be taken seriously, perhaps because Angelica had given him a sexual confidence that he hadn't felt in years.

'Why do you put on the camp manner?' he asked.

'Because it's expected of me, I suppose, and I hate to disappoint. Want me to pack it in?'

'Please.'

'I'll try.'

'I was wondering where you were between seven and eleven last night,' Greg said.

'Here, in my darkroom, developing and printing, as I think I mentioned.'

'I also wondered why, when you told me about your conviction for gross indecency in a public lavatory in Banbury, you didn't mention the one for corrupting a minor.'

'There, I knew there'd be tears before bedtime.' Hamilton sat down on a chair, perched high on a pile of clean washing with a laundrette scratchiness, his feet barely touching the ground. 'The lad was *twenty* – that was when the age of consent was still twenty-one, obviously. I ask you, how can a boy, a *man*, of twenty, old enough to vote and die for his country, to marry and father a football team, not be old enough to consent to sucking another man's cock in the privacy of his own home?'

'So what happened?'

'The privacy turned out to be illusory,' Piers said with a grin, 'in that his mum came home unexpectedly. She was Italian. If you think being a policeman's dangerous you should

83

try confronting an irate Italian mama who's just found out that her only son is unlikely to make her a grandmama.'

'I'm surprised you got out intact.'

'There was a moment when I thought I might be singing soprano for the rest of my life.' Hamilton was suddenly serious. 'I know what you're getting at, Gregory, but I'm a homosexual, not a paedophile. And, don't you see, I'm the last person in the world to go after little girls. They come way down my list of sexual turn-ons, somewhere below Vietnamese Pot Bellied pigs.'

'Anyone confirm your alibi?'

'No.'

'You haven't got a "partner"?' Greg said, audibly putting the word in inverted commas.

'I like to play the field. With so many lovely men in the world, why spend more than one night with any of them? Look, let me show you the pictures I was developing. I know it doesn't prove anything but it shows that there are pictures, and you might be able to work out that they were taken yesterday afternoon if you employ your cunning black arts of detection.' Kenneth Williams was back in the room with them. 'Ooh, hark at me! Talk about come up and see my etchings.'

'What are they of?' Greg asked.

'Didn't I say? The gypsy encampment. The fair.'

Greg knew nothing about photographs but he thought these were good, full of energy and light.

'Very different from posed studio work, of course,' Piers said, sitting down next to him and rather close, reverently handing him the prints one by one, holding them by the edges so as not to get greasy paw prints on them. 'It's what I like best, but the studio portraits are my bread and butter.'

'Much of a living in it?'

'Enough, just about. I live over the shop, as you see, and my tastes aren't particularly expensive.' Except for cashmere coats, Greg thought, and what were probably designer jeans. 'Weddings, Christenings. Not funerals, though. I wonder why that is. Surely if hatched and matched are worth recording for the family album, then dispatched should be too.'

'Would I be right in thinking that you've never had anyone close to you die?' Greg asked quietly.

'Few casual friends dead of the dreaded "A" word, but otherwise no. Was I being tactless? You don't want to mind me. My tongue often babbles without engaging my brain.'

'I've noticed.'

Greg turned his attention to the pictures and paused for a long time on each one. The Town Crier, actually the proprietor of a garage on the Bath Road, had opened the fair, as always, cheerily ruddy in his frock coat and stockings, his garters and buckled shoes, his tricorn hat, ringing his hand bell and chanting 'Hear ye' at the top of his voice.

Everybody needed a hobby.

But it was the Romanies who interested him, as they had Piers. He saw Rufus Lee who would never, he was sure, be induced to smile for the camera. He was dealing with his horse – a tough, old carthorse by the look of it, a shaggy bay, its hooves the size of dinner plates – peering into its eyes as into the eyes of a lover. They belonged together, these two, and were old friends. From the angle of the shot it looked as if they were kissing.

Not a tender man, he thought, except with his horse and his mentally challenged son. Some ten feet behind him, out of focus since he was the subject of the photo, was a striped tent with the words 'Let Gypsy Lee See Your Future' discernible on it and an ornately robed figure, presumably Rufus's wife, visible in the flap.

'The gypsies don't mind you taking their photos?' he asked.

'What? Afraid that I might be stealing their souls? These are twentieth-century gypsies, Gregory. They've got transistor

85

radios and portable TVs in those vans. The old lady who tells fortunes has got a mobile phone hidden in those medieval robes. I caught a glimpse of it as she moved. Perhaps she phones the Fates to get the latest gen.'

'Did you have your fortune told?'

'Sort of.'

'How, sort of?'

'I went in and handed over my fiver, then she took my left palm and stared at it for a while. Then she glanced up and held my eyes for a bit, then she dropped my hand and shook her head. Bit unnerving.' He laughed unconvincingly. 'Maybe I haven't got a future.'

'I hope you asked for your money back.'

'You know, I was out of the tent and it didn't occur to me. That's a damn good act.' He turned over another picture. ''Course,' he added practically, 'some of the gypsies wanted paying which is why I mostly photographed the crowds.' He riffled through a few. 'So many young lovers, look, of all possible genders. So much sexual energy.'

People wore brighter colours in summer, Greg thought, especially women – blossoming forth in fuchsia dresses or buttercup shoes. In winter they were grey and brown, like the world. Surely it should be the other way round.

He took another picture and gave a quick exclamation. He'd never to his knowledge seen Jordan Abbot alive, and the photo Josie had lent him was, as Piers had pointed out, very posed. Here she was, not twenty-four hours ago, a joyous child who knew the world to be a good and happy place. She wore a full-skirted dress, demurely knee-length, sleeveless, dotted with such flowers as were not seen in nature, a ramble of purples and mauves and violets. Her legs were bare and ended in flat sandals. A leather purse on a thong hung from her shoulder, perching on one girlish hip. She kept her hand on it, protecting the few silver coins that were her Saturday pocket money.

She was talking to Lashlo Lee, as one child to another, his face ruddy with pleasure and sunshine. To one side, almost out of shot, Josie stood guard over her most precious possession. He examined her face which he'd seen only in the terror of the night. An ordinary woman such as an ordinary man might love, had loved. Careworn but kindly. Pinched but proud. Not happy but surviving.

'That's her, isn't it?' Piers took the picture back from him and he relinquished it most reluctantly. 'I'd forgotten she was there. There were a lot of people on the downs yesterday, a fine Saturday afternoon. Ye Oldee Englishee Summer Fairy. I took that because I liked the composition, the looming presence of the mother, the guardian, offside, neglected – even, for the moment, forgotten.'

All that in one six-by-four snapshot.

In the next photograph Jordan and Lashlo were holding hands and he was pointing to one of the caravans, Huwie Lee's van. Later he was giving her a piggy back and you could almost hear the squeals of glee from her open mouth with its matching rows of unfilled white teeth. Now she was perched, tiny, on the shoulder of a great shire horse that looked incapable of movement, like a monument, like one of the sarsen stones he glimpsed in the distance behind them.

Here she was later with the face paint on. There'd been nothing like that around when he'd been a child and he thought what fun it must be to be made up like a clown, like a rabbit, like a cat. No wonder she hadn't wanted to take it off.

'Can I have prints of these?' he asked. 'They might jog people's memories better than the portrait, especially where we see her with the face paint on.'

'Sure, take these. I can print some more. Can you get them copied?'

'No problem.' Piers put the prints in a stiffened wallet for him to keep them flat and Greg thanked him profusely and put them in his inside pocket. 'So the gypsies saw her,' he said.

'Half the town saw her.'

And wanted her for their own?

As he was leaving, having refused tea, coffee, croissants and fellatio, he said, 'Do you ever wish gay men were allowed to marry?'

'What a strange man you are, Gregory, with your impertinent questions – and I mean impertinent in its true sense in that I don't see to what your question pertains. However, to answer you, I can't see the point and, as I told you, I like to play the field.' He held the door open for his guest. 'What I wouldn't say no to, though, funnily enough, is a pretty little daughter of my own. You got kids?'

'I did have.'

'Lost touch after divorce?'

'Something like that.' He couldn't bear people's reactions if he told them, couldn't face the pity that made it so much worse. Poor Josie, he thought, you have that to come, for the rest of your life, as if you are tainted, as if someone had given you a priceless jewel to safeguard for them and you had stupidly destroyed it.

Piers lost interest in the subject, admiring himself in a mirror by the front door. '"The child that is born on the Sabbath day is bonny, and blithe and good and gay." Three out of four ain't bad.'

'Ah, but are you good?'

'I've never had any complaints.'

Greg noticed an array of photographs on the wall at the top of the stairs and paused to study them. They were what he thought of as real portraits: not posed, cheese-ing studio work but black and white natural shots, all of young men, some in profile, some with their heads turned away, most in a state of undress though none obscenely so. Some of them looked sheepish at being caught on camera; one held his hands up, laughing, in protest. They were good looking, dark-haired as far as one could tell in monochrome, not too tall. That must be how Piers liked them.

He'd always thought that women's bodies were roundedly superb while men's were absurdly and angularly grotesque. But in some strange way these boys were beautiful. He realised that his host was watching him with amusement and he recollected himself and said, 'Don't bother to come down. I'll let myself out.'

Piers pursed his lips into a pout and lisped, 'Goodbye, darling, be sure to come up and see me again sometime.'

Greg, tiring of this game, turned back to say something sharp but the door had closed in his face.

As he parked his car on the common, the door of one of the camper vans flew open and the hippie man jumped out, wearing nothing but a pair of skimpy blue underpants and a tee shirt. He had legs like pipe cleaners, not meeting at the thighs; his arms were weedy and pale, his hair the way hair goes when you've slept on it badly. He was a most unappetising sight. The dark-haired girl peered out from the van behind him, equally unclad, a towel clutched to her small bosom. A considerably more appetising sight if she took a shower.

'Well, that was quick,' the man said. 'I'm glad to see you're taking my complaint seriously.'

'Eh?' Greg said.

'My complaint. About the nutcase with the gun.'

'What is your name, anyway?' Greg said. 'I'm damned if I'm going to call you Ozymandius, or even Ozy.'

'Mr Clive Peel.'

'All right, Mr Clive Peel. I haven't got the faintest idea what you're talking about and I haven't got time at the moment to –'

But Clive Peel was prepared to remedy his ignorance. 'We were going about our lawful business, carrying out a Druidic ceremony at the stone circle at sunrise, when that big gippo came out and threatened us with a bloody shotgun, said we were making too much noise.'

At any other time Greg would have burst out laughing at the bourgeoisely aggrieved tones of this householder, but the mental picture of Jordan's body, so soft and silent on the canal bank, was still too acute. He said, 'I'm a superintendent, I don't deal with disputes between neighbours.' He turned away.

'Now look here –'

'I said, bugger off!'

He banged on the door of John Smith's caravan.

Smith was the commonest surname in the country and, although John wasn't a fashionable forename at the moment, the John Smiths of England must number in their thousands or tens of thousands. God forbid that they should ever get together and stage a revolt.

So why was it that a man who said his name was John Smith was automatically disbelieved, subject to the suspicion of shop-keepers and the derision of hotel receptionists?

Not that this John Smith would have seen many shops or hotels in the last twenty-five years. Greg had noted his pallor, compared to his compatriots, the entrenched greyness of skin you saw in a man who'd spent most of his adult life behind bars, locked up for anything up to twenty-three-hour a day.

From the depths within somebody called, 'It's open.'

'So your name really is John Smith?'

'Come in.' Smith greeted him from the far end of the van, moving easily amid the junk to offer his hand. 'Sit,' he added, clearing books from a stool. Greg obeyed. He introduced himself.

'I know who you are,' Smith said. 'The head *muscro*.'

'I think Huwie Lee used that word. Dare I ask what it means?'

'Just policeman.'

'Just policeman? Or rotten bastard policeman?'

Smith laughed. 'Just policeman. The rest is implied. Coffee? I was going to make some. It's out of a bottle but it's not half bad.'

'All right.'

'You look as if you could use some, as if you were up early this morning.'

'I didn't get to bed.'

'Is that the way of it?'

Greg watched as Smith lit a primus stove and began to heat a small pan of water. 'Did you hear what I said when I came in?'

'I heard. It seems to be my official name now, at least. I was born a Petulengro, which is Romany for Smith. I was Jan Petulengro for the first twenty-nine years of my life. But my parents didn't register my birth with the authorities and, when the police came twenty-five years ago to arrest me for the murder of my wife and two small daughters, they found I didn't exist. Which didn't stop them from sending me for trial, nor deter the jury from finding me guilty on all three charges, nor prevent the judge from giving me Life, nor the newspapers from calling me a monster.'

He straightened up, satisfied that the water was beginning to stir, the top of his dark head just shy of the ceiling. 'But you know about that: you found my file, or whatever it is they have these days.'

'You're on the Police National Computer, of course, and I checked our archives. You'd be amazed at the long memories some of our men have.'

'No, I wouldn't. I too have a good memory, and I would have no difficulty in recognising the faces of the policemen who beat me to a pulp in the cell on the night of my arrest.' He looked Greg over calmly. 'But you were not one of them, not even with twenty-five years of wrinkles and grey hair stripped from you.'

'I should think not!'

'So you know I was released on Life Licence six months ago.'

'I also know that one of the terms of your Licence, naturally, is that you keep the Home Office informed of your address.'

Smith gestured round the caravan. 'I have no address. Third caravan from the left under the by-pass? Until Tuesday week?'

'Exactly.'

'So what are you saying? That you could snap your fingers and have me recalled to jail, although I haven't done anything?'

'I could.'

'I know you could. Believe me, no one understands that better than I. I took an external degree in law while I was inside and have made criminal law my speciality.' He looked at Greg closely and in silence for a moment then, apparently satisfied that he wasn't about to produce a pair of handcuffs, continued. 'You wouldn't think it possible for somebody not to exist for the first thirty years of his life, would you? Not in this day and age.'

'Difficult, certainly.'

'Not so very, not if you don't have to play by the rules. I never went to school, never had the sort of job that needs a National Insurance number, never had to go down on my hands and knees to a bank manager for a mortgage, never went abroad so I never needed a passport.'

'What about when you got married?'

'Are you married?'

'I was once, briefly.'

'Then you must have noticed that the authorities are strangely trusting on this point. You're allowed to embark on the most important step of your life without so much as producing a birth certificate. Not that those are hard to come by, of course: you go to St Catherine's House in the Aldwych, find a suitable entry in the register and buy a copy.'

Greg considered the matter. What Smith said was true but there had to be more to it than that. 'People knew me, though, and my wife. They'd known us both for years, and our families, our friends.'

'They knew who you said you were when they first met you and gradually it became a part of your folklore. Anyway, what's in a name?'

Greg decided to leave this topic since he found it oddly disturbing, touching as it did at the core of identity. He was Gregory Philip Summers and always had been, because that was the name his parents had given him when he was five days old, Gregory after his maternal grandfather and Philip after the young Princess Elizabeth's husband. It was the name by which everyone knew him and somehow that was important to him. But who had he been for the first five days of his life?

He was getting off the point. He cleared his throat. 'Where did you serve your sentence?'

'All over: The Scrubs, Durham, Parkhurst, last five years in an open prison in Suffolk.'

'It must be extra hard – for a Romany.'

Smith looked at him in silence for a moment then said coolly, 'You could say that.'

'I mean it's hard enough for me to contemplate – being locked in a cell, having no privacy, no freedom, no autonomy, never being allowed to go for a walk in the woods, or a quick pint down the local – but for a Romany, a man with travelling in his blood –'

Smith interrupted him and there was pain in his voice. 'Yes! . . . I had to live it and now I don't want to think about it any more.'

'I'm sorry.'

'I could have got out after fifteen years, you see. All I had to do was admit to the murders and tell the Parole Board how

93

sorry I was, how full of remorse and regret; but all I would tell them was that I was innocent, that I hadn't killed anyone, let alone my own flesh and blood, that that woman and those baby girls were my life. So they kept me in for twenty-four years and then they gave up in disgust and let me go. Do you think I'm crazy?'

The water boiled and he poured it onto a puddle of brown liquid in an earthenware mug, stirred it once with an index finger which seemed oblivious to the heat and handed it to Greg. 'Sorry, no milk. I could probably coax some from the goat.'

'Don't bother!' It was hot and Greg blew on it for a while. He'd tasted bottled coffee with chicory as a child, long ago. It didn't smell bad at all. He sipped tentatively and, feeling he could no longer avoid answering the question, said, 'Some might say so.'

'Some might say so,' Smith agreed, 'and many did: fellow prisoners, warders, members of the Parole Board. But what do *you* say?'

Greg hesitated and Smith continued, 'If you'd been locked up for fifteen years, far away from the smell of the countryside, the patter of rain on the roof of your van in autumn, the moss for your bed in the summer and the stars themselves for your canopy; and all you had to do to get out was to tell a lie – a handful of words that would haunt you for the rest of your life, that would murder your wife and babies over again – would you do it?'

'I don't know that I would.'

'Then you and I are two men who think alike, and perhaps the only two in this God-forsaken country.' He raised his earthenware mug in salute. 'Good health!'

'If it came to the point,' Greg murmured, not returning the toast, 'if I was tested, I don't know if I would have your strength.'

'Honour. Do you know what that means?'

'I like to think so.'

'Good.'

They drank coffee companionably for a while. Then Greg said, 'It must be hard to adjust to life outside after so long.'

'That's what everyone thinks but I don't find it so. People say England's changed – that the *world's* changed – out of all recognition in the last twenty-five years, and so it has, but they don't keep prisoners in lead-lined caskets. I had TV, radio, newspapers, books –'

'How would a man stay sane without books?' Greg commented.

'Indeed! My last year in the open prison I went out every day to a job in the local B&Q, stacking shelves. I wasn't expecting to find Ted Heath still in Number Ten and Rod Stewart top of the pops. I didn't faint the first time I bought a loaf of bread and it cost seventy-five pence.'

'Yes. No. I hadn't thought.'

'No one thinks about what it's like. They don't want to.'

'What are you living on now? The dole?'

He shook his head. 'Never stay anywhere long enough to claim it and I don't want to because that would be another form of prison. I can catch a rabbit if I'm hungry and I have a little money. They don't exactly pay you well for work you do inside but it's surprising how it adds up over twenty-four years, with compound interest. When that runs out I shall find some work to do, but I'm not fussed about it. Do you know the legend of the Romany ancestry?'

'Can't say I do.'

'We're not descended from Adam and Eve, like the rest of you, but from Adam and his first wife Lilith. Thus we were born without original sin and are not doomed to work and suffer as other men are.'

'How convenient.'

'Isn't it? Although I seem inexplicably to have done my share of both.'

'So you didn't kill your family?'

'I did not.'

Greg looked at him for a moment. A man who'd spent half a lifetime in prison had learnt to give nothing away, as a man who'd spent half a lifetime in the police force had learnt to give nothing away. 'Do you know who did?'

'Not for sure. That's one of the reasons I'm here, one of the reasons I've come back to the people who cast me out, who would have strung me up in an instant as your law hadn't the guts to do.'

'You're not . . . going to do anything stupid, are you?'

Smith laughed. 'Why change the habits of a lifetime?'

'Because the law takes a dim view of personal revenge.'

'I know it.'

'Have you got a gun?'

'Me? A lifer out on licence? Are you serious?'

'That's not an answer,' Greg said. 'Just the imposition of an assumption.' He gave him the benefit of the doubt. 'How old were your daughters?'

'Six and four.'

'I'm sorry.'

'Yes, so am I.'

Greg felt in his pocket and took out the carved whistle. 'Your handiwork, I believe.'

Smith didn't need to examine it. 'Yes, that's mine. Where did you get it?'

'You gave it to a girl at the fair yesterday. When her mother tried to pay you for it you said it was a gift because you'd once had a little girl like her.'

'I remember. She was a dear little thing with long blond hair and the smile of an angel.'

'You once had a daughter of six, the same age as Jordan. That was her name – Jordan Abbot.'

'And she gave it to you? There's no gratitude among the young these days. I suppose she prefers the Teletubbies or whatever the latest craze is.'

'Jordan Abbot is dead,' Greg said. 'Taken from her bed in Hungerford and murdered some time last night, her body dumped by the canal. Like your daughter, she will never be older than six.' Smith took in a sharp breath. 'Oh, don't worry. I've not come to accuse you, although there are some in the town who would blame the gypsies.'

'Naturally. It's so much more convenient to blame the stranger, the outsider, than to contemplate the possibility that it was one of your own.' He looked up and said sharply, 'What's going on?'

'Good question.' Greg became aware of a growing noise outside, aware that he'd been aware of it for some minutes without its really registering. His mind analysed it in a flash: people, angry people, lots of them, furious, shouting people. Horses neighed in panic. Dogs barked impotently. Not far away, a woman screamed.

Smith pulled the door open and stared out for a moment. Then he turned back to Greg and said,

'It's the lynch mob.'

7. The Longest Morning

Gregory raced to his car and used the telephone to call for back up. It would take a while and meantime he was going to have to handle this as best he could, although he knew from experience that a rabble bent on summary justice does not listen to the calm voice of constabulary reason. Control assured him that a couple of patrol cars in the area were on their way and that somebody should make it there within ten minutes, but ten minutes was a long time when a pack had scented blood.

There must be forty men in all, although eight or ten of them were the enthusiasts, the ones who were inciting and exciting the rest, some of whom looked uncomfortable now that the hot rhetoric of half an hour ago – the banging on neighbouring doors, the whispered phone calls, the massing outside the Town Hall – had become a cold reality on the common. These latter were the ones he would have to work on.

He recognised near the front the three boys who'd found the body, the first accusers, their eyes still haunted by what they'd seen. Most of the mob was made up of last night's searchers, in fact – sensible, responsible men, family men, men with so much to lose from this idiocy, but urging each other on with a conviction of their righteousness, a distrust of the state's law, a demand for what they saw as justice. Above all, with an overwhelming sense of outrage. Their faces were blank, almost vacant. They were on a mission and had emptied their minds of any obstacle to it.

It was one of the most frightening things he'd ever seen, since he knew that there was, at this moment, no atrocity of which they were not capable. Glancing back the way he'd come, he saw that John Smith had vanished, his caravan left open and abandoned. Sensible man.

It was Mrs Lee who'd screamed, Lashlo's mother. Since it was for Lashlo that these men had come.

Their ringleader was a tall, fair man of forty whom Greg knew by sight but could not at that moment name. He was overweight, red-faced, his pale eyes disappearing into the thread-veined flesh of his cheeks. His chins folded into his neck like a flight of well-trodden steps. He wore fawn corduroy trousers and a brown tweed jacket with leather patches on the elbows, but was nothing like a benign schoolmaster.

'Give us the queer boy,' he called out in a ringing tone, 'the one that's not right in the head, and no one else'll get hurt.'

The rest of the Romanies came to their doors or windows but they were outnumbered and playing a waiting game. There was a fatalism on their weathered faces, the legacy of generations of persecution. If the sacrifice of one would save the whole community then there had been times when such sacrifices had been made.

Greg sought about for a weapon, although he couldn't hope to take on this mob single-handed. He picked up his torch and a round-headed walking stick that he kept in the boot. They were better than nothing. Possibly. What he must manufacture out of nowhere was time.

Enlightenment came to him and he shouted, 'Mr Templeton!' The leader spun round and stared at him, his eyes ablaze with a temporary, dumb madness. 'George Templeton,' Greg said again, walking a few steps towards him, the cane clenched in front of him with a fist at either end, speaking slowly and clearly. 'You know me. I'm Superintendent Summers from Newbury CID. I live in Kintbury. You mended my garden fence for me after the storms last autumn.' He was trying to look like an authority figure. Half of police work was bluff, although it wasn't always clear which half.

'This is an unlawful assembly,' he continued, 'and I must ask you and your followers to disperse peacefully.'

Templeton spat deliberately on the ground. 'You're not needed here, copper. The time for your sort is past, since if you'd an ounce of gumption you'd have arrested the boy hours ago. We, the honest people of Hungerford, will deal with this matter as it should be dealt with.'

His pomposity, his verbose rhetoric, might have been funny if it hadn't been so chilling.

A metal wrench whizzed past Greg's head, missing his left ear by inches and bouncing across his car bonnet with a clang – one, two, three times, like a demented peel of church bells. The mob jeered, bayed and whistled, and he knew that he'd lost them.

As he stood, more helpless than he'd felt in his life, weighing up his options, Greg heard Mrs Lee shout, 'No! No, Lashlo, no!' He saw the boy lope across the open space from his parents' van towards the one belonging to Huwie Lee, the one where he'd been sleeping for the past two nights. The mob was after him in an instant, a yapping, ululating pack of hounds after this most graceless of stags as it ran for home. He reached the van just ahead of them and slammed the door shut behind him, crashing the bolts to. Unable to break it in, the rioters began to rock the van back and forth, smashing the windows, heaving it to an angle where it must surely topple over at any minute.

Around them animals were beginning to panic, sensing hate, smelling fear. A grey horse wrenched free of its tether and kicked out in all directions before bolting across the downs, pursued by two cursing gypsy lads. The nanny goat spread her back legs and pissed long and hard on the ground.

Greg could hear sirens now but far away, much farther away than he would have liked.

He couldn't just stand there. 'Please!' he yelled desperately, hurling himself into the thick of them. 'Please! Stop this madness. Think.' They buffeted him from side to side, punching, bruising, scratching and biting. He lost hold of his pathetic weapons in the first thirty seconds. He clung on to passing arms, knowing that if he fell he'd be trampled beneath their heedless feet. Dimly, he heard the camper vans start their rackety engines. The hippies were getting out of here. Fast.

'Help me!' he yelled at them futilely. 'Peel, you bastard, help me.' Clive Peel's van backed into one of the standing stones with an almighty crunch, then broke away from it, back bumper parting company with the bodywork, licence plate crumpling to the ground, leaving the upright swaying like a Saturday-night drunk at Casualty, as his van led the stampede away.

The Romanies exchanged looks, sighed, and launched themselves into battle. They were so distinctive in appearance that they might as well have been wearing the uniform of an opposing and wearyingly outnumbered army. Greg saw one of them smashed in the face and kicked as he fell to the ground; another became a punchbag. A third was a more doughty fighter, kicking his assailant in the groin, then bringing his knee up in his face as he doubled over, bloodying his nose.

Attaboy! Greg thought before three heavyweights dropped on the man from differing directions.

'Fire the van!' someone in the mob shouted. 'Burn him!' And the rest took up the chant, a sinister litany. 'Burn him! Burn him! Burn him!' Cooking fires smouldered around them, built to simmer all day, and the men began to kindle lighted brands from them, as the van fell back into an upright position once more and Lashlo's terrified face could be seen at one of the shattered windows.

'No!' Greg yelled. 'It's murder. Murder. Do you hear me? Murder!'

The firebrands burnt invisible but deadly in the clear June light.

'This isn't right.' A lone voice, the undersized newsagent who'd provided the maps last night, demurred, but was shouted down. A bigger man seized him by the collar and threatened him, drawing him up face to face. Who wasn't with them was against them. Greg saw panic in the shopkeeper's eyes, panic and apology. He tried to make his way towards him, in an attempt to rally the more sane members of the mob, along with any gypsies who were still standing, but a foot hooked deliberately round his ankle sent him staggering, clutching.

And then Rufus Lee was on the steps of Huwie's van, pointing his shotgun at the crowd. He was an impressive figure and they hesitated for a moment until George Templeton threw back his head and laughed, a sound wiped clean of mirth. He swept his hand round, indicating his followers. 'How many of us can you shoot, gippo, before we take you?'

'Only two,' Rufus said smoothly. 'So who's volunteering?' He levelled the gun at Templeton's head. 'I'll start with you, shall I, fatso?'

It gave the builder a moment's pause, time enough for Greg to regain his balance. He gave up his attempt to unite the voices of reason into a sane song and began to force his way through the crowd towards the van, desperate to prevent the bloodshed that now seemed inevitable. He stalled in amazement as John Smith appeared from nowhere, slithering across the roof of the van, and seized Rufus from behind, pushing up the barrel of his gun as his finger tightened automatically on the trigger, discharging it harmlessly into the air.

'Damn you, Jan!' the gypsy leader yelled. 'Damn you to hell forever.'

The crowd cheered Smith as he wrested the gun from Lee and pushed the man off the steps onto the grass with his foot. He was much smaller and lighter than Rufus and yet he had no trouble in gaining the ascendancy. He stood for a moment looking down at him, the conqueror, sweat fresh on his face and muscular forearms. With the gun cocked over his shoulder he was like a soldier doing drill.

'What the hell do you think you're doing?' Greg demanded, now fighting his way forward again.

Smith broke open the shotgun, pocketed the ammunition and let it fall to his feet, then held up his hands for silence and, amazingly, got it. He had the voice of a preacher, a Billy Graham. It was a voice that commanded respect, carrying easily over the heads of the townspeople. 'If the boy dies here today you will all of you, individually and together, be guilty of premeditated murder. You will serve a life sentence for murder. Does any of you know what that is like?'

He was losing his audience. His quiet authority, his audacity, had captured them for a moment, but now that moment was passing and angry murmurs ran among them like will-o-the-wisp. This was just another dirty, murdering gippo and he wasn't going to tell them what to do.

Until he said, 'Because I do.' They fell silent again. 'I know the days that are as long as a week, the weeks that are as long as a year, the years that are, each of them, a decade. I know the dismal loneliness of one man trapped among a thousand uncongenial souls, the haunting nights of his thoughts. What man of you here has the courage for that?'

There was complete silence for perhaps ten seconds, then, 'I do!' Templeton shouted and the cry was taken up around him. Even the ones Greg had earlier identified as less certain were now swept up in the adrenalin of the bloodlust, even the newsagent, banging his fist repeatedly in the air, chanting.

'I do! I do! I do!'

The men struggled once more towards the van and its terrified occupant, falling over each other in their urge to kindle the ultimate bonfire from the common's brown grass.

But Smith had delayed them long enough. Two police cars and a van screamed to a halt on the downs at that moment, disgorging a dozen men in riot gear with helmets and shields. More sirens were clearly audible now, coming from the other direction, heading their way. The crowd dispersed in a noisy panic, bumping into each other, crashing into the ditch, heading for railway line and canal and gate, their adrenalin drained now that they were the ones who might get hurt. A handful stayed to put up a fight, quickly subdued.

'Thank you, God,' Greg murmured. 'Dear God, thank you.'

He bent and picked up his torch which had been kicked under the nearest van. He clicked it on and off in vain. Broken, but at least it wasn't his head. He retrieved his walking stick and resisted the urge, rising in his gorge for a second, to swipe the nearest mobster across the back of the neck with it. He settled for venting his frustration on the ground.

'Stupid, fucking bastards,' he muttered, as clumps of earth and grass skittered up around him.

'Good job you were here, sir,' a PC said cheerfully as he frog-marched a chastened man away.

'Oh, yes. I was a great help.'

But he'd summoned assistance and a truly brave man knows when he's outnumbered. He went to the aid of a couple of fallen Romanies. They were cut and bruised but walking wounded. They muttered incomprehensible curses at him as he tried to help them, making no distinction between him and the murderous rabble. The *gorgio* was the enemy and the *muscro* was the worst of the *gorgios*.

Another siren disturbed the peace as an ambulance pulled off the road and two men emerged with a stretcher, but the Romanies were having none of it and wouldn't go with them and they soon gave up the struggle. 'I've had worse,' one of them said in a deep bass voice. 'I'm not going to no fucking *gorgio* hospital.' They took the man with the bloody nose in the end, although he had nothing worse than a messy face and sore balls.

Within a few minutes two-thirds of the mob had run away. A die-hard core of perhaps twenty had been arrested and taken off to Newbury.

Smith, who'd been watching the scene with a slight smile on his face, now jumped gracefully down from the steps and held out a hand to the still recumbent Rufus, who ignored it pointedly and got up by himself, brushing grass from his clothes.

'You're a stubborn old sod, Rufus,' Smith said. 'You could have got yourself killed then, but I don't expect thanks.'

'Good!' Rufus said. 'Because you'd wait until hell freezes over.'

Smith banged on the door of the caravan. 'Lashlo? It's all right. You can come out now. They've gone.' There was no reply. 'Tell him, Rufus. You're the only one he'll listen to.'

'Lashlo?' Rufus's voice was gentle, as Greg hadn't heard it before, like a horse coper handling a fearful mare. 'It's all right, boy. Come out.'

The door slowly opened and the frightened face of a child, superimposed on a man's features, looked out at them, its eyes swollen red with tears. Rufus silently held out his hand and the boy took it and followed his father down the steps.

'*Daya?*' he said.

'I'm here, Lashlo.' Mrs Lee stepped forward from the shadow of her van and hugged him. Her head reached barely to his chest and her arms were level with his waist but there was no doubting who was the stronger here. After a moment she released him and looked up at him. 'It's all right. Everything will be all right.'

'I'd like you to come down to the station with me, Lashlo,' Greg said, 'and answer a few questions about the death of Jordan Abbot –'

'No!' Lashlo yelled and dived back up into the caravan. 'No!'

'You're as bad as they are!' his mother snapped. 'There's no difference between you.'

'Are you arresting him?' Smith demanded.

'Not unless I have to. I thought he might like to come voluntarily and make a statement like a good public-spirited citizen.' Greg nodded to two of the policemen who remained with him and they went into the van without ceremony and dragged the boy out.

'Oh, very voluntary,' Smith said.

'He's got a few questions to answer. And it's also for his protection.' Greg turned to Rufus who was silent, lost in uneasy thought. 'Although he's seventeen, he can have a responsible adult with him, given his mental handicap.'

'Yes, I'll come.'

'I'll come too,' Mrs Lee said and Rufus answered curtly, 'This is man's work.' Husband and wife looked at each other and something unspoken passed between them and the woman acquiesced.

'And get yourself a solicitor,' Greg said. 'Do you know one?'

'What do you think?'

'Then we'll find you one. Do you need a lift to Newbury police station?'

Rufus said simply, 'I'll follow you to the station under my own steam.'

'I'm not doing it,' Josie Abbot said, 'and that's that. I've seen them on TV and they're obscene.'

'It really can help,' Barbara told her. 'When viewers see the photograph of Jordan, see you, hear that you're a widow, that Jordan was all you had –' Josie began to cry silently. 'Sorry,' Barbara said. She sat down next to Josie on the sofa and put her arms round her. Josie laid her head on Barbara's shoulder and sobbed. 'But they pull out all the stops then,' Barbara went on, 'and somebody must have seen something.'

'I've seen them,' Josie repeated, making a visible effort to compose herself. 'I've seen the mothers and fathers crying on TV, cried with them, eaten my heart out with pity for them, cursed the sick strangers who prey on children. Then, a week later, I hear that the police have arrested them, that mother and father, and charged them with the crime, with the murder

106

of their own child.' She turned her pink eyes up to Barbara. 'That's what you think, isn't it?'

'Certainly not.'

'But it's in your mind, as a possibility.' Barbara didn't answer, but glanced quickly away, unable to meet her gaze. 'Thank you for not lying to me any more.'

Barbara seldom felt confused but at that moment she couldn't make out if she was dealing with a cruelly wounded mother or a calculating murderer. An instinct in her guts told her that she hadn't yet heard the full story, that something more was buried deep behind this nondescript woman's sad eyes. There was guilt here, terrible guilt, that was certain. Yet mothers whose children died *did* feel guilty, however helpless they might have been to prevent the tragedy.

'If . . .' Barbara began. 'If there was anything you wanted to tell me . . .'

'There isn't.'

'It's so much easier in the end, Josie. Such a terrible weight taken away.'

'No.'

'If you were protecting someone, some man –'

'No.'

'Then what shall I tell them?'

'All right!' More calmly. 'All right. I'll do it.'

'I'll be with you,' Barbara said, 'every minute,' and squeezed her hand.

'Thank you for filling my cells to bursting point,' the custody sergeant grumbled, 'and making my life a misery.'

'They're facing serious charges,' Greg said. 'Riot, affray and unlawful assembly for starters. GBH, if I can persuade the Romanies to give evidence. I might charge them with attempted murder if I'm in the mood and I shall certainly charge them with assaulting a police officer.'

'Who?'

'Me!'

'Oh, you. Do you want to see a doctor?'

'Of course I don't need a bloody doctor.'

'Not much of an assault then. Still, nasty business. Lucky we got there in good time, by the sound of it.'

'I called it in as soon as I could.'

The sergeant shook his head. 'We got a three-niner a bit before that. Didn't you know?'

So that was why help had arrived so quickly. Perhaps somebody back in Hungerford, some wife or daughter, had feared for her husband's stupidity and summoned help. 'Get a caller number?' he asked.

'No. Mobile.'

Greg shrugged. 'Meanwhile,' he went on, 'I'm going to let them cool their heels in a cell for as long as possible.'

'You do know there's something like fourteen different solicitors on their way here right now?'

'Good, and I hope every last one of them's been dragged off the golf course. What have you done with the gypsy boy?'

'Interview Room One, like you said.' He tapped his forehead, 'Not all there, if you ask me.'

'Nothing gets past you, does it? Whatever you do, don't let him near the others. We'll need to get the duty solicitor out for him.'

'Sir, have you got a moment?'

He looked round and saw a uniformed constable standing there, one of the ones who'd come to his aid at the camp. A handsome young man of twenty-five with an easy grace about him that Greg envied.

'Constable . . .' He searched his memory. He knew almost everything about this man except, at the moment, his name. A good policeman who'd expressed an interest in becoming part of CID, married not eighteen months ago to a pretty blonde called Tina who won prizes at showjumping. A brother who was in the fire service. He must be getting old. He finally found what he was looking for. 'Constable Whittaker?'

'Yes, sir. I found something up on the downs at the gypsy encampment that I heard you might be wanting to see. A blue button.'

'What!'

'Torn off something, a bit of white thread still in it.'

'Where?' Greg croaked.

'That's the odd thing. It wasn't anywhere near any of the gypsy vans – right on the other side of the hawthorn hedge, in fact – but the ground was churned up as if something had been parked there recently and one of those big stones had taken a battering. Oh, and there was a twisted car bumper nearby and a broken licence plate.'

Ozymandius and his harem. The public-spirited hippies who'd fled at the first sign of trouble, leaving him to struggle on alone.

'I left everything where it was,' Andy Whittaker went on. 'I was afraid with all the people milling about it might get moved so I left Chris there –'

'Chris?'

'Clements. My partner.'

'Okay. Good. Well done.' He turned to the sergeant. 'Do you know where Sergeant Carey is?'

'Hungerford, with the deceased's mother.'

'Of course. DCI Stratton?'

'Still in bed with the papers if he's got any sense. Oh, no, he goes God bothering on Sunday morning, doesn't he?' He warbled tunelessly, '"Oh, Gawd, our 'elp in ages past."' He glanced at his watch. 'Should be back by now. Shall I call him out?'

'I'll give him a ring myself. Whittaker, can you go and pick the chief inspector up at his house? He'll come out with you and organise a proper search of the area.'

'Right.'

109

The young man turned away, but Greg called him back. 'By the way, did you pass some camper vans on your way to the common – Dormobiles and a mobile kitchen – painted over with graffiti?'

'No, the roads were pretty empty and I'd have noticed anything like that.'

So they'd not been heading for Newbury. He put out a call to cars in the area to apprehend Clive Peel and his lady friends on sight. They had some questions to answer.

Rufus Lee arrived at the station an hour later, accompanied by John Smith. Greg raised his eyebrows. 'Rufus is a practical man,' Smith said, 'and he loves that boy more than anything.'

'Feel free to talk about me as if I wasn't here,' Rufus grunted.

'Sorry we took so long,' Smith added. 'Not easy finding somewhere to park horses.'

'Jesus! I'm not going to ask.'

'Anyway, I'm Mr Lee's legal adviser. Mr Lashlo Lee, that is.'

'You got a practising certificate?' Greg asked.

'Of course I haven't.' They looked at each other challengingly. It was Greg's decision whether or not to allow Smith to act as Lashlo's legal advisor and both of them knew that. What would be in the boy's best interest? Finally, Smith said, 'Failing which I'm Mr Lee's responsible adult and we waive our right to legal representation.'

'You're not a relation, though.'

'I'm his uncle.'

'You told me he was no kin of yours,' Greg reminded Lee senior.

'I lied.'

'My wife was Rufus's sister,' Smith explained. 'In case you'd been wondering why he hates me so much.'

Life hadn't been kind to Rufus Lee, Greg reflected: a murdered sister, a murdered daughter and a mentally handicapped son. He must bear the mark of Cain. 'Come on then,' he said. 'I do want to ask Lashlo a few questions, but I've got him here mainly because I shall have to let those maniacs out on bail in a few hours and I think he'll be safer here until I find out who killed that poor little girl. Are you going to start demanding I let him go, because I can't guarantee his safety once he's outside these four walls?'

'But why does poor Lashlo have to stay in jail?' Smith demanded. 'Why not the mob who threatened him?'

'Because another mob is waiting to take their place,' Greg said. The real answer was that it was less trouble.

'On balance,' Smith said finally, 'my client is prepared to remain here *voluntarily* until further notice.'

'No!' Rufus yelped. 'They must let him go. He is my son, my responsibility, and I will take care of him.'

'It's for the best, Rufus. We'll have him out as soon as the hysteria's died down.' Lee looked mutinous but, Greg realised, he was afraid of Smith, as a strong man might well fear a ghost. 'You want him kept safely, don't you?' Smith said. 'You don't want any harm to come to him.'

'No,' Lee snapped, 'of course I don't.'

Lashlo seemed subdued, not so much frightened now as resigned, his thick, square-topped fingers toying non-stop with the red and black neckerchief he'd taken off. Greg asked if he was feeling better, able to answer questions and, after a glance at his father and a nod from him, he signalled that he was. Greg held out a copy of the studio photo of Jordan and Lashlo stopped fidgeting and reached out, taking it between thumb and forefinger.

'Pretty,' he said. 'Jolly.'

'Yes, she was lovely, wasn't she? You saw her, didn't you?'

'Yes. Jolly.'

The repetition surprised Greg, then light dawned. 'Is that what you called her? Her name was Jordan. Is that what you called her, Lashlo?'

'Yes. Jolly.' A child's thing of taking an unrecognisable word and corrupting it into a known one.

'When did you see her?' The boy looked unhappy. His days were much the same and time was a difficult concept. Greg prompted him. 'Was it yesterday, Lashlo? Saturday, when lots of people came to the common for the afternoon. To the fair.'

'Yes,' Lashlo said gratefully, and Greg knew he would have agreed to any day out of politeness.

'You talked to her for a while,' he stated. 'You gave her a piggy back.'

'Who says?' Smith asked sharply.

'I do, in fact.'

He explained about Hamilton's photographs, remembering that he still had the folder Piers had given him in his inside pocket. He took it out and spread a number of them across the table. Rufus picked them up and slowly looked at them, his face unfathomable. 'The camera never lies,' he said at last, although modern technology had rendered that cliché obsolete. Now alien spaceships blew up The Empire State Building and dinosaurs rampaged through twentieth-century woods and nobody thought it strange, while only those with a tenuous grip on reality thought it true.

'I talked to her myself,' Smith said, 'as you know. I gave her that whistle. I imagine dozens of people passed the time of day with her.'

'Was that before or after? Lashlo, did Jolly have a whistle? One of your Uncle John's whistles?' He shook his head. 'What did you and Jolly talk about?' Silence. What did children talk about? He couldn't remember, if he had ever known.

'It must have been about three when I talked to the mother and child,' Smith said after a while, 'say a bit after when they linked up with Lashlo.'

'You have a watch?' Greg asked, noticing his bare wrist.

'I don't need one.'

'Had she been made up as a rabbit by that time?'

Smith shook his head. 'There was a long queue for the face painting.' He nodded at the last photograph. 'I never saw her like that.'

'I daresay they went home for their tea about four,' Rufus put in, 'and that was the last my son saw of them.'

'I daresay.'

'Is that right, Lashlo?'

The boy nodded.

'Mr Lee, I am conducting this interview, if you don't mind. Lashlo.' He leaned across the desk and put his hand on the young man's wrist, feeling the black hairs like wires erect against his skin, the tremble like the breast of a captive pigeon. He spoke slowly and clearly. 'Lashlo, did you see the blonde girl – Jolly – again after you'd given her the piggy back?' He shook his head vehemently. 'Not later that day?' Shake. 'That evening?' Shake. 'Did you arrange to meet her at any other time?' Lashlo shook his head till it might fall off.

'*Mande kinyo,*' he said, '*nastis jalno durroder.*'

'What?'

'He says he's tired,' Rufus translated, 'that he can't take any more.'

Greg looked a query at Smith who nodded confirmation. He was going to have to take their word for it that what he'd heard wasn't a confession. He could call on interpreters for a number of languages but Romany wasn't one of them and finding someone reliable might take days.

The two adults exchanged a few sentences in their liquid tongue, impossible to tell if they were angry, weary, acceptant. Funny thing about languages, Greg thought, as he waited patiently. Italian invariably sounded emphatic, although even Italians must be asking sometimes if you fancied a nice cup of tea. At seventeen he'd protested undying love to a big-breasted

German exchange student, feeling all the time as if he were barking orders. She'd laughed at him and said, 'You English, I love your sense of humour.' No wonder he'd failed the A level.

The conversation ended and, 'Can we stop?' Rufus asked.

'Soon. Lashlo, can you tell me one thing you talked about?'

Lashlo, suddenly coherent, almost eloquent. 'She wanted to run away with the gypsies!'

Barbara was in his office when he got back, apparently trying his desk for size. His secretary wasn't there on Sundays and anybody could wander in and out, and often did since he never remembered to lock the door. She got up as he came in.

'Good fit?' he asked.

'Lovely. And you a hero again, I hear.'

'Bollocks.' He brought her up to date with what he'd been doing and she reciprocated, neatly and logically.

'Josie's agreed to the TV thing,' she concluded, 'and I've fixed it up with the press office. You coming?'

'Yes, I suppose.' Sometimes he wanted to slit himself in half from head to foot so he could be in two places at once. 'Where? What time?'

'They'll come to us but in plenty of time for the early evening news. Four at the latest. Hungerford Town Hall.'

'Four it is. Is she still on your list of suspects?'

'Sentiment cannot override method.'

'Was that a yes?'

'What about the gypsy boy you rescued from the lynch mob?'

'Oh, Lashlo's an innocent, a kid in a teenager's body. He's done nothing. And if anyone rescued him it was the man Smith.' He explained quickly and clearly who Smith was and his bizarre history, his doomed relationship with the Lee family.

114

'I saw two gypsies at the front desk on my way in,' she said. 'One built like a brick shithouse and a smaller one who had the big one on a leading rein – metaphorically speaking – and did the talking. Which is which?'

'Lee is the big one.'

She nodded, as if he'd confirmed her surmise. 'Who else then, apart from Josie?'

'What about Piers Hamilton?'

'I don't know who he is.' Greg explained. 'Ah, your new friend from last night. Why him?'

'I've absolutely no idea. Can't you use your imagination? How's this? There's not much money in weddings and christenings and he has expensive tastes, so he takes child porn pictures as a lucrative sideline. He enticed Jordan back to pose for him in secret after he'd done her studio portrait for her mum, seeing that she was the sort of subject these weirdos salivate over. She was threatening to tell, so she had to be silenced.'

'What can I say? It's not impossible but then few things are. Why have you taken such a dislike to Hamilton? Because he's gay?'

'I didn't say he was gay, did I?'

'Blimey! Do you think I can't tell? And I know how you are about them.'

'I'm not any way about them so long as they don't get behind me. And I haven't – taken a dislike to him, that is. Actually, I like him. Then there's John Smith himself.'

'Yes, I like him for it. Mr Enigmatic. One life sentence under his belt. Brooding. Rather sexy.'

'Is he? I'll take your word for it.'

'There's something seductive about people who've suffered and that's a face ravaged by suffering.'

'Ghoul. He's Lashlo's uncle. Spent half his life in jail for a murder – *three* murders – he insists he didn't commit. Lost a six-year-old daughter of his own a quarter of a century ago.'

'Not a blond moppet, though, not by the look of him. Do you like him?'

'I find him a little frightening. No, *unnerving*. When someone's served a long life sentence and been released, it's as if they've come back from the dead.' Which tied in with what Rufus had called him: bo weevil, boval something. What was it? Some sort of ghost. 'And he has that self-containment that long-term prisoners have,' he added, 'although I can't help wondering if it's native with him.'

'And what would his motive be?' Barbara asked, but as if she were humouring him.

'Suppose he wanted a replacement for his lost daughter. Jordan wanted to run away with the gypsies, so suppose he said "Run away with me, little girl" and she thought, "Fair enough", then panicked and tried to leave. He restrained her, didn't know his strength. One dead girl on his hands, knowing that with his record they'd lock him up and throw away the key.'

He patted his pockets, checking for car keys, the action triggered by his last word, remembering with a wince the noise of that iron wrench on his paintwork. It was constabulary paintwork, of course, and wouldn't cost him a penny, just a lot of paperwork, but vandalism was vandalism and he was agin it.

'You off out?' she said.

'I sent Harry to the downs to check the place where they found the button from Jordan's dungarees, assuming it is her button. It would be too much of a coincidence if it wasn't, but I'll get it tested against the one she was still wearing. I'm going to see how he's getting on and if there's any sign of the hippies yet.'

'Don't forget. Four o'clock.'

'I won't.'

But before he left he had one last thing to do. He gathered the chastened rioters together with their gaggle of solicitors. It was perhaps the first time he'd seen lawyers looking shocked. They knew these men, did their conveyancing and updated their wills periodically, played golf with them and swapped risqué jokes at the Rotary Club. How could they have turned into the slavering mob that the police alleged?

And yet they believed it.

'Have you any idea what you almost did this morning?' Greg asked them quietly. One of the teenage boys who'd found the body burst into tears. He was shivering, although it wasn't cold, in a state of shock, and Greg made a mental note to make sure he saw the doctor before he left. Allegations that he'd mistreated teenagers in custody were the last thing he needed.

'Think,' he went on, 'if you'd burnt that boy alive in his caravan, you'd be facing murder charges now, every one of you. You think he killed a child but you, too, would have killed a child this morning, because a child is what Lashlo Lee is, however physically hefty he may be.'

'But he killed Jordan Abbot,' Templeton burst out, 'we all know it, and you're going to let him get away with it. And she was such a . . .' He swallowed hard. 'Such a dear little thing.'

A man, Greg thought, who would never admit he was wrong. 'I'm releasing you on police bail for the moment,' he said, while I confer with the CPS over what charges you're to face. 'Your solicitors will explain it to you, if it isn't clear. You'll report here once a week until further notice. None of you will go anywhere near the gypsy camp, nor any of the gypsies if they leave it. Is that clear?'

They nodded.

'Attempted murder and conspiracy to commit murder both carry potential life sentences,' he concluded. 'I suggest you go home to your Sunday dinner now and think about that.'

Josie had five hours to kill. Despite her promised press conference, a number of reporters were waiting outside the house and she couldn't sit in her living room without their peering in at her, and she wouldn't draw the curtains, not in the middle of the day. She'd seen them knock on her neighbours' doors, seeking dirt. She couldn't believe that they'd found it.

She sat alone at the back, in her cramped kitchen, and tried not to think about what she was going to do with the long rest of her life. For six years and three months Jordan had been her life, full time, and now the house was empty and she had no life left. They'd not been parted for more than a few hours since she'd brought her home from the hospital. She hadn't spent years getting her baby to pass her over to the care of strangers.

Marriage and motherhood had been Josephine Pierce's ambition in life, so she'd left school at sixteen, done a year's secretarial course, and got a job in a solicitor's office to fill in time until the right husband and father came along. She was patient. She'd met Peter at the local amateur dramatic society four years later. She hadn't joined looking for a husband because women outnumbered men ten to one at such events. She'd joined because she loved to act, because being some-body else gave her confidence.

She glanced at the clock, marvelling at how slowly the time passed. Sergeant Carey would call for her in the car at 3.45. Sergeant Carey was so different, with her high-flying career and her breezy self-confidence, and yet not unsympathetic. She was a woman who would choose to remain childless, Josie guessed, and for the first time in her life she could understand that, comprehend how a woman could refuse to open herself to that pain.

Pete had been a rarity, a working-class man who wanted to ponce about on stage in his spare time. In costume he was transformed. He was the Master Builder. He *was* Mr Sloane. He was also twenty-four, lithe, with blonde good looks and eyes like cornflowers, and Josie had longed for him at once. Some of the older women – married women – had eyed him up, fancying a bit of rough, but he'd laughed off their overtures, polite but certain. In the pub with Josie later he made fun of them, taking off their airs and their ghastly good taste.

It was a swift courtship. Pete knew exactly what he wanted in life and his wants matched hers. She thought humbly that he could have found a beautiful wife – a long-limbed, big-eyed, talented wife – but he wanted someone ordinary to love, someone undemanding, safe. Someone who would be kind to him. He was working for a big firm then but his ambition was to be his own boss. He was an independent man, an only child whose elderly parents had retired to their native New Zealand – a place, he claimed, laughing, that prepared people efficiently for death.

They'd bought the cottage in Inkpen cheaply as it had been almost derelict. Pete was good with his hands, not only plumbing but electricity, tiling, decorating. The only thing they'd had to call someone in for was the plastering.

Eighteen months ago they'd got everything they'd ever dreamed about: the cosy house, the flourishing business, the longed-for child. Then the telephone had rung that December night and he'd answered it in the hall and she'd heard him arguing quietly with somebody. She remembered thinking dispassionately that it was hard to quarrel in whispers. He'd banged down the receiver with a stifled exclamation of annoyance then come into the sitting room to find her, all easy smiles, to say he had to go out on a quick job and why couldn't frozen pipes be more considerate?

'Still, a few extra bob for my princess's Christmas,' he'd said, shrugging on his bomber jacket. 'I won't be long.'

She knew that he'd been trying to protect her, but she didn't want to be protected.

8. The Longest Afternoon

'Don't go too near that stone thing,' Harry warned him, 'unless you've a lifelong ambition to be squashed flat as a pancake. Haven't seen anything at that angle since the Leaning Tower of Pisa.'

Wonderful, Greg thought. These stones had been here for more than two thousand years, the open-air church of a long-dead religion, standing against wind, rain, snow and, probably, the best efforts of the Luftwaffe, until Clive Peel had come along as a one-man demolition team and ruined it. It would have to be safely taken down some time soon.

And how could three gaudy camper vans have vanished into thin air within an hour of leaving this spot? The same way anything got out of the Newbury area in a hurry – in any conceivable direction. He picked up the torn-off licence plate, bent rather than broken. At least the van could be stopped for failing to display it.

He saw that the gypsies were packing up, also preparing to leave. They would do no more business in this place and Angie would miss her afternoon at the fair. What with murders and riots, you might say that the festive mood had been dispelled. But they were philosophical: tomorrow was another day and also, when you were a nomad, another place. He could see no reason to detain them, assuming that Rufus and his wife would stay where they could be near Lashlo. Probably Smith too.

A number of people in estate cars turned up with their trestle tables, not having heard the news. They would look about them, puzzled at the lack of activity on what should be the busiest day of the fair, call out a polite query to a curt gypsy, look shocked at his reply, go closer for a more detailed account, shake their heads in dismay, confer for a moment, then get back in their cars and drive away.

PC Whittaker had led them to the spot where he'd found the button and a good area had been taped off. From Greg's memory and the faint wheel marks on the grass, he concluded that it had been underneath Peel's van, the one with the male/female signs plastered over it. If the van had been parked there for a few days the ground under it might be damp, explaining the grass stains on Jordan's shirt.

Had someone dragged Jordan's body under there? Left it for a while, perhaps while they waited for the first panic to pass and a cool, clear intellect to offer a solution of what to do with the body. Peel himself? If not, could it possibly have been done without Peel's knowledge?

He watched dispassionately as a finger-tip search of the ground proceeded, a line of men, not three feet apart, walking methodically, trained to miss nothing, not a blonde hair, not the whisper of a footprint. He glanced at his watch. 'I'll leave you to it, Harry, if that's all right.' He sighed. 'I'm on TV again tonight.'

'Could be the start of a whole new career,' Stratton said sourly.

The gypsy woman intercepted him on the way back to his car, Rufus's wife. What was her name? Not Orlando, but something like it. Orlenda. She was still in her costume and he had a moment of doubt. Perhaps she really did dress like that all the time. Presumably she was worried about her son, perhaps coming to ask for him back. She had eyes like sherry.

'I'm in a hurry,' he said apologetically as she was somehow blocking his way with her slight body. 'Lashlo's all right. We're looking after him for a bit for his own safety. Rufus and John have gone with him to see him settled at the hostel and I expect they'll tell you about it when they get back.'

'I bet you're a man who's always in a hurry.' Her voice was ordinary now that there was no drama. If he'd heard it on the telephone, he'd have taken her for a suburban housewife. He felt disappointed. 'It's my daughter's things I want,' she added.

'Her things?'

'Whatever she had with her at that boarding house.'

'It wasn't much. Old clothes. Nothing valuable.'

'That's not the point. The Zingari are wanderers and carry nothing of value with them through life.' Oh, no? Greg thought cynically. He'd never known a gippo turn down a valuable. 'But I must burn what she left behind her in the material world, so that her spirit may be free.'

'I see,' he said, and did. 'I'll make sure everything's turned over to you.'

'It was you, wasn't it, at the boarding house that night? The policeman who disarmed Huwie?'

'Yes.'

'Thank you.'

'I'm only sorry I didn't get there in time to prevent the tragedy.'

'No one could have.'

He turned away but she seized his left hand and spread the palm out under her stooping face. She was short-sighted, he thought, and you couldn't do her act with a pair of NHS specs balanced on your nose. He waited patiently. He knew the drill: Do you know someone called Elizabeth? Have you ever been disappointed in love? Have you a creative talent you feel is undervalued?

Yes, yes and yes. Don't we all? Haven't we all?

Instead she stared at the hand for a full minute, then glanced at his face. He began to feel uncomfortable. 'I do have to rush off.' He wanted to look at his watch, to emphasise that he had an appointment which wouldn't wait, that he was an important man, but she had too firm a grip on him. Then she dropped his hand as abruptly as she'd taken it and turned to walk away.

'Well?' he called after her, feeling foolish, but as if he'd crossed her palm with silver and been short-changed.

She paused. 'Well what?'

'What do you see?'

'I was looking for my benefit, not yours. You're not a believer, not in anything.'

'Looking for what?' he persisted.

'To see if you are the man to solve the secret of the little girl's death. If you know truth when you see and hear it.'

'And am I?'

'Don't you know?'

'I usually do – solve murders, that is.' Most policemen did since they were not usually difficult to resolve, the old motives, the old methods, the obvious suspect. She nodded slowly, and walked away. He called after her, 'If you foresee something – something bad – is there anything you can do to prevent it?'

She stopped and looked back at him for a moment, then laughed and walked away shaking her head – not as a negative, he thought, but mocking the sheer stupidity of the question.

It was, as Piers had said, a damn good act.

The Town Hall was full, with newspaper, TV and radio reporters in attendance. Murdered children were headline news. There would be breast-beating editorials about the state of a nation where a six-year-old girl could be snatched from her bed, her life snuffed out by one strong hand. Josie was a single mother but, as a widow, would escape the usual censure that implied fecklessness as a contributory factor in her personal tragedy. Hamilton's portrait of Jordan would grace the front pages of every newspaper tomorrow, tabloid or broadsheet, even the *Financial Times*, whose readers had different priorities.

He recognised some journalists, and not just local ones. In more than twenty-five years in the job, he'd attended many such events, though becoming the leading player only recently, and probably knew them better than they knew him. Still, they were trained to recognise faces, and voices called out to him by name – be it 'Superintendent', 'Mr Summers', or plain 'Greg' – as he made his way through the crowd and the automatic doors parted before him with a barely perceptible whoosh. He waved them away. They knew the drill: let their questions wait until the cameras were rolling.

A uniformed PC stood aside and opened the door to let him into the back room where Barbara was chaperoning Josie. She was dry-eyed at the moment but he knew how quickly the most innocuous questions brought tears to a susceptible eye, let alone the ones they were *really* eager to ask.

'Be prepared for some stupidity,' he warned her. 'Some idiot will ask you how you feel, for sure, as if they can't work that out for themselves.'

'What should I answer?' she said. 'I'm not sure what I feel. I don't know if I shall feel anything ever again.' Barbara put her hand on Josie's shoulder and squeezed. She looked neat, as always, in a navy blue skirt and tailored jacket with a cream silk blouse, businesslike. Josie was more casually dressed, tousled and tearful. It didn't do for the bereaved mother to look like a merchant banker, even if she was one.

Greg sat down beside her and took her hand. It was hot and sweaty and his impulse was to let go and wipe his own, but he resisted it. 'Tell them what she was like,' he said, 'what her favourite toys were and the things she liked to do, her favourite subjects at school. Don't let them treat her like another statistic. Make her come . . . come alive for them.'

How he wished at times like these for a greater facility with language. Come alive for them! But she didn't seem to mind, or even notice the slip. How his tongue tripped over words, instead of words tripping off his tongue. Did the articulate lead simpler lives, the ones who could ask and tell, convey exactly what they meant to say? 'Try to speak clearly,' he went on. 'Don't make them ask you to repeat things. It's worse the second time round.'

Normally the tragic mother had some family member with her, usually a man, to speak for her if she lost the power to do so, but Josie was an only child and an orphan, and her in-laws were twelve thousand miles away, their presence in Wellington vouched for throughout the crucial hours.

'Are your in-laws coming over?' he'd asked.

She said coldly, 'No.'

'It's a long way and I expect they're getting on.'

'They'll live forever,' she said. 'I don't want them here. They didn't like me. I wasn't good enough for their only son. They tried to take Jordan away from me when he died. They asked me to let them have her and bring her up in New Zealand. They claimed she'd have a better life there. As if I would.'

'I expect it was just a suggestion.' Greg would have to speak for her if necessary, protect her from this new mob, as vicious in its way as the one he'd dealt with that morning, and as single-minded. Like him, they were doing their job and he wouldn't do theirs for a hundred thousand a year.

'When can I have her body to bury?' Josie asked.

'Not yet, I'm afraid. If we make a quick arrest, as we hope, then the Defence may . . . may . . . may ask for a second autopsy.'

Barbara said, 'I think they've finished setting up,' and her voice seemed to come from far away.

'You go first,' he said.

The crowd fell silent as Barbara opened the door onto the platform, made her way quickly to the furthest chair and sat down. Greg held out the middle chair for Josie to sit, then took the last of the three chairs himself. A gaggle of microphones bristled on the table in front of each of them.

'I am Superintendent Gregory Summers of the Newbury police,' he said into the silence. 'This –'

'Could we have a test for sound, please?' someone on the ground below him interrupted, his voice a little bored.

125

Greg glared at him, a young man, twenty-something, with long hair in a pony tail and dressed in black. He wasn't going to sit there reciting 'Mary had a little lamb'. He said, 'How's that? Is that all right? Can you hear me?'

The man adjusted the microphones, pressed his earphones into his head, frowned and said, 'I don't like the acoustics in here but that'll have to do. Go ahead.'

Greg started again. 'I am Superintendent Gregory Summers of the Newbury police. This is Mrs Josie Abbot, whose six-year-old daughter Jordan was found dead by the canal in Hungerford this morning. My colleague is Sergeant Barbara Carey. Mrs Abbot has a short prepared statement to make.'

As she took a piece of lined A4 paper from her pocket and unfolded it, he recognised Barbara's handwriting, neatly flowing and without corrections. Her voice was steady as she read the few sentences, clear enough to be easily heard throughout the room. The small space was lit like a lightning storm by the constant flashing of camera bulbs.

'Yesterday I had the best daughter a mother could wish for. Her name was Jordan and she was six years and three months old. What can I tell you about her? She was pretty, but every daughter is pretty to her doting mother. She was bright but every child is an Einstein to its parents. She was strong and good and funny. She was Jordan Abbot and I loved her.

'My husband, Peter, died in a senseless accident eighteen months ago. Jordan was our only child, born after long and complicated medical procedures when we'd been told we could never have a child. She was all I had. Yesterday evening somebody took her from her bed and killed her for reasons that I cannot begin to imagine and hope that you can't either.

'Somebody watching this programme knows who that killer was – your husband, your brother, your son. Perhaps you suspect or perhaps you know. Perhaps he's confessed to you or perhaps he's done it before.' Her voice began to fail at the end, a choke coming into it. 'Please, don't let this happen to any other girl, any other mother. Please, if you have any doubts, call the police. I shall not sleep again until the murderer of my baby girl is caught.'

She folded up the piece of paper and put it tidily away, breathing a sigh. Greg nodded approbation at Barbara. 'I will take questions briefly,' he said. 'I know you understand and appreciate what Mrs Abbot is going through so please direct your questions to me.' He pointed at a TV journalist in the front row, recognising him from the night of the siege. 'Mr Chaucer?'

'Was the child sexually assaulted?'

'No.' Sometimes they withheld information like that but he and Barbara had agreed that now was not such a time.

'Then what could the motive for this abduction have been?'

'Your guess is as good as mine. Mr Curry?'

But Adam Chaucer didn't give way so easily and he forestalled his colleague with a further question, his confident voice drowning out the other man, a mere newspaper reporter who needed to remember his place. 'Is it true, Mr Summers, that a mob attempted to apprehend and possibly murder a suspect at the gypsy encampment on Hungerford Common this morning, and that you yourself prevented a lynching?'

Greg saw Josie Abbot give a start of surprise and glance sideways at him. He sighed. How fast news travelled. He would have to answer this question despite the reporter's queue jumping or the incident would get blown up out of all proportion. 'This sort of crime arouses strong emotions, especially in a small town like this. Happily, the crowd came to their senses before any damage could be done.'

'So it wasn't a riot?'

'It was an unlawful assembly.'

'And were arrests made?'

'Some, but the men involved have been released on police bail and no charges have yet been brought.' He turned to another reporter. 'Now I think –'

But Chaucer was determined to hold the floor. 'And is it true that one of the gypsies has been taken into custody since this riot?'

'One of them is helping us with our enquiries. It's still early days.'

'Is he under arrest?'

'No.' It was someone else's turn and Chaucer seemed finally satisfied. Greg pointed to a small, thin woman with a long nose, dressed in black. He almost said, 'Woman with the big nose?'

'Lady in the black suit?'

She had a nasal voice, either that or a bad summer cold. 'Have you liaised with other police forces about unsolved crimes which might be connected to this one?'

'That is in hand. So far I've heard of nothing that compares with this case in *modus operandi*, victim profile, whatever. My sense it that this was a one-off crime, an opportunistic crime, but I'm keeping an open mind.'

'Mrs Abbot,' the woman said, turning her attention without warning, and asked her question before Greg could stop her, although it was not quite the idiotic question he'd warned Josie against. 'Mrs Abbot, what are your feelings towards the person who abducted Jordan?' Josie Abbot stared at her as if she were mad. 'Mrs Abbot?'

She got to her feet, her chair falling clumsily away behind her, her voice rising rapidly to a shriek. The pony-tailed sound man looked annoyed. 'I think he is evil, vile and wicked. I think he's a monster. I hope whoever did it, that a lynch mob does get to him first, because he doesn't deserve to live!'

Barbara had her arm round her by now and Greg retrieved her chair, glaring at the long-nosed woman who looked back impassively. Josie slumped down in her seat, spent. He struggled to contain his anger.

'That's enough questions. I repeat the appeal Mrs Abbot made. Jordan was taken from her bed between seven and eleven last night. Her body was dumped on the canal towpath sometime before three a.m. Somebody must have seen something, or suspect something. Somebody came home late, hyped up, frightened, behaving bizarrely. If you know who that someone is then call the police.'

He and Barbara helped Josie from the platform, ignoring the additional questions that were coming at them from every part of the room.

'I want to know exactly what that was about a riot,' Josie said. She was sipping tea in the back room – quick slurping movements as if she didn't taste it but was a tea-sipping machine.

'There's not a lot to tell,' Greg said. 'Some of your friends and neighbours appointed themselves judge, jury and executioner on a simple-minded gypsy boy they'd elected scapegoat.'

He filled in the details when she pressed him. He expected her to exclaim at their folly, but she didn't. Instead, when he'd finished, she said, 'If they did get the right person, if they did string him up . . .'

'Yes?' he said after an unbearable minute.

Her eyes were cold. 'Then they'd have my lifelong gratitude.'

'Josie!'

'*You* stopped them?'

'Actually I didn't, but I would have done if I could. No one takes the law into their own hands, whatever the crime, whatever the temptation.'

As they were leaving Barbara turned to Josie and said, 'I'll call at your house first thing tomorrow, Josie, and every morning. Would you do something for me? Would you not open any post you receive, either via the postman or by hand? Let me deal with it.'

Josie placed a hand over her mouth. 'Oh!'

'Please. There are some sick people about and that's the last thing you need at the moment.'

She nodded weakly. 'Thank you.'

'Yes, thank you,' Greg murmured. 'I should have thought of that myself.'

'What about the telephone?' Josie said after a moment.

'I've arranged for the exchange to intercept calls since this morning. Your friends will get through but anyone else will be put off by getting the operator. I've also arranged for the loan of an answering machine, since I notice you haven't got one. That way you don't have to talk to anybody unless you feel like it.'

Josie excused herself and went to the lavatory. Greg and Barbara looked at each other for a moment. 'You're a marvel,' he said.

'And don't you forget it when you're doing my annual report.'

'I shan't.'

'And don't describe me as "painstaking" like my last guv'nor.'

'Blimey, you must have upset him. Okay, Babs, run Josie home and make sure she's okay, then what we both need more than anything is some sleep.' A clear, fresh mind tomorrow would be worth any amount of plodding work tonight.

Josie returned and Barbara told her to wait out of sight at the back while she fetched the transport. As she and Greg walked round to the front of the building to retrieve their cars, Adam Chaucer was doing his piece to camera, finishing with a flourish, 'This is Adam Chaucer for Newbury Newsround in a devastated and vengeful Hungerford.'

'Fucking ghoul,' Barbara said under her breath.

As he came in the front door she was waiting for him, in a short skirt the colour of forget-me-nots and a tee shirt that

130

emphasised her small breasts, her hair freshly washed and swinging free. Her voice was mocking. 'On the news *again*, Gregory. A riot *and* an emotional appeal.'

'Yes, dear. Sorry, dear. I'm trying not to make a habit of it. Truly.'

She reached her face up to his and kissed him. 'I don't mind you getting into trouble. I don't mind you taking risks – that's part of your job – but I don't want to be kept in the dark about it.'

'No. Understood.'

'I heard about this riot you quelled. People are talking about it in the street in Kintbury.'

'Wow! Tell it in Gath. Publish it in the streets of Ashkelon. It wasn't me that quelled it in the end, as it happens. I was just there. And I was stupid. I could have been badly hurt.'

'It's better to live one day as a tiger,' she said, 'than a thousand years as a wuss.'

'Wuss? Is that the original quotation?'

'Yes.'

'Sure?'

'Certain.'

He pushed her back against the overflowing bookshelves of the hall and kissed her passionately. Through the kisses he said, 'Whatever you say.'

Barbara followed Josie into the bungalow. The reporters had left, satisfied with their words and pictures. She thought how empty the place felt as she went into the hall, as if no one lived there.

'I'll make you some tea,' she said.

'I'll make it.'

'Are you sure?'

'I don't want to be fussed over. It doesn't help.'

'I suppose not.' She followed Josie into the kitchen and stood with her hands in her pockets. She never carried a bag if she could help it, finding it restricting, and her knuckles grazed against keys, a handkerchief, a dictating machine and a ball point pen. Her mobile phone was strapped to her belt. She decided to make herself at home and sat down as Josie filled the kettle. 'Do you want to talk about it?' she asked. 'Or not.'

'Do people want to, usually?'

'Some do and some don't, which is I why I ask. Some people find it helps and others . . . want to keep it to themselves. Just as some need to be alone with their grief while others crave company.'

'Perhaps later,' Josie said. 'Maybe tomorrow.'

'Whatever you say.'

She picked the tea caddie up and put it down again. 'Why am I making this tea? I don't want any more. It's for something to do. Do you want tea?'

'Not really.'

Josie switched the kettle off again. Barbara examined the cork board on the wall next to the telephone. There was a calendar, one month to a view, not many entries. Jordan had a dentist's appointment next week, to keep those perfect white teeth free of fillings. A shopping list prompted Josie to buy washing powder and eggs. A snapshot showed a man of about thirty proudly holding a white-draped baby in his arms, nervous, new at this.

'Peter,' she said, with certainty. 'He was handsome.' She got up for a closer look. The picture was overexposed and his blonde hair looked as white as the baby's wrappings, his eyes a watery blue, his red sweatshirt washed out. 'Jordan takes after him,' she said.

'Yes, she does. Did. No one ever doubted they were father and daughter.'

'Josie, have you thought about going to see your GP? I know that people don't want –'

'I'll go tomorrow,' she said.

132

'Oh! Good.' She was used to argument. Most people took the suggestion as an insult.

'I'm not afraid to ask for help. When Pete died I was able to cope, just about, but when the house was repossessed and we had to come to this . . .' she gestured, 'this dump, I got very low. Dr Tabor was kind and understanding and he gave me some pills that helped. Better than that, he let me talk, however much of his surgery time it took up.'

The telephone rang. 'Shall I get that?' Barbara asked. Josie nodded and she picked up the receiver, said, 'Sergeant Carey,' and listened. 'The operator wants to know if she can put a Mr Adam Chaucer through.'

Josie gave an exclamation of annoyance. 'Didn't he get his pound of flesh at the Town Hall?'

'No,' Barbara told the operator. 'Mr Chaucer is not to be put through.'

She hung up.

Over supper he told her about John Smith. She listened with a frown of careful attention, not interrupting. 'Do you think he's telling the truth?' she asked, when he'd finished.

'Not necessarily. It may be that, even after twenty-five years, he can't face what he did, can't admit it to himself.'

'Still, if what he says about the Parole Board is true –'

'It is. I made discreet enquiries, called in some favours in the Home Office.'

'Then it argues strongly for his innocence.'

'Some would say so,' Greg said for the second time that day.

'And the Parole Board? They can't see it?'

'They're in an impossible position, dearest, to be fair. In theory a lifer can't be let out until he's paid his debt to society, is no longer a threat, and is truly sorry for what he's done. It's not the Parole Board's brief to accept that he can't be sorry for something he didn't do. Supposing they did? Chaos. They're not the Court of Appeal. They'd be declaring him innocent

133

without having the power to quash his conviction. The case would have to be re-opened . . . it doesn't bear thinking about.'

'God damn the law then,' Angelica said robustly, 'and the system – the lawyers and policemen and judges and smug gits on Parole Boards who'll uphold the status quo rather than admit that an injustice has been done.'

'Point taken, Angel, but Mr Smith himself is a lawyer, did the studying in jail. God knows, he had the time for it.'

'Are you going to turn him in?'

'I should, if only to stop him doing something stupid, assuming that he's come back here looking for the real murderer of his pretty chickens and their dam.'

'Should, Gregory?'

'Should, but shan't. Yet.'

They watched the late news, side by side on the sofa. She didn't seem to mind seeing it again and he had to stop her videoing it. He thought his face looked horribly red on the screen, as if he was about to have a stroke, although he knew himself to be a pale man.

In Hungerford parents were keeping their children in that night, boys as well as girls. In Hungerford, in Kintbury, in Froxfield, in Chilton, in Inkpen. In Portsmouth and Norwich and Exeter, in Aberdeen.

'She was so pretty,' Angelica said, her voice full of sorrow.

'They say the good die young.'

'Yes,' she said. 'How can she bear it? The mother?'

'Because she must. Because we have to bear things that seem unbearable. Because there's no alternative to bearing them.'

'Except suicide.'

'Except that.'

After a moment, she said, 'You need a hair cut.'

'And the police are appealing for witnesses,' the reporter concluded, as Greg's office telephone number came up on the screen. 'This is Adam Chaucer for Newbury Newsround, in a devastated and vengeful Hungerford.'

'I don't like him,' Angelica said.

'Who?'

'Chaucer.'

'Well, you can't tell what someone's like on TV, you know.'

She shook her head, impatient at his condescending tone. 'He comes in the shop. He's rude and snappy and overbearing and he calls me "Love", which is bad enough, but he says it not in a nice way but in a patronising way, like he thinks I'm beneath his notice, that everyone is, because he's on the telly.'

'I'm surprised he does his own shopping,' Greg said, after digesting this.

'Oh, his sort live alone. They don't let a girl stay the night at their place in case she gets ideas. What he does is pick up some woman at some do in London, go back to her place, give her one, hang on half an hour out of bored politeness, then get dressed and drive back up the M4 at a hundred miles an hour in his big, red, shiny car with leather upholstery.'

He was surprised at her vehemence. For a moment it sounded as if she hated men. All men. 'I'll tell the traffic boys to look out for him.'

'Takes a long, hot shower to wash her yucky stickiness off him. Says he'll call. Doesn't.'

He knew nothing of her sexual history before Fred, didn't want to. There must have been men, probably lots of them, from what he knew of her generation. Men who left after half an hour and didn't call.

'Tell him your boyfriend's always on the telly these days,' he said.

John Smith came down the steps of his caravan, pulling the door to behind him. The sun was setting over Hungerford town, a washed red on the grey buildings. Getting on for half past nine, he thought. He glanced across the common and the road to the pub, the Down Gate, wondering about a pint of beer, but he'd lost the habit in prison and knew that the townspeople wouldn't welcome one of his complexion tonight.

Instead he turned away, needing to stretch his long legs, wanting the taste of the dusk air in his lungs. Rufus's depressed dog raised its head from its paws and gave a whining noise in its throat.

Smith laughed. 'Come on then, if you must.' He unravelled the dog's rope from the wheels of the van and let the creature free. It hobbled a few yards, as if cramped, then began to bound ahead of him, a new animal, silly.

He rounded the stone circle, the overgrown copse, running down the slope of the ditch so that he'd have the impetus to get up the other side. He could see the railway track and the canal beyond, no trains, no boats, no walkers. How well he knew this place, after all these years. It had been the last place he and his family had stopped before disaster had come for them. 'But I am still alive,' he said aloud, though not loudly. 'I was the one who survived.'

The dog chased a rabbit, but was outclassed. He realised that he didn't know its name, or if it had one, let alone if it would answer to it. It differed little from the dog Rufus had had then, one of a long line, and he'd never understood why his brother-in-law kept the creatures, unless for the pleasure of ownership. Certainly he showed them neither friendship nor affection.

He'd been out walking that other night, though dogless. It had been a Friday, he thought, although it was no longer as clear as it had been. In prison you had nothing to do but remember. Outside there was the struggle of life. That night he hadn't been to the pub either, not from choice, but because the landlord had barred him the previous night, after the row, calling him names, the usual names: thief, vagabond, dirty gippo.

He wasn't dirty. He'd never been dirty. His father had laughed at him for his fastidiousness as a child. You could wash perfectly well in a pot of water boiled over an open fire or a primus stove and, for the unrivalled pleasure of immersion, there were rivers and lakes and rainstorms.

The dog returned and sniffed his boots. He rubbed its floppy ears and it responded with a look akin to love. 'We could both use some exercise,' he said, walking briskly on. 'Heel, boy.' They'd had gyms in prisons for the past few years: running machines, rowing machines, electric staircases, weights, punchbags. They were taken by hangers and floggers as a sign that prison was soft, giving criminals facilities they wouldn't have been able to afford outside, but they performed the useful task of dissipating the energy and aggression of caged men, rampant with testosterone.

He'd used them daily, kept himself in shape, but it wasn't the same. Running and getting nowhere, rowing without water; was that a sane man's pastime? Running without getting anywhere was like life, one of his cell mates had claimed, running as fast as you could to stay in the same place. The gypsy life was travelling hopefully without ever arriving, he'd replied.

He'd walk up to the lock and back. He'd have done a full circle, coming back along the canal, but he knew that the towpath was still shut off. He thought about the blonde girl at their one meeting. How unlike his dusky daughters she'd been, and yet how similar. The same age as Syeira who insisted she was Sarah, going through a childish need to conform. The same trusting expression in the eyes, be they blue or black, the trust of a child who has not yet encountered adult viciousness.

He'd kissed her goodnight before he went out that night. Kissed them all, all three of his beloved women, because the fight in the pub had been over before it had begun, like all their fights. 'I won't be long,' he'd said, and he hadn't been. But long enough.

He'd returned from his guilty walk shortly after sunset.

He'd not understood for a moment. A strangled body lying tidily on a bed is not immediately sinister, not with the blankets drawn up to the chin, even on a hot night. He'd said, 'Early night?' then, 'Not sulking, are you?' and shaken her when she hadn't answered him, and seen it at last.

Stumbling across the van on plasticine legs, praying, not the children, please not the children too.

Yes, the children too. Yes, the children.

He'd bolted from the van and run, leaving the door wide open, run half way to Kintbury before realising it was no good, that the world wasn't big enough for him to run away from what he'd seen, and he'd called the police from a wayside call box. They'd been there by the time he'd got back and he'd gone with them without a murmur, with none of the protestations of innocence that the blameless make, and the blameful too.

He'd never known what happened to that van, but suspected that Rufus had burnt it along with everything in it, as a total erasure.

After his second abortive parole board they'd suggested he see a psychiatrist and he'd agreed; any break from routine was welcome in prison. Besides, he was interested in the human mind and glad to meet a man who held the key to it. But if Dr Paterson had ever been entrusted with that key, he'd long since lost it.

He spoke a great deal about denial. Sometimes, Smith had said, when a man denies something, it's because it isn't true. But Paterson hadn't wanted to hear that. Smith had continued with their meetings all the same: they made a change from his cell mate's banal and obscene conversation. At the end of their last session Paterson had shaken hands with him and said, 'It sometimes takes a man years to learn to forgive himself, John. It may be that you don't think you've been punished enough yet.'

He'd politely agreed.

Syeira would have been thirty now, or thirty-one, he couldn't quite remember. She might have rejected the travelling life, he thought dispassionately, married out, become housebound. He wouldn't have minded, not the way Rufus and Orlenda did.

At the lock, he picked a dog rose from the hedge for her, for all the little girls who would never be women, and pulled its white petals off one by one and dropped them in the water. The lock gate tugged them into its mouth and shredded them.

It was dark by the time he got back but he had no trouble in recognising the shape in the night as Orlenda. It was as if she was waiting for him.

'You all right?' he asked.

'I'm all right.'

'Nothing ever surprises you, does it, Lenda? It must be so boring, being able to see the future.'

'Don't let Rufus see you with his dog,' she said. 'There are limits to how far forgiveness will stretch.'

'Take him.' He picked up the discarded rope and tethered the animal to the wheel again as she watched.

'Been walking, Jan?' she asked.

'Up to the lock and back. It's a good walk.'

She said, 'I remember.'

9. Monday, 22nd June

'Have you ever thought of escaping?' Greg asked at breakfast, 'of running away?' Angelica spat a mouthful of coffee inelegantly back into her mug and pantomimed incomprehension.

'Running off with the gypsies,' he elucidated.

'Oh! No.'

'Never? Never wanted to hitch your horse to the wagon and take to the open road, stopping where the fancy takes you?'

'Or where the police will let you. Thanks, I'll stick with mains sewerage and a supply of electricity. Where would I plug my hairdryer in?'

'The four winds would be your hairdryer,' he said dramatically, 'and the thunderclouds your power shower.'

'And a patch of nettles my toilet?'

'You have no poetry in your soul, girl.'

'And you have too much, old man.'

'You look nice,' he said as they were going out of the front door a few minutes later. She wasn't wearing her overall. Normally she wore jeans or short skirts but today she had on the charcoal-grey, knee-length skirt she'd worn to Fred's funeral, part of a suit, and a moss-green, short-sleeved silk sweater that slid through his fingers like river water. There were proper shoes on her feet: not trainers but black, low-heeled court shoes

She patted her bulging canvas bag. 'The overall gets too sweaty in summer. I'll change at work.'

He left her in the Savemore carpark as usual, by the staff entrance, and drove to his office. He had to be at the Coroner's Court at eleven, where the inquest into Reyna Lee's death would be opened and immediately adjourned. Because he had this immutable appointment he couldn't seem to get on with anything else. He drank three cups of coffee, read the reports that were piling up in his in-tray, dictated enough things to keep his secretary happy and looked out of the window for five minutes. He had a commanding view of the inner ring road.

Barbara came hurrying in at 10.15. 'One,' she said, 'Forensic have found traces of motor oil on the front of Jordan's dungarees – presumably from Peel's van.'

'It looked the leaky sort,' he agreed. So she'd been lying on her back . . . unless there was already a pool of oil on the ground, in which case she'd been lying on her front.

'Two, there are no fingerprints on the bedroom window or sill except Josie's and Jordan's.'

He waited for three or four or more, but they weren't forthcoming and he said, 'Thanks, Babs,' and she sped away again. He decided to nip over to Sainsbury's for his newspaper. There were perfectly good underpasses to get him across the roundabout that cut the police station and magistrates court off from the town centre, but it was a point of honour to dart through the tail end of the rush-hour traffic instead. He arrived a little breathless at the other side and stopped to catch his wind.

As he stood by the traffic lights a green and white minibus with the Savemore logo came to a halt at a red light. It was a courtesy bus provided for staff and customers, making a round of the train station, bus station and market place every half hour. In a forward seat, her head bent over a Penguin Classic, he could see Angelica in her moss-green jersey. She read only classic novels since Fred's death: she said modern ones made her too sad. She didn't look up and he stood staring as the lights changed and the bus pulled away towards Newbury railway station.

His paper forgotten, he braved another grand prix of cars and thundering lorries to take him into Station Approach. The minibus was pulling away, empty, and he went cautiously to the station entrance and peered in, feeling like a spy. She had her back to him, buying a ticket, rummaging for her wallet, exchanging a word – perhaps a joke – with the man behind the window.

As she paid over her money the London 'turbo' train slid noiselessly into the station and, with her ticket and change still in her hand, she broke into a trot, clumsy on her unaccustomed heels and hobbled by the straight skirt. She boarded the train at the nearest open door, her fat, cream canvas bag banging against her haunches. There was a whistling noise, a verbal warning of closing doors, an actual closing with a pneumatic 'schtum' and the train left the station as efficiently as it had come.

On automatic pilot he turned away and plucked a newspaper from the display rack at random. He would be puzzled to find later that he'd selected the *Daily Telegraph.*

'Mister.' He ignored the small voice but it was insistent, and soon added an impatient tugging at his sleeve to its antics. 'Hey, mister. Wake up.'

Recalled to life, he glanced down. 'Romy?'

'Oh, you remember me then.'

'Of course I do.' She looked neater than when he'd last seen her. Her hair had been cut, though not professionally, and her clothes were clean and tidy – a pair of grey jeans and a blue shirt, trainers, although not a brand name he'd heard of.

'That one's boring,' she sneered at his paper. 'This one's much better.' She indicated a lurid newssheet with colour pictures of a soap-opera star who'd become more famous than his character by committing adultery with the wife of a bishop. Allegedly. Jordan's picture vied with it on the front page as if the stories were of equal importance, the soap star running hunch-shouldered from his house to his car on the left side of the page, watched by Jordan's laughing eyes on the right.

Oh, the foolish antics of adults, the eyes said. *How glad I am I shall never be one.*

'I think I'll stick with this all the same.' He paid for his paper and bought her a Kit-Kat which she accepted with demurely lowered eyelids and a murmur of thanks, thrusting it in her breast pocket. 'Are you out on your own?' he asked.

She nodded and raised a finger to her lips, making him part of the conspiracy. 'Don't tell,' she said.

'You're not supposed to be here in other words.' He glanced at his watch. 'Especially as it's now school hours. Where're you living? At a hostel?'

'Nope. We're with some people in Thatcham.'

'Both of you together?' She nodded. 'That's good. That's very good. Are they nice people? Are you happy there?'

'Yeah, they're okay. Bit fussy. You know clean your teeth, change your knickers, eat up your greens. They tried to get me to go to church yesterday morning but I told them no Romany sets foot in a church, and they got a bit snotty, but I told Jude, the woman from the social, and she says they've got to respect my beliefs, so that showed them.' She made a face. 'And they've got a cat.'

'Is that bad?'

'They're unclean animals. *Mochardi.* They lick themselves all over.'

'I see.'

She said in disgust, 'The other night it got in my room and I woke up and found it asleep on my bed.' Cats sensed when someone didn't like them, he knew, and exploited it. 'Still,' she continued, 'I reckon I can get them sorted out given time.'

'I'm sure you can,' Greg said with a faint smile.

'And there's school, of course.' She sighed.

'I don't think you'll be able to get out of that, Romy. You might find you get to like it. Bright girls like you usually do.'

143

'Maybe,' she agreed, apparently willing to accept the inevitable. 'But my mum taught me to read real good and she said if you can read you got access to all the knowledge in the world.' She was right, he thought. Teach an intelligent child to read and let her loose in a library and she'd learn everything she needed to. 'They won't let me see my dado,' the girl went on. 'Jude makes excuses when I ask, fobbing me off like I was some little kid. Can you get me in to see him?'

'No, I'm afraid not. It's not my decision.' Huwie Lee was still in prison in Reading, awaiting trial. It was doubtful that social services had any plans to let him see his children. 'He'll be away for a long time, you know, Romy. You'll probably be grown up when he gets out.'

She nodded philosophically. She was pretty much grown-up now. 'It's just that he needs looking after.'

'Do you know Lashlo Lee?' he asked.

She looked at him as if he were stupid, as he apparently was. 'He's my uncle, inne?'

'Of course. Well, did he ever . . . touch you or your sisters in any way?'

'What? Hands in knickers you mean. No, 'course not. He'd never do anything like that. I don't think he'd know how. Or why. He never showed me his *cori* either.'

'His . . . ?'

'You know.' She was unexpectedly coy. 'His *thing*.'

'Oh. Right.'

'He's a big harmless old carthorse. It wasn't him killed that girl on the telly. It couldn't have been.'

'No, I don't think so either. Good, thanks.' He paused, thinking he'd done enough questioning of a minor without a responsible adult present; besides, he couldn't think of anything else to ask.

'I gotta go now,' she said. 'You couldn't lend me a couple of quid for the train, could you?' Wheedlingly she added,

'You looked dead good on the telly last night. Bit like Mel Gibson.'

She would go far. Greg took out his wallet and gave her a five pound note. 'Keep the change,' he said.

'Coo, ta.'

'You've missed the Thatcham train, you know.'

'Doesn't matter. There'll be another one.'

'Yes.' There would always be another one.

'Here,' she said, 'can me and Bonnie come and play with your little girls one day?'

He hesitated. 'That might be tricky.'

'You made them up,' she said matter-of-factly. 'I thought so. Why?'

'To make myself seem more of a real person to your father, a man with children and responsibilities like himself.'

'So he'd be less likely to shoot you. That's clever. That's very clever.' She looked at him with respect. 'Mrs Cluxman – that's our foster mother – she says you mustn't tell lies under any circumstances. I told her she was talking a lot of bollocks.' Romy looked hurt. 'She wouldn't let me have a choc ice that evening. T'isn't fair.'

'I expect she'd have let you have one if you'd apologised for using rude language.'

'No need,' she said. 'I took Bonnie's when she wasn't looking. Mrs C, I mean, not Bonnie.' Greg laughed. He hoped the Cluxman's cat knew what sort of adversary it was taking on. She turned away towards the platforms. 'See yer.' She hesitated. 'What about the mother?' she asked.

'Sorry?'

'The mother, your wife, with the blonde hair and the green eyes. Make her up too?'

'. . . Yes. I made her up too.'

'Oh. I thought that bit was for real.' She shrugged. 'You did have me fooled then.'

'I had everyone fooled. See you, Romy.'

'Give us yer 'and,' she said, 'and I'll tell yer yer future.'

'No thank you, dear,' Greg said. He wasn't falling for that one again.

'Sure? I'm good at it. Gran says I've got the gift and she should know 'cause there's no one like her for the *duckering*. No charge.'

'Quite sure.'

Romy shrugged and skipped off onto the platform. A moment later he saw her crossing the stairs to the down plat-form, the service to Kintbury, Hungerford and Bedwyn. He opened his mouth to call out to her then let her be. He was certain it wasn't a mistake and that she'd find her way back again when she felt like it. From the far platform she saw him watching and waved. He returned the salute. She'd begun the Kit-Kat and there was chocolate on her cheek. The train arrived as he stood there and when it pulled away she was gone.

'My future?' he murmured. 'Thanks, but I prefer not to know. Sufficient unto the day is the evil thereof.'

He walked slowly back to his office. He passed two girls at the junction with Carnegie Road, teenagers, maybe sixteen, fresh out of school and unemployed, even unemployable. Both wore heavy black eye make-up and short skirts, sweaters with deliberate rents in the elbows, bare legs in plimsolls. They ignored him completely; at least he wasn't going to have to run them in for soliciting. They were leaning against a concrete wall, handing a cigarette back and forth between them. Neither of them knew how to smoke it and one of them almost choked as he went by.

'She's not my sister,' the other was protesting with the endemic sulkiness of her years. 'She's my mother's boyfriend's stepdaughter from his second marriage. She only lives with us 'cause her mum buggered off. She's not my problem.'

Am I my mother's boyfriend's stepdaughter's keeper? It was only in the last thirty years that family relationships had got that complicated.

He glanced at his watch and swore out loud, making the girls stare at him censoriously. He was late for Court. He ran.

Back at his desk, three quarters of an hour later, he picked the telephone up and dialled. A polite woman told him, unasked, that he'd got through to Savemore supermarket, Newbury, which came as no surprise since that was the number he'd dialled; that her name was Pauline, which seemed more than he needed to know; and that she wondered how she might be of service to him.

When he'd told her how she might be of service, she said that Mrs Summers had taken the day off and that they didn't encourage personal calls to staff on the shop floor since it meant fetching them away from their work station. He thanked Pauline courteously and she said he was welcome and suggested that he have a nice day. He thanked her again and hung up. He wondered if he would ever see Mrs Summers again.

Can I – may I be – my dead son's widow's keeper?

'Anybody home?' Barbara poked her head round his office door.

'Where've you been?' he asked, not as a reprimand but in a spirit of genuine enquiry.

'To Josie's, to see about the post.'

'Of course. I forgot. Anything?'

Barbara took a clear evidence bag out of her pocket and placed it on the desk in front of him. It contained a white, unstamped envelope with no address and a sheet of paper with a neat – too neat – handwriting in black ink. He read it through quickly and wrinkled up his nose in distaste.

'He didn't waste much time,' Barbara said. 'You see how he's picked up on the fact that Jordan was an IVF baby, calling her abnormal and an abomination which didn't deserve to live, and that can only have come from this morning's papers. Josie didn't go into detail on TV.'

'Why "he"? Isn't it received wisdom that anonymous letter writers are usually female?'

'Yeah, and Chief Constables are usually blokes. Call it a hunch. Men are less understanding about fertility treatment than women are.'

'Is it anything to do with the case?' he asked.

'I doubt it.' She picked the packet up and reread the letter herself. 'Odd: no block capitals, undisguised writing. He's not afraid that Josie will recognise the hand so –'

'A complete stranger.'

'Presumably.'

'Who thinks he has the right to attack a woman he's never met when she's at her most vulnerable because of some pathetic bee he's got in his bonnet.'

In this great age of communications, everyone was public property.

Barbara said, 'The other side of the coin is that there are about a hundred bunches of flowers on the pavement outside the bungalow. A hundred well-wishers against one sicko.'

'That seems a hopeful ratio.'

The towpath was still cordoned off but bunches of flowers had been left on either side of the barrier. Waterless, cellophane-wrapped flowers that would be dead within hours. A poignant but pointless tribute. People did it because they'd seen it on TV and thought it was the right thing to do in the circumstances, that it was some sort of tradition that you neglected at your peril. He couldn't remember when the first time had been.

'I took the nicest ones in,' Barbara said, 'and arranged them in vases. But it seemed like . . . what? What's the word I'm looking for?'

'A mockery?'

'Yes. As if a nice vase of carnations would cheer her up and make everything all right.'

Greg gestured at the letter. 'She hasn't seen this?'

148

'Not likely!'

'If it were me, I'd want to see them. Anything's better than being kept in the dark.'

'You think you do but you soon forget you *haven't* seen them, whereas once seen never forgotten.'

He opened his mouth to dispute this but the telephone rang.

'Summers. Where? What, now? All right. I'll send someone down.' He hung up. 'Babs, can you go down and fetch me up a Mr Cameron who says he saw Jordan in Hungerford on Saturday night. Alone.'

She was half way out of the door saying, 'I'll drop this letter off at Forensic on the way.'

Douglas Cameron was in his late thirties, Greg guessed, a fit-looking man, smart but comfortable in a good blue suit, a man at ease with himself and not afraid of the police. A little below average height and slightly stocky, he had the dark Celtic good looks that his name suggested, although there was no trace of Scotland in his voice.

He gave Greg his card as he came into the room, along with a firm, dry handshake. The card announced in plain black lettering on white that he was a surveyor, a partner in a large and prosperous firm of estate agents in Newbury. Greg offered him a seat and he declined coffee. He was explaining, but not apologising for, his delay in coming forward.

'I drove my wife and children to her mother's in Southampton on Saturday evening. My wife doesn't like to drive long distances. They're to stay there for a few days as her mother's just come out of hospital.' He crossed one leg neatly over the other, revealing well-polished brown shoes and navy wool socks.

'I dropped them off, had supper with them and got back to Hungerford at about ten. I didn't read a Sunday newspaper or watch TV – when my wife and kids are away I take the opportunity for a bit of peace and quiet, catch up on my reading. So it was only when I got to work half an hour ago and saw a colleague's paper that I recognised the little girl. There seemed no point in phoning as my office is the other side of the roundabout, so I came straight over and here I am.'

Greg made a note of his home address. 'You're not far from the town centre,' he remarked.

'The other side of the canal.'

'And you didn't hear any of the noise Saturday night? The search parties out looking for Jordan?'

'My bedroom's at the back and I'm a heavy sleeper.'

Obviously a man with a clear conscience, Greg thought. 'And you're sure it was Jordan Abbot you saw?'

'Oh, yes. I was aware of a small person crossing the road ahead of me and I slowed down to give her plenty of time to get safely across and looked at her carefully.'

'She was taking a risk in crossing? Showing poor road sense?'

'No, there was plenty of time, but you can't be too careful. No, the reason I looked twice was that there seemed to be something odd about her face, then I realised that it was face paint, the sort of thing my Victoria had done at a birthday party a few weeks ago. Clowns, rabbits, whatever. They seem to love it, especially the girls.'

There seemed no doubt that it was Jordan he'd seen, but Greg asked, 'What was she wearing?'

'Blue jeans. No, wait, there was a bib thing. Dungarees. A pale tee shirt or blouse.'

'You knew her?' Barbara asked.

He shrugged a negative. 'We haven't lived in Hungerford long – barely a year – and I don't remember her. I might have passed her in the street. My children are younger, pre-school.'

'And this was what time?' Greg said.

'Ten o'clock. I had the radio on and the pips had just gone.'

'You didn't think it was late for a child so young to be out on her own?'

'Actually, I did, which was one of the reasons I looked at her carefully, but it was still barely dark – midsummer, you know – and people let their kids run wild these days.' He smiled the smile of a man who had his own children well under control.

'It must have been only just light,' Barbara pointed out.

'Yes, but I could see her well enough. The streetlights were on too.'

They said that dusk was the worst time for human judgment, more deceptive that full dark. 'You didn't stop?' Greg said. 'Ask her if she was okay, offer her a lift home?'

'Of course not!' Cameron looked shocked. 'We drum and drum it into kids that they mustn't talk to strangers, let alone accept lifts from them. It would have been downright irresponsible.'

But Jordan Abbot hadn't been afraid of strangers.

'Can you show us on my map exactly where this was?' Barbara said, opening out a plan of the town.

He pointed. 'I was coming down the Salisbury Road. Just as it becomes the High Street, here. She came out of a side road, here –'

'Atherton Road?'

'Presumably.'

Not two hundred yards from her home.

'Then she crossed, as I said, and went into the road opposite and a few yards down the hill. More like an alleyway than a road.' He squinted at the map upside down, then picked it up to read the cramped writing. 'Barnard Court, it must be.' There was a complex web of residential roads, lanes, avenues and closes off that side of the High Street, some council, some private, passing both schools, the recreation ground and swimming pool, and with footpaths out to the common. There were a dozen possible routes she might have taken, a hundred permutations.

151

'And you're sure there was no one with her,' Greg said, 'nobody who might have slipped into the hedge when they saw your car coming?'

'She was alone, skipping along the pavement, like she had something important to do. Her mouth was moving so I think she was singing. If she'd been older, I'd've said she was on her way to meet her boyfriend.'

There seemed little doubt that she'd been on her way to the common. And that she'd been passionate about something, not a boyfriend, not at six, but something that got little girls passionate. Adventure.

'So, she dressed and climbed out the window of her own accord,' Greg mused when Cameron had gone, 'deliberately gave her mother the slip.'

'Does that let Josie off the hook? 'Barbara asked. 'If Jordan was alive and well outside the house at ten o'clock.'

'Unless Josie looked in and found her missing earlier than eleven o'clock. Loving mothers like to look often at their sleeping children.' So did loving fathers and some of his happiest memories were of watching the infant Frederick sleep, his tow hair unruly on the pillow, breathing as deeply as a cat. 'Suppose she found her missing and ran around looking for her. Perhaps she suspected she was heading for the gypsy camp and caught up with her, then started to hit her –'

'Why?' Barbara asked, startled.

'I can tell you've never had anything to do with children. It's what women do when their kids have frightened them.'

'Beat them?'

'*Slap* them to say, "Don't ever frighten me like that again". Then sometimes it gets out of hand.'

'Jordan must have known Josie looked in on her last thing,' Barbara said, 'even if she was usually asleep when it happened. She must have known she'd be in big trouble.'

Did that mean she'd never meant to come back?

152

'Children don't think of the consequences,' Greg said. 'They have the gift of living in the moment that most of us adults lose. She'd had a wonderful time at the fair that afternoon and didn't see why she shouldn't have an equally wonderful time with the gypsies for always. She wasn't going to let her mother act as spoilsport.'

'But did she get that far?' Babs asked, 'or was she waylaid, among those hundreds of houses?'

'Can we check for known offenders living on the estate?'

'Of course, but it'll take a while.'

'Do it. And do house-to-house in the Priory Road estate again. I know they've been seen already but we're asking something specific this time: did anyone see Jordan shortly after ten that night?'

'It's a bad time,' Barbara said. 'They'd have drawn their curtains. On a Saturday night people are out at the pub or cosily set in front of the telly.'

'But someone must have been out, or looking out, getting round to closing their curtains for the night. We must find out how far she got.'

'We know of one convicted child killer in the area for sure,' Barbara pointed out. 'Your friend Smith.'

'I know,' Greg said moodily.

'A jury found him guilty of murdering two children in cold blood – his own daughters – and no one has proved otherwise, however much you don't want to believe it of him.'

'I know. God forbid that the lynch mob should find out about him.'

'What about a reconstruction?' Barbara suggested.

'I think that's not a bad idea if the house-to-house doesn't throw anything up. If we can find someone to lend us a blonde six-year-old for such a gruesome task.'

'She might have been stopped on the common,' Barbara said, 'clear of the houses but before she reached the gypsy camp.'

153

Waylaid by whom, Greg wondered? By a late dog-walker? Some drunk on his way home from the pub? By Clive Peel and his odalisques? But their new-age mumbo-jumbo was just that, a nonsense. They weren't the types to be looking for a human sacrifice.

He'd found a Clive Peel on the PNC. He couldn't be sure it was the right one but it was promising. He was listed as being twenty-nine, which tallied, the right height and colouring. He'd been a schoolmaster in Poole, but been sacked for having a sexual relationship with one of the fifth-formers, a girl of fifteen. Her parents had refused to press charges in the end, not wanting the inevitable publicity, so it hadn't come to court. Probably the girl had refused to give evidence against him.

'A biology teacher,' Barbara said, reading the printout he'd given her. 'What was that then, her biology practical?'

After that there'd been a conviction for shoplifting and arrests for criminal damage in the course of trespass. His flat had been repossessed in 1996 and his current whereabouts were unknown.

Nasty bit of work, Mr Peel, Greg thought, although the man's record was innocuous enough and the schoolgirl probably old enough to know what she was about, no six-year-old girl. Greg would very much like to speak to him but his whereabouts, as the computer reminded him, were still annoyingly unknown.

10. Monday Afternoon

'Did Josie tell you about her husband's death?' Barbara asked.

'Yes.'

'All the details?'

'Quite a bit. I got the impression that she needs to talk about it.' He cast his mind back. Emergency call before Christmas, drunk driver, world ends with a bang. 'Can't remember the other driver's name,' he said.

'Frank Meldrew of Froxfield.'

'Oh. Your memory's obviously better than mine.'

'No, I've been making some enquiries, had a chat with the two lads who were first on the scene, Whittaker and Clements.'

'Why?'

'It struck me as odd that she didn't get any compensation. If the accident was entirely the fault of the other driver then surely she should have taken his insurance company for thousands – hundreds of thousands – for the death of the breadwinner.'

'Perhaps he wasn't insured.'

'No, he was. He was a perfectly decent, law-abiding bloke and his car was insured, MOT-ed and had recently been serviced. He'd been drinking, yes, but not all that much, a quick Christmas drink with colleagues, half an hour in the pub at knocking-off time.'

'You can drink a lot in half an hour.'

'Whittaker says they breathalysed him at the scene and got a marginally positive reading. They thought that by the time they did the blood test back at the station he'd be okay, but he was unlucky. Either his metabolism was slow or the doctor was quick getting there, but he still showed positive. He insisted that Abbot's car had veered across the road towards him – that it'd been Abbot's fault, essentially – but you know how it is when you're over the limit, they threw the book at him. He was charged with causing death by dangerous driving and the jury convicted him.'

He thought himself hard done-by, Greg remembered Josie saying bitterly, to do time at all.

Barbara went on. 'And another interesting thing is that the investigating officers never found any trace of this emergency call Peter Abbot was supposed to be answering.'

'Didn't Josie act as his secretary, take phone messages? That's what usually happens in these one-man companies.'

'When they asked for details so they could check what sort of state Peter was in when he set off home – if he'd complained of feeling ill, maybe – she said he'd answered the call-out himself and she didn't know where it was. But he had no handsome cheque on him as payment for work done, nothing but five quid in his wallet. I don't think there was a call-out.'

'She wouldn't be the first person whose spouse was playing away to be in heavy denial,' Greg said gently, 'if that's what you're getting at. It doesn't make her a liar.'

'Infidelity is one possibility, perhaps the first that springs to mind. And then there's the compensation. Because there *was* a payment from Meldrew's insurance company after the conviction. The Abbots senior, Peter's parents, employed a hotshot London lawyer and the money was put in trust for Jordan, with the grandparents as trustees and the lawyer having day-to-day charge of the investments.'

'I see.'

'As if they didn't trust Josie to have access to it.'

'What sort of money are we talking about?'

'Two hundred thousand at the time: probably grown by now in a rising stockmarket.'

'And who gets the money now she's dead?'

'Isn't *that* the sixty-four thousand dollar question!'

'It's not possible,' he said after a long pause. 'A woman doesn't kill her own much-loved child for *money*.'

'You middle-aged men are all the same,' Barbara said. 'You think women are *better* than you are, that we're nicer, that we don't do cruel and wicked things the way men do. That we're fluffy bunny rabbits.'

'Oh, yeah!' He thought about Diane, about Angelica, about Barbara herself. He could see no fluffy bunnies in his life. Nor did he want any.

'Look at it this way,' Barbara went on, 'you're a married woman who wants badly to give your husband a child. No –' He'd opened his mouth to object. 'Let me run with this one. You go through years of humiliating tests and fertility treatment before you succeed. Five years later he dies in a car crash, coming back from we-don't-know-where, but you know, or suspect, from a visit to another woman. The compensation goes to the kid, but locked up by your hostile in-laws so you can't touch it. Resentment builds up, festers over eighteen months and one day, one night, something snaps.'

'I think we'll go and have a word with her,' Greg said, 'although I don't believe a word of it. Then we can check the route Jordan took that night while we're about it.'

'I don't believe this!' Josie said. 'Don't you think it's bad enough to lose your only child without the police making it clear that you're their number one suspect?'

'Nobody's saying anything like that –' Greg began.

'Aren't they? It bloody sounds like it.'

'I wanted to check a few details of the trust fund that was set up for Jordan. It's standard practice in cases of sudden death, of . . . of murder, to look at the victim's finances.'

'Well don't ask me,' she said bitterly, 'because I had nothing to do with it. You'll have to ask the Abbots' solicitor.'

'You should have got your own lawyer,' Barbara said, 'to represent your interests, as distinct from Jordan's.'

'Do you know what lawyers cost?'

'Legal aid.'

'Yes, and then they claw the court costs back out of your settlement. And what if I'd lost? I couldn't take that risk. The Abbots keep saying that the money's to pay for her to go to a good school eventually – by which they mean a boarding school, away from me – while it would be more to the point to buy her a new pair of shoes occasionally, or pay for us both to go on holiday.'

'Don't you know who gets the proceeds if the trust is wound up?' Barbara slipped in.

'Yes.' Josie flushed. 'I do. I'm her sole heir.' She began to cry. 'I can't bear it. I can't bear it that you think I'm the sort of person who would do that to my child.'

'There isn't a *sort* of person,' Greg said softly. 'Bringing up children is terribly hard work, especially on your own, and sometimes people can't cope, sometimes they snap.'

'Oh, get out!' she yelled. 'If you're not arresting me you can get out of my bloody house now before I throw you out.' As they were leaving, she wiped her eyes and said, straight to Greg, 'I'm going to make you so sorry for this.'

'She's hiding something,' Barbara said as the front door slammed behind them. 'I'm sure of it. I just can't work out what.'

They left Greg's car in Fox Close and followed the route the girl had taken that night, according to Douglas Cameron. At the bottom of Atherton Road a made-up path took them across the edge of the green, past a red postbox and a wooden bench, to the top end of the High Street.

'There's a streetlight overhead, as Cameron said,' Greg remarked.

There was no traffic coming and they walked across and turned sharp left into the narrow pathway called Barnard Court. This took them past a terrace of well-tended cottages with white shutters at the windows, hearts cut in the wood. 'With our luck theyll have had their shutters closed on Saturday night,' Greg grumbled.

'I don't think they're meant for function, just decoration.'

'They'll have to be seen again with our new information.'

Barbara had a dictating machine with her and made notes into it constantly. Greg let her get on with it. Detail was what she was good at. On impulse, he rapped at the front door of the last cottage in the row. They stood waiting. There was no reply and wasn't going to be one. Funny how you could tell if someone was coming to answer you or not.

The path curved round, past three newish houses, and into an unnamed footpath rising steeply, so steeply that the council had provided a handrail for ageing detective superintendents. Greg paused to take his jacket off as Barbara sped up the hill ahead of him. On their right they could make out bungalows but the wooden fence was high.

'Old people's homes, by the look of it,' she said, waiting for him to catch up. She was standing on tiptoe to see over the fence.

There was streetlighting in the pathway but no houses to overlook it.

At the top of the footpath they stood looking at the varied buildings of the Hungerford County Primary School for a moment, before crossing into South View. 'She knew this route well,' Barbara remarked, 'took it to school every day.'

'I know it well too, better than I like.' Greg shivered and put his jacket back on. To their left was the place where Michael Ryan's house had stood until he'd burnt it down. In this narrow cul de sac seven people had been shot dead, one of them a uniformed PC from Newbury, a man of Greg's age, a face he knew well. He'd stood here that day amid the carnage, with the stench of decaying flesh in his nostrils, at a time when Barbara was a girl of seventeen, still in school, miles away in Hertfordshire. He envied her her lack of memories.

He pulled himself together. 'More possibles,' he said, 'but this route could hardly be better designed to let her get out of town unseen.'

The road gave way to a footpath and a metal kissing gate took them out to the common. Greg shaded his eyes with his hand. Barbara was equipped with sunglasses. Fields of crops beyond the canal shimmered blue in the midsummer light.

'She could have gone anywhere from here,' he said, 'in any direction.'

'Assuming she got this far.'

'I'm going to leave you to go back and try those houses we passed.'

'Sir.'

He walked her back as far as the first house and left her. 'See you back at HQ later.'

Greg glanced up from his desk a couple of hours later as a shadow fell across it. It was Barbara again. Lost in thought, he hadn't heard her come in although she must have opened and closed his office door to do so.

'Did you just materialise there?'

'Sorry?'

'Doesn't matter. Finished that house-to-house?'

'Almost all no replies. No luck where there were replies. Everybody wants to have seen something but no one did. I'll go back this evening, do the rest.'

'Good.'

'Meanwhile I've got the data you wanted.' She placed three sheets of computer printout in front of him, sat down in the chair opposite him, crossed her right leg over her left and balanced an identical sheaf of paper on the upper knee. Her leg bobbed up and down as if an invisible physiotherapist were hitting it with a hammer.

'Unsolved child murders in England and Wales in the last five years,' she explained as he looked blank.

'Yes. Sorry. I was miles away.'

'I also got children missing in suspicious circumstances even where no body's been found.'

'Any pattern?'

'I've not much more than glanced at them but if there is it's very abstract.'

'Modern art?'

'Quite.'

He read the topmost paper. Amelia Adams, aged five, blonde, dead of a broken neck two years before in Banbury. No sexual assault. He glanced up. 'Sounds promising.'

Barbara was ahead of him. 'Uh, uh. Read on.'

He did so. Amelia's stepfather, Christopher Keen, had been arrested three weeks later and charged with the crime.

'I said unsolved murders,' he said acidly.

'*Mea culpa.* I should have read it before I brought it in but whoever input the outcome to the computer didn't update the "Case Closed" field.'

'Evidently,' he said, thinking how ugly this language of inputs, outcomes and updates was.

'Computers are only as good as the people who use them.'

Keen had pleaded guilty to manslaughter and was now serving an eight-year sentence.

Greg turned the top sheet of paper face down on his desk and scanned the second one. A six-year-old boy, Derek Fielding, had been sexually assaulted and strangled in Northampton a year ago, the naked body dumped by the river Nene. He looked hopefully at Barbara but she was shaking her head.

'I've never heard of a serial murderer killing both men and women, boys and girls. And Jordan wasn't sexually assaulted, or naked.'

'But the river,' he said, 'the towpath. Isn't that too much of a coincidence?'

'A quiet place to take a frightened child.'

161

'And he was blonde too.' Children were fairer than their adult selves, he'd noticed, so that a golden-haired toddler turned into a sulky teenager with hair the colour of treacle toffee and just as sticky. Why was that?

'I'm inclined to agree with you,' he conceded. He took the third case. Anita Adobah, seven, of mixed parentage but IC2 – black – in appearance. She'd disappeared on her way home from school in Streatham, South London, six months earlier. No body found. He picked up the telephone, called Streatham and asked to speak to the officer in charge of the case. After much whispered discussion at the other end he was put through to an Inspector Cavendish and placed his telephone on loudspeaker so that Barbara could hear.

'Oh, little Anita,' Cavendish said cheerfully, when Greg explained his errand. 'We're morally certain that the biological father abducted her and took her back to Nigeria, but the authorities there aren't being co-operative so we're keeping the case open for the time being. I wouldn't say it was exactly active.'

'Morally certain?'

'He'd been telling people he was going to do it and there was a sighting at Heathrow that same night.'

'Okay. Thanks.' He pressed the button to cut the connection and crossed his arms. 'As we thought, a one off.'

'Or just the first.'

'No!'

'All right. I shall dematerialise again and get back to Hungerford.' She got up. 'One unsolved child murder in the whole country at the moment, sir. You could call that good news if you were a bottle-half-full sort of person.'

'Except that now there are two.'

Smith, sitting on his doorstep as usual, watching the world go by, recognised the woman who walked purposefully towards him across the common that afternoon and rose at her approach, an instinctive mark of respect to a woman who'd lost the most precious thing a woman has.

'Mrs Abbot,' he said when she was in earshot. 'I was so sorry to hear –'

She pulled her arm back and slapped him hard across the face. He was too stunned to try to stop her, even to react. Her fingers tore at his flesh next as, recovering his sense of self-preservation, he struggled to grab her wrists. Fortunately the nails were sensibly short and inflicted little damage but he still felt the sting, the trickle of blood as one clawed home.

Then she collapsed down on the steps of his caravan, her strength gone, and began to weep. 'I can't take any more,' she wailed. 'I can't take any more.'

Smith, ignoring the curious stares of his few remaining fellow gypsies, bodily picked her up and hauled her into his van. 'I'm not sure what I've done to deserve that,' he said mildly as he installed her on his sofa-bed and stood looming over her, hands on hips, a red patch on his left cheek testimony to the force with which she'd struck him. He wiped the back of his hand down his chin and examined the smudge of blood on it.

'You stopped them from taking that boy who killed my girl. You stopped them from stringing him up as he deserves. How can you live with yourself?'

'I see.' He sat down beside her. 'Have you ever heard of miscarriages of justice?'

'I know what they *say*.'

'You don't believe that people can be wrongly convicted of a horrible crime, spend years of their life in prison?'

'The juries hear the evidence,' she said stubbornly, 'and they discuss it and they reach their verdict. Then years later some smart-arsed barrister comes along and gets them freed on a technicality.'

'But there was no jury in this case,' he said gently, 'no evidence against Lashlo. You saw him on Saturday afternoon as he played with Jordan. Did he seem violent to you?'

'Not then, but such people are unfathomable. We can't understand them, their wants, their frustrated sexual desires.'

'He's like a child –'

'It's all very well to say that,' she said passionately, 'but children are cruel and selfish and uncivilised until we make them different. And when somebody has a man's strong body and a man's urges, and a child's irresponsible and undisciplined mind then I say he's horribly dangerous.'

It was unarguable, Smith thought. People didn't want to admit it but children *were* irresponsible, uncivilised, which was why nature had given them parents to keep them under control and paint a veneer of culture and enlightenment on them. Children took what they wanted if they could and never paid for it.

'If they get him to court,' she went on, 'some smirking man in a black gown and a stupid wig will say he isn't responsible for his actions and they'll find him not guilty and put him in a nice cosy hospital.'

He got up. 'I've got a bottle of brandy somewhere. I think a small glass might calm you down.'

'And while no one is under arrest for the crime,' she went on, as he glugged the comforting brown liquid generously into a mug, 'I'm the one they're trying to pin it on.'

'Do you want to tell me about it?'

She did so, leaving her brandy untasted. 'Why do they do that?' she broke out in the end. 'Why blame the person who loved her most? What sort of sick, cynical world do we live in where your nearest and dearest are automatically the obvious suspect? I would have given my life for her.'

'Yes. I know.'

She was downing the brandy in one gulp and almost choked at his words. 'Have you ever lost a child?' she demanded when she'd recovered. 'Because nobody who's never lost a child has the right to tell me they know what I'm going through.'

'I lost two,' he said, 'and a wife with them. And they pinpointed me at once as the obvious suspect, because that's the way the world is.'

It silenced her. She listened to him for a while, as if in a daze, as he told her his story without elaboration or self pity, her eyes darting occasionally to fix his face. She drank more brandy, knowing that she needed it. Then she got up and said, 'I must go. I have a phone call to make.'

'Got time for a quick one?' Harry Stratton asked at seven o'clock.

Greg didn't go through the charade of looking at his watch. 'Not really, Harry. I want to get home.'

'It's been ages since we had a quiet drink.'

Greg sighed. Clearly his subordinate wanted a private talk, but why couldn't he simply say so? 'Just a quick one then.'

They found a peaceful corner in a pub nearby, a scruffy place, not much frequented by anyone and not a regular haunt of the police. Greg was a patient man and he knew it would take Harry a while to get round to what was troubling him so he sipped his pint of bitter and waited.

'Is it work?' he asked when the silence threatened to become oppressive.

'No, nothing like that.'

'Personal?'

'You remember what I was saying the other day about Ruthie, about her having a boyfriend?'

'Sure.'

Harry took a deep breath. 'Only I've found out that she's been to our GP and he's put her on the pill.'

Greg was shocked but he said, 'Oh, I see.'

'It doesn't seem right!' Harry burst out. 'She's not fifteen until October, way below the age of consent. Surely it can't be legal. Surely it's aiding and abetting a crime, or something.'

165

'It's a grey area, I think,' Greg said. 'Doctors have to do what's in the best interests of their patients and her GP would presumably argue that if she's becoming sexually active then safeguarding her against pregnancy is in her best interest.'

Harry snorted. 'If he didn't encourage her by giving her contraceptives, then it probably wouldn't happen.'

'Wishful thinking, mate. Kids do it, safe or not. Look, are you sure he hasn't done it to regulate her periods or something, because –'

'Quite sure! She says they haven't slept together yet, that she's being on the safe side. But why should I believe her?'

'Why should she lie? She's had the aggro from you, so she's probably telling the truth.'

'I thought of forbidding her to see him –'

'Then she'll see him on the sly and lie to you about it. You've got to face facts.'

'The worst of it is . . .' Harry downed the rest of his beer and picked up the whisky chaser he'd bought to go with it. 'The worst of it is that Prue knew about it all along, went with Ruthie to see the bloody doctor.' The dull brown liquid disappeared down his throat after the beer in one gulp.

Greg noticed that Harry had reverted to his daughter's childish name, Ruthie, instead of the more grown-up Ruth that she'd insisted on for the past four years. 'It's good, surely, that she could trust her mother,' he said.

'But why didn't she discuss it with me? Prue, I mean. Aren't I her father? Don't I get a say? I've done my best to be a good father, Greg.'

''Course you have, mate.'

'It isn't easy in the job, we know that, and there were inevitably times when I had to let her down because of work, when I didn't turn up at her birthday party like I'd promised or had to cancel some treat we'd arranged at short notice. But I thought she understood. I thought they both did.'

'I'm sure they do. I'm sure it wasn't a deliberate slight. It's that teenage girls are embarrassed to talk to their fathers about things like that.'

'You're lucky you only had a son . . .' He checked himself. 'Sorry!'

'It's all right.'

'Oh, God, I'm so sorry! What was I thinking?'

'It's all right,' Greg repeated. 'Harry, it's hard for parents to come to terms with the fact that their children are growing up, becoming sexually active – worse with girls than with boys, I'm sure.'

'I feel as if trust has been destroyed between me and Prue, as if all these years when I thought we were friends and partners as well as husband and wife, that we discussed things, that we had no secrets, were a . . . a sick joke.'

'I guess there are always secrets.' Greg finished his pint and said lamely, 'I'm sure you'll feel better soon. Look at it a different way: she's being responsible by getting herself fixed up *before* she starts . . .'

'Fornicating?' Harry gathered up their glasses 'Another?'

'No, I must be getting home.'

'Thanks for listening.'

'What are friends for?' He got up but Harry stayed where he was. 'Not coming?' Greg asked.

'I'll hang on for a bit. Home feels like . . . I feel like I don't belong there at the moment.' He added, almost to himself, 'I moved out here from London because I thought it'd be a better quality of life for my family and now this.'

'Take it easy if you're driving.'

'Yeah, sure.'

Greg was half afraid to open his front door in case the big house sang out its emptiness to him, but he could hear her voice on the telephone in the hall as he pulled his key from the lock and she nodded a greeting to him, said, 'Righto then. Gotta go. Thanks. Bye,' and hung up.

'My mam,' she volunteered, unasked.

'How is she?'

'All right.'

'Are you going up to see her?'

'Yeah. Soon. Perhaps you might come with me.'

'Perhaps.'

Apparently satisfied with this reply, she wandered off into the kitchen.

Rita Lampton was younger than he. A well-preserved forty at the time of the wedding, she'd flirted with him relentlessly and it embarrassed him to confront her as her daughter's acknowledged or unacknowledged lover.

He looked at the telephone for a moment. Last number redial would tell him who she'd called; 1471 would tell him who'd called her. He'd recognise her mother's number either way. He turned his back on the treacherous instrument and went upstairs to change. If I speak with the tongues of men and of angels but have not trust, he told himself, then I am nothing.

Half an hour later they sat down in the dining room to microwaved freezer pizza and a supermarket salad. Some of the crust of Greg's pizza was still frozen but he wasn't going to complain, just put it to one side to thaw. There was nothing domesticated about Angelica: like most women of her generation she could see no reason to clean up after a man or cook his meals. A suggestion from Diane shortly after the wedding that she might like to iron Fred's work shirts had been met with a peal of genuinely incredulous laughter.

'We're pushing the boat out tonight, aren't we?' he said, looking at the table with its linen cloth and best crockery laid. 'I can't remember the last time we used the dining room.'

'I bought you flowers too,' she said with a laugh. 'Carnations. Not even past their sell-by date.'

'So I see. They're lovely. I've never had a woman give me flowers before.'

168

'The sexes are equal these days, haven't you heard?'

He'd bought flowers for Diane when he felt guilty.

She'd opened a bottle of wine and he poured himself a glass and sipped it slowly. 'You know, when Fred was dying, he never said to me, "Take care of Angie", or anything like that. You'd think he would have done.'

She laughed. 'That's because he told me, "Take care of Dad".'

He was doing the washing-up when he heard her calling him urgently from the sitting room. 'Greg! Greg! Come quick.'

He ran in. She pointed at the TV screen, but all he could see was an advertisement for the Renault Clio. 'I don't want a new car,' he said. 'I'm perfectly dissatisfied with the one I've got.'

'It's the local news. They said, "After the break, stay tuned as bereaved Hungerford mother, Josie Abbot, talks to Adam Chaucer about her daughter Jordan's tragic death and about the harassment she's been suffering at the hands of the Newbury police" – or something like that.'

'Oh, no!' Greg slumped down on the sofa next to her. Josie's threat to make him sorry had not been an idle one. 'I don't deserve this,' he said, and she took his hand and squeezed it.

The commercials ended two minutes later and dramatic music heralded the return of the news. The handsome face of Adam Chaucer filled the screen, talking directly to camera, with his blonde-streaked hair, hazel eyes, straight nose – like the ones you saw in magazine adverts for plastic surgeons – his even, white teeth prominent as he spoke. He wore a smart black jacket but with a white tee shirt under it, although it looked like silk. It seemed to say, I am young, I am thrusting, I am going places.

Not as young as you're painted, Greg thought, observing the crow's-feet around the man's eyes, or perhaps too many

169

Caribbean holidays. He had a number of unshakeable prejudices and one of them involved men who dyed their hair.

'Slimeball,' Angelica said.

His voice was low-pitched and oozingly sincere as he ran quickly over the facts of the murder and spoke of the great sympathy he and his viewers must have for his guest. Then the camera drew back as he introduced Josie sitting, like Chaucer, in a beige easy chair, the other side of a coffee table piled with magazines. There were bookshelves behind them with leatherbound books by the yard, a fake sitting room.

She sat upright, wearing an expensive-looking dark suit – courtesy of wardrobe, he assumed. Her short curls had been tidied, pearl studs put in her ears, make-up applied. She was composed, dignified, different from at the appeal yesterday.

If she'd killed her daughter then she was a bloody good actress.

'I've suffered the worst loss any parent can suffer,' she said at Chaucer's invitation. 'There is no nightmare like losing a child. It's bad enough if it's to disease or an accident, but to a deliberate and callous act of murder, it's – well, it's something you never get over.'

'But your ordeal has been made worse, Josie,' Chaucer said, 'by the attitude of the Thames Valley police.'

'They've made it clear from the first that I was their prime suspect. They've neglected other lines of enquiry, pestering me with endless questions, irrelevant things about my late husband.'

'What other lines of enquiry do you think the police should be concentrating on?' Chaucer prompted her.

'There was a gypsy boy who took an unhealthy interest in Jordan at the fair on Saturday afternoon. He's an obvious suspect but the police haven't arrested him.'

'No, but we've questioned him pretty bloody thoroughly and are keeping him in custody,' Greg barked at the screen, knowing that only mad people talked back to the television.

'This was the same boy that a group of your neighbours from Hungerford attempted to apprehend in a citizen's arrest yesterday morning?'

'Citizens arrest?' Greg yelped. 'It was a lynch mob.'

'That's right,' Mrs Abbot said, 'and that man Summers stopped them.'

'I should add,' Adam Chaucer turned back to the camera, 'that we invited Superintendent Gregory Summers of the Newbury police to join us this evening to put his side of the story but were refused.'

'You bloody liar,' Greg said, stunned, as Chaucer concluded, 'Make what you will of that.'

'You called me a hero on Friday night, Chaucer,' he muttered.

Josie went on calmly, 'There's also a man, another gypsy – he calls himself John Smith –' Chaucer gave an appreciative snigger. 'Who is a convicted child killer. Twice over.' Greg gaped at the screen. 'Why is he not under investigation?'

He buried his head in his hands. 'I can't believe she did that. I can't believe she'd put a man's life deliberately at risk like that. How did she know about him, anyway?' He picked up the remote control and killed the sound so that he could think what to do, but he couldn't bring himself to switch the set off. The interview ran on for two or three minutes more and Josie's strain was palpable.

'She's near breaking point,' Angelica said, 'and he doesn't care if he pushes her over the edge so long as he gets his story.' The telephone rang at that moment and she answered it. 'Yeah? Hello, Babs. Yeah, we're watching it. Yeah, ballistic. Hold on and I'll put him on.' She handed the receiver to Greg. 'Barbara Carey.'

'Barbara? I'm not going ballistic. I'm going nuclear. What? Damage limitation? Where do you get this bloody jargon from? Whatever happens, I'm not giving that little wanker an

171

interview. Yes, okay. I'll see you tomorrow. I've got to call HQ about Smith.' He hung up.

The interview had ended. A girl in a yellow dress pointed at a weather map. It was going to be hot again. Greg picked up the receiver, dialled the number of Newbury police station and asked to be put through to the inspector in charge of the night relief. He explained the situation succinctly.

'I'm afraid we'll have another lynch mob on our hands,' he concluded. 'I want a patrol car out at the gypsy encampment at once and I want it to stay there until further notice. They're to explain the situation to Smith and put him on his guard, and they're to call for back up at the first sign of trouble. Is there anyone on duty tonight who's authorised for firearms? Yeah? Make sure he's standing by. Thanks.'

He hung up. 'Oh, Josie,' he said with a heartfelt sigh, 'why did you let them manipulate you like this? Why can't you see who your friends are?'

'Buy a lady a drink, kind sir?'

'Barbara! Long time no see.' She slid onto the stool next to him, her skirt riding up to show a measure of taut thigh, unstockinged, and he asked, 'What're you having?'

'Spritzer.' He nodded to the barman. 'This still your local then, Jonathan?'

'I'm a creature of habit.'

'Yes, I know. Killed many patients lately?'

'Oh, I leave that to specialists.' He looked at his watch. 'You've left it late. Nearly closing time.'

'Long enough for one drink.'

Her wine arrived and he paid for it. 'What brings you to Hungerford?'

'Work.'

'Still in the same business?'

She nodded. 'Detective Sergeant now.'

'Congratulations. I knew you'd go far. You told me so often enough.' She laughed. He looked her over carefully. 'You're looking very good, Babs.'

'You're not looking so bad yourself.'

Dr Jonathan Tabor was a tall man and his thinness made him seem taller, along with his slight physical clumsiness which miraculously disappeared when he made love or when he was dealing with his patients, especially the children. He was thirty-two, a good age for a man, before physical decline set in. He had a blaze of auburn hair which looked as if he never brushed it. She remembered with a small smile that he had a similar excrescence down below.

'What's amusing you?' he asked.

'Nothing. Just thinking.'

She didn't normally fancy redheads but she'd been prepared to make an exception in his case, attracted by his dry, freckled skin and pale blue eyes. He was a nice man; too nice, which was why she'd ended their affair after a few weeks. That had been three years ago. She knew that she'd hurt him badly and hoped that he'd had time to heal, since she needed his help.

'So, how are you, Jonathan? Still living in the same place?'

'Yes. It suits me and I've had no reason to move.'

'There isn't a Mrs Tabor now?'

'Oh, no.'

She wouldn't have minded if there had been except that it would have raised logistical problems. She downed her spritzer in one gulp and said, 'Your place, then?' and got up.

Unfazed, he emptied his glass. 'I'll, er, pop into the gents.' He felt in his pocket for change.

'It's okay. I've got some.'

11. Tuesday, 23rd June

Greg loitered over breakfast. One of the pleasures of being a superintendent was that you'd served your time on the streets, on the slog. Besides, he didn't like the sound of what he had waiting for him this morning. After Barbara's call he'd unplugged the telephone and left the Ansaphone on. He hadn't checked his messages this morning, however redly the machine winked at him.

As he buttered toast, happy that Angelica had never tried to boss him into low-fat margarine, he heard the post plop onto the mat.

'I'll get it,' she said, and was out of the room before he could put his knife down. She was gone a longer time than seemed necessary, perhaps five minutes, and he thought he heard the barely perceptible squeak of the sitting room door. She came back into the kitchen with a number of long, white, boring-looking envelopes, reading from them as she came and handing them to him one by one. 'Mr G. Summers, Mr G. P. Summers, Gregory Summers Esq. – how posh. Oh! Mr Frederick Summers.'

It still happened often which was why he liked to be first to the post. 'Shall I deal with it?' he asked.

'No, just junk mail.' She opened it and scanned it quickly. 'Does Fred want a Diners Club card, d'you think?'

'I don't think so somehow.'

'The ambrosia is free where he is.' She tore the letter across with one swift movement and threw it in the bin. 'And the nectar.'

'And the angel cake,' he said.

Junk mail was bad enough without them sending it to dead men.

Dr Jonathan Tabor lay on the bed, uninhibitedly naked, his arms folded behind his head, watching Barbara dress. She did it slowly, knowing that a woman dressing could be as erotic as a woman undressing if she did it right. Her small breasts vanished into the coffee silk and lace of her bra and she said, 'Do me up,' sitting down on the bed so he could fasten the hooks.

'Early start,' he commented, fumbling. 'Are you working on the Jordan Abbot case?' She nodded. 'That's a dreadful business.'

She said casually, 'Of course, she was your patient, wasn't she?'

'How did you know that?'

She got up and put her matching pants on, taking a pair of tights out of her jacket pocket and checking them for ladders. 'Josie mentioned that she was coming to see you yesterday morning, to get some tranquillisers.'

'Anti-depressants,' he corrected her automatically.

'Isn't that the same?'

'Not at all.'

'I've never tried either.'

'No, I can imagine.'

'It's good, though, that she was prepared to come to you. So many people in her situation refuse medical help, as if soldiering on made their grief more valid.'

'That's a woman who's suffered a lot,' he said, 'more than any one person should suffer.'

'Does she come to you often?'

'You know,' he said, 'that doctor-patient confidentiality is absolute.'

'Of course.' She pulled her skirt up and fastened it, sensing that he had something he wanted to entrust to her and that he wouldn't let it be bullied out of him. She would play the waiting game, pretend she wasn't that interested, while he found a way of squaring it with his conscience. 'Sorry,' she added. She tucked her blouse into her skirt and tidied her hair in the mirror with her hands.

'It can't be germane,' he said.

'No? Well, you're the best judge.' She put her jacket on and flipped her hair loose from the collar. She found one shoe easily and put it on, then began to hunt for the other, lurching drunkenly round the room on different-length legs. 'Have you seen my other shoe?'

'Under the bed?' He rolled over and peered, emerging with a paperback book. 'Oh, I've been looking for that.'

'Here it is, in the corner.' Symmetry was resumed. 'Better be off.' She made for the door, waiting for him to call her back. She knew she wouldn't have to screw it out of him.

No pun intended.

Jonathan said quietly, 'I called her in for a smear test three months ago. She's thirty-five and she'd never had one done.'

She paused with her hand on the door knob. 'Oh?'

'I can't be a hundred percent sure, of course, but it seemed to me that she'd never had a child.'

Barbara stood like a statue for a few seconds, then she let out a long satisfied breath. 'So that's it!' *No one ever doubted they were father and daughter.* That statement hadn't struck her as particularly odd at the time; now it did.

'Vaginal birth is pretty traumatic –'

'I can imagine.'

'And there was no Caesarean scar either.'

'She told me Jordan was born by IVF.'

'For heaven's sake, Barbara. They're conceived in test tubes, not born in them. This isn't *Brave New World.*'

'Sorry, my brain's not in top gear at this time of the morning.'

He sat up, understanding, more sad than angry. 'That's what this was about, wasn't it? Last night. You came looking for me deliberately in the pub. You just wanted information out of me.'

She wouldn't deny it. 'I never turn down a decent fuck,' she said, 'and you're a decent fucker.'

'*Decent!*'

'Nine out of ten.'

Slightly mollified, he said, 'Do you meet many tens?'

'None, but I keep looking. Did you ask her about it?'

'What? Oh, no. It didn't seem relevant. Jordan was healthy and well cared for. I mean, so what if the child was adopted and she preferred not to say? She wouldn't be the first and I could be wrong. I'm not a specialist. Perhaps some women heal up like new.' He took a tissue from the bedside table and blew his nose copiously. 'You hurt me, you know, back then.'

'But you got over it.'

'. . . Yes, I suppose I did, now you come to mention it.' But he needed her to understand how painful it had been at the time. 'I was . . . I could easily have fallen for you, Barbara. I could imagine myself married to you.'

'If I wanted to wash a man's socks and iron his shirts, I'd start a laundry.'

'It doesn't have to be like that.'

'I must get off, Jonathan. It's been nice.'

'Can I call you?'

'Yes, do. And thanks for trusting me with the info. It might be important.' She bent over and kissed his genitals, sleeping on their auburn nest. 'You should be struck off.'

Greg drove past a newsagent on a suburban corner on his way to work. There was a *Daily Mirror* billboard outside and he read 'Hungerford Mother Blames Police for Mental Anguish' as it flashed past.

There were journalists waiting outside the station when he arrived. He had to lower his driver's window and insert his electronic card to open the shudderingly slow gates into the car park.

'Superintendent, what do you say to Mrs Abbot's allegations?'

'Mr Summers, is she your only suspect?'

'Inspector, is the gypsy boy in custody?'

'What about this man Smith, Summers?'

'Aren't you ashamed of yourself?'

He ignored them, finally got through the gates and entered the building. There was a similar clamour in here but at least it was on his side and Harry Stratton punched him on the arm, muttering, 'Don't let the bastards grind you down,' on his way out, through the door before Greg could ask him where he was going.

Bob Holman, the inspector from the night relief, intercepted him as he was half way up the first flight of stairs, calling up to him. 'Hey, Sunshine.'

He was Greg's age and they'd been constables together all those years ago. Sunshine had been his nickname back then, long forgotten by everyone except Holman.

'You're here late,' Greg said, glancing at his watch.

'When you didn't answer your phone earlier I thought I'd hang on and make sure you got my message.'

'I didn't.'

'I left one on your machine a good three hours ago.'

'I didn't check.' He didn't like the set of the man's mouth. 'Just tell me, Bob. I'm a big boy. I can take it.'

'Smith . . . he's gone, done a bunk.'

Greg came slowly back down the stairs. 'I'm listening and it had better be good.'

'I got a car out there within minutes of your call and they spoke to Smith, put him in the picture, then took up position a bit away from the camp where they'd have a good view along the road in either direction, see trouble coming in plenty of time. Only, when dawn came . . . they found Smith's van had gone.'

'They fell asleep, in other words.'

'No way! Or not both of them together.'

'Wasn't a boy/girl combo, by any chance?'

'Yes, as it happens, but they know better than to sit snogging on *my* time.'

'So how do you explain his sneaking away like that? They're a good size, those vans, and then there's the logistical problem of getting the horse across the cattle grid at the gates with no one there to unlock the barriers.'

'I'm not explaining it, sir. I can't. I'm telling you the way it is.'

'All right,' Greg snapped and started upstairs again.

'Do we want me to start a search for him?' Holman called after him.

'No. He's not wanted in connection with any crime and your constables would obviously be wasting their time if they're that incompetent.'

He knew that wasn't fair but he didn't feel like being fair this morning. Who was being fair to him? Clearly Smith didn't trust the police to protect him and preferred self reliance. What a nuisance that man could be.

His secretary seemed relieved to see him. Susan Habib was Jewish and her husband Arab – a walking détente. He didn't know what sort of Arab: he'd once asked her where her husband came from and she'd replied in her nasal voice, 'Peterborough.' She was of average looks and average competence like all police secretaries. Presumably women with above-average looks or secretarial skills didn't work for Civil Service wages.

She told him that the chief superintendent would like to see him at his earliest convenience and that the deputy chief constable's office had been on the telephone.

'Did you take a call yesterday, Susan,' he asked, 'from a Mr Chaucer?'

'No. Wait, someone – a man – rang about four but you were out of the office and when I told him that he hung up without leaving a name.'

How convenient. He'd slipped out for coffee or a pee and Chaucer could legitimately claim that he'd tried to reach him and failed.

'Here's Sergeant Carey for you,' the woman said, and glared at Barbara who was inclined to enter the superintendent's office without awaiting the permission of his secretary cum guard dog.

'I've got to go and see the chief in a minute,' he told her. 'At my "earliest convenience", which means half an hour ago.'

'You've not arrived yet.'

'Oh, so I haven't.' He called after his secretary's departing back, 'I'm not here for the next few minutes, Susan, if anyone asks. I'm still on my way in.'

'Yes, Mr Summers.'

When she'd gone he asked, 'Where was Harry off to in such a hurry?'

'DCI Stratton's dealing with another murder case,' Barbara said.

'What!'

She was succinct. 'Two blokes in a pub last night, with a drop taken, words exchanged, "Step outside and say that", very macho. Both took their glasses with them and broke them, one got the other across the carotid artery by mistake, dead on arrival at hospital.'

'My God!' Greg said, although this was the sort of murder he usually got on his ground, no mystery about it, only a deadening inevitability.

'The perpetrator's been hospitalised with shock,' Barbara went on. 'DCI Stratton's gone to the hospital to make his day when he's been pronounced fit for questioning. He said it was all morning and possibly longer if you asked. We'll manage perfectly well without him.'

'Okay. I thought a press release, Barbara.'

'I've drafted one. I'll print it out for your approval.'

180

'You're wonderful.' He got up and gave her smacking kiss on the cheek on his way out of the door.

'That's sexual harassment, that is,' she called after him.

'I don't care. I'm in enough trouble. Make a formal complaint, why don't you?' She laughed. He turned back. 'Have you been to Josie's to see about her post this morning.'

'No, I'm going now. I don't feel well disposed towards Mrs Abbot at the moment.'

'See you later.'

It wasn't like Barbara to be indecisive, but she honestly didn't know what to do with the information she'd gleaned that morning and she needed to think about it for a while. She didn't want to damage Jonathan, who was a damned good doctor, especially as she couldn't see what bearing it had on the case, if true. Josie might be proved a liar, which wouldn't make her a murderer. Unless they were all murderers.

The logical thing, the obvious thing, was for her to gain the same information by a different route. It was easier to find something when you knew it was there to be looked for.

Apologising mentally to her superior officer, Barbara set off in her car for Hungerford.

Via Inkpen.

Chief Superintendent Barkiss was liked by his men for one reason above all: he stuck up for them, took their side, be it against his superiors, the public or the media. He listened to Greg's explanation without interrupting. 'Okay,' he said at the end, 'let me see this press release before it's issued. I'll speak to the DCC myself.'

'Thanks, Jim.'

Barkiss had got back from his golfing holiday in Portugal that morning and looked brown and fit. He was a short man who must only just have met the height requirements when he joined, perhaps designated LTG – Likely To Grow – a ruse used to slip promising cadets in under the limbo pole.

That had changed, of course: any shortarse could get in now.

'What's this about a siege?' he asked, leaning comfortably back in his black leather swivel chair – the *Mastermind* chair, as Barbara called it – and folding his arms behind his head. 'We back in the Middle Ages? Sometimes feels that way.' Greg explained. 'Oh, that'll make a dent in the budget,' the superintendent said cheerfully. 'Still, can't be helped. Coffee?'

'I've got a suspect to interview,' Greg said. 'Maybe later.'

Peel had a blankness about him which was hard to feign. He'd been stopped west of the Severn Bridge heading, so he said, for Fishguard and a few days holiday in Ireland. It was a free country, wasn't it? He'd lost his retinue in that his van was now a convoy of one, and he'd mislaid eighty percent of his harem, accompanied now by the averagely attractive girl who gave her name implausibly as Topaz Jones. One thing he still had was his fake accent, but he knew his rights and refused to say anything in it until a duty solicitor was fetched for him, which took about half an hour.

'Been arrested often?' Greg asked pleasantly as they waited. 'Know the ropes?' He got no reply.

'We split up this side of Bristol,' Peel explained once suitably chaperoned, 'for whatever business it is of yours. The van the gippo damaged was too crocked up to go any further and the other one was making a funny noise in the engine and my van only sleeps two.'

Presumably he'd gone eeny, meeny, miny, mo.

'I think it is my business,' Greg said. 'Firstly, because you ran out on me at the riot when I was yelling to you for help –'

'Yeah? We didn't hear you. Lot of noise, mate. Sorry.'

'Really?' In France they had a 'Good Samaritan' law which meant you could be prosecuted if you didn't to go to the help of someone in distress. Greg thought they could do with a bit of that here.

Peel smiled faintly. 'You had just told me to bugger off,' he pointed out, 'and I was brought up to obey nice policemen.'

'More importantly,' Greg went on, ignoring this lie, 'because I need you to explain how part of the dead girl's clothing came to be under your van.'

Peel was speechless. Authentically so, Greg thought. 'You're stitching me up,' he said in the end. His voice rose hysterically as he turned to his solicitor. 'This is a frame up.'

'No one's accusing you of anything at the moment,' Greg pointed out, 'but I'd like to know your exact movements between the hours of, say, nine o'clock on Saturday night and about three on Sunday morning.' Peel glanced at his brief who shrugged. Life was harder since the days when you could advise your client not to say anything until he'd had time to come up with a plausible story, if then. 'Not long ago, last Saturday,' Greg said, 'or have drugs destroyed your memory, Mr Peel?'

'I don't do drugs,' he snapped. 'Bit of grass, maybe.' The solicitor sighed audibly at this admission. They hadn't found any drugs in his van, to Greg's disappointment, since it would have been something to hold him on. There was a faint odour of marijuana, true, but they'd apparently smoked the lot and it wasn't illegal to reek of the stuff or to be obviously high on it, only to have it in your possession.

'So?' he said. 'Last Saturday night?'

'We hung around the fair till it ended about seven, then bought ourselves hamburgers from one of the other canteens before it left.'

'You're not a vegetarian yourself?' Greg asked. 'You surprise me. You being so much in touch with nature and all. Or maybe not. No doubt the real thing tastes better than that soya crap of yours.'

You fucking hypocritical fraud.

'What's my client being accused of?' the solicitor asked. 'Selling food you wouldn't want to eat?'

'Ever hear of the food chain?' Peel said. 'That's what nature's about. The strong prey on the weak, birds eat insects, men screw women.'

Adults break kids' necks.

'Lovely,' Greg said.

'We drove one of the vans to a place called Shalbourne where there's a pub – The Plough – hung out there until closing time, then got back to the common around eleven-thirty, midnight –'

'Which?'

'I don't know. I wasn't late for a board meeting.'

'You stayed in the same van then?'

'No, Cathy stayed in my van with me and the other girls . . . let me see. I think they went into one van. I told them not to go to sleep, to be sure to be ready at dawn.'

'Dawn?'

'For our ceremony,' Peel said impatiently. 'The solstice. The sacrifice to the sun god.'

'Sacrifice?'

'Figure of speech. The sacrifice is naturally symbolic.'

'Imaginary?'

'If you like.'

'I certainly hope so. So Cathy can alibi you from about midnight until dawn and all of them before that.'

'Yup.'

'Did she sleep at all?'

'No.' He grinned and shoved his thumbs into his belt buckle, thrusting his pelvis forward in brazen youth. 'I didn't give her a chance to sleep.'

'And you were doing what exactly? Playing scrabble?'

'How much detail d'you want? Let me see. I think she gave me a blow job to start with –'

'No, all right,' Greg said. 'I don't want details. This is the van with the symbols painted over the windscreen – yin and yang, Mars and Venus?'

184

'That's right.'

'Which is where the button from the girl's dungarees was found after the riot the next day.'

Peel had recovered his *sang froid*. 'If you say so.'

'Is it not possible,' the solicitor put in, 'that the item in question got moved – kicked about – in the course of what I understand to have been a considerable affray and found its way accidentally under my client's van?'

Greg didn't bother to answer, largely because he could think of no reply he wanted to make. There was nothing more likely and it would take a while to check the oil of Jordan's clothing against any likely leak from Peel's van. He continued to address his suspect. 'Would you and Miss . . . what's her other name, this Cathy?'

'Um . . . Jacobs, I think. Yeah, that's right.'

'Am I right in thinking that you and Miss Jacobs would have been too preoccupied to notice if anyone had been hanging around outside the van or messing about under it.'

The Dorset accent reappeared, redolent of the farmyard. 'I reckon we would at that.'

Greg changed tack. 'Are you the Clive Peel who used to live at 3a Tobruck Road, Poole?'

He glanced at his solicitor. 'Do I have to answer that?'

'What's the purport of this question?' the lawyer asked.

'I'm trying to establish if Mr Peel is the same Clive Peel who appears on my computer with a number of previous charges and an offence against a minor female which never went to court.'

'She was fifteen!' Clive objected.

'I think that answers my question.'

'It's absurd to say that a girl that age can't consent. If her dad hadn't come home unexpectedly . . .' He sounded so like Piers with his twenty-year-old boy that Greg had to stop himself from laughing. Let's form a club, he wanted to say, for those of us sleeping in the arms of those we shouldn't be sleeping with. 'There's a world of difference between a fully-grown woman of fifteen and a kid of six,' Peel pointed out. 'I'm no paedophile.'

'No, all right.'

'Anyone who rapes a kid that age –'

'Who said she was raped?'

Clive looked taken aback. 'I assumed . . .'

'Did you?'

'I think my client's answered your questions to the best of his ability,' the solicitor said. 'He's been most co-operative as a *witness* in this distressing case. If you wish to detain him, I suggest you come up with a charge.'

The trouble was that Peel had no fixed abode, which made Greg reluctant to release him, but he couldn't keep people in custody because it happened to suit him. Finally, he said, 'Let's go for a walk, Mr Peel.'

'Eh?'

'If you can spare me five minutes of your valuable time, I'd like you to stroll across to the mortuary with me.'

12. Tuesday Morning

'Have you known desperation, Sergeant Carey?'

'No,' Barbara conceded, 'I can't say I have. Unless you count desperation to have a large gin after a hard day at the cutting edge . . . No,' seeing Josie Abbot's face, 'I didn't think you would.'

'Then don't condemn me.'

'Mrs Abbot.' They'd been Josie and Barbara to each other the day before but that was gone now. 'I know you think you were using the media, but the truth is that they were using you, to get a good story. I bet Adam Chaucer was charming and polite wasn't he, probably a teensy bit flirtatious, allowing for your present sadness?' Josie flushed. 'I bet he took you out for a stiff drink after and made like he was your special friend.'

'He took me to dinner after the recording,' the older woman said defiantly.

'Very nice. Was it good, a bit of male company, after all this time? And such a good-looking man too.'

'Yes,' she said, 'it was nice, as it happens.'

'But in two days' time, when the story's cooled, he won't return your calls.'

'Look,' Josie said after a minute's silence, 'I didn't mean to make it sound like a personal attack on Mr Summers –'

'That isn't much consolation to him this morning.'

'He's been . . . kind. But he distorted what I said – Adam – he blew it up into something much bigger and then it was too late to stop it, the train had run away with me. I was afraid he wouldn't do the interview at all if I tried to back down and I'd be left with the same feelings of helplessness I've had these last few days, these last eighteen months. Maybe all my life. I'll know better next time.'

'I don't suppose there'll be a next time,' Barbara said. 'I'll be back later.'

'There's no need,' Josie said quickly.

'There might be,' Barbara said with deliberate obscurity. The person she most wanted to speak to in Inkpen had been out and she'd promised herself another visit later that day. She also had some enquiries to make in Lambourn. She collected Josie's post, two more letters that were certainly abusive, one incongruous in a pink envelope with red flowers on it, and left. She didn't take the phone bill.

Clive Peel turned his head away and put his hand across his mouth. He was suddenly much younger and a lot less full of himself. He was also an unsavoury yellow colour. When he could speak, he said, 'If I got my hands on the bastard who did that to her –'

'Oh, the pathologist did *that* to her,' Greg said mildly, pulling the sheet back up. Slashed her open from neck to crotch and across from right to left, sliced open the top of her head, removed her entrails. Eat your heart out, Jack the Ripper. They'd also wiped her whiskers, floppy ears and black bunny nose away. 'The murderer,' he concluded, 'hardly touched her, snapped her neck in two and left her neatly and reverently on the tow path.'

Peel said, 'All right, Summers, you win.'

'What do you mean, I win?'

'I saw her, Saturday night, in Hungerford, about ten, talking to a man in a car. I saw the man who abducted and murdered Jordan Abbot.'

'This is sudden,' Greg said evenly, although his heart was beating fast. 'Why did you lie to me before?' Peel shrugged. 'Because it's as natural to you as breathing?' Greg went on. 'Because I'm the enemy? Because you're on one side of the great divide and I'm on the other?'

'Something like that. Never tell the cops anything unless

they can find it out for themselves, that's always been my motto.'

Greg laid a hand on his arm. 'Let's get back to the station and go over your statement again, shall we? And this time we'll have the truth.'

Rufus Lee was standing at the front desk as they reached the door. He had his back to them but his shoulders were glowering. Greg, seeing him, wheeled round and went in the back way, through the car park. Whittaker and Clements were coming out and held the door for him and his witness.

'All I'm saying,' Clements was telling his partner, 'is that if you travel through the galaxy at warp speed, you'll be bound to crash into things – stars, planets.'

'God, you're sad,' Whittaker said. 'Sir, there's that big gypsy asking for you at the front desk. It's about his son, I think.'

'Not now, Whittaker.'

'No, sir.'

Barbara joined them in the interview room and listened with interest as Greg took Peel through the events of Saturday evening again. Now that he'd decided to tell the truth, the hippie didn't seem to want a solicitor present. It made Greg wonder what people thought solicitors were for.

'You said in your original statement that you were at The Plough in Shalbourne until closing time.'

'I left earlier than that. Two of us, me and Cathy, we decided to leave the others and get off by ourselves. We left the pub about quarter to ten.'

'What were the other four girls supposed to do?'

'I told them to hitch a lift back to Hungerford and walk from there.'

'Proper little gent, aren't you?'

'That stuff – gentlemen, ladies – it's prehistoric. It's an insult to women, right?'

189

'You're an insult to women. So you got to Hungerford at what? Ten?'

'Must have been about that. I was driving down the hill and I saw a big car stopped on the other side of the road – he'd pulled across to the right, I mean, he was facing in the same direction as us – and he was talking to a kid through the open window, a girl, about so high.' He demonstrated with his hand at chest level. 'Blonde. I'm not saying it was Jordan Abbot – I saw her for maybe five seconds – only that it might have been.'

Too much of a coincidence if it hadn't been, Greg thought. 'You said "he",' he said. 'Could you see that the driver was a male?'

'That was the impression I got. The street lamps were on but I tell you it was fast. Empty, open roads, bowling downhill. Blink and we were gone.'

'Was he alone?'

'I didn't see anyone else in the car.'

'Can you describe him?'

'It was almost dark and he hadn't put the inside light on. I could make out a shape, maybe, average sort of shape. Not bald, not fat.'

'Did you see Jordan get into the car?'

'Nope.'

'You said at the mortuary that you'd seen the man who abducted and murdered her,' Greg pointed out.

'Poetic licence.'

'A big car?' Barbara said. 'Can you be more specific?'

He turned to look at her, acknowledging her presence for the first time, and smiled. His eyes shifted deliberately down from her face to the v-neck of her blouse and back again. She didn't react although Greg, sitting close beside her, felt her body tense. 'Travelling salesman's car,' Peel said with a sneer. 'Family man with 2.4 kids and a mortgage sort of car.'

'Colour?'

'Dark.'

'Black? Blue? Grey?'

'Might have been dark red, come to think of it. A purplish-red or maroon.'

'Saloon, hatchback?'

'Estate.' His eyes moved back down to her breasts and he licked his lips.

Barbara got up, said, 'Sergeant Carey leaving the room at 11.37' into the tape recorder and murmured, 'See you upstairs in a few minutes,' to Greg.

After Peel had signed a new statement and Greg had warned him to keep himself available for the time being, he went up and found Barbara at his desk, typing into his computer. 'He was even flirting with you,' he remarked.

'Thanks for "even".'

'You know what I mean. He's in a police station, giving a statement about a horrible murder, something he's previously lied about, and he's flirting with a female officer.'

'I don't call it flirting. I call it leering. Flirting has a touch of subtlety about it, a sense of humour, a sally between equals, whereas I'm a human being and he's pond life.'

'What on earth do women see in him?'

'He's got a cheeky, boyish smile.'

'What!'

'Are you familiar with the concept of sarcasm? I told you. He's a slimeball. Those women of his must have low self-esteem.'

'Is that why you left the room?' he asked.

'Nope. Not such a tender flower as that.' She spun the computer screen round in his direction. 'Douglas Cameron is the registered keeper of a Volvo 940 estate, P-reg, June 1997, owned by Collins and Mather, estate agents, Market Place. What you might call a "travelling salesman's car" if you were an arsehole like Mr Peel. "Blackberry wine" is the colour, which I take to be a purplish-red or maroon, as advertised.'

'He's good, isn't he?' Greg said after a pause. 'Cameron, I mean. All that righteous indignation when I asked if he'd spoken to her. Made me feel guilty and irresponsible for suggesting such a thing.'

Barbara looked at her watch. 'Almost noon. Presumably his office is the best place to look for him.'

'Well . . .' He stopped as the door opened and Harry Stratton came in. He looked tired and rather grim.

'I hear the Jordan Abbot case is breaking,' he said.

'Christ!' Barbara said. 'You can't keep a secret in this place.'

'Why would you want to?' Stratton asked.

'Barbara,' Greg said, 'go round and ask Mr Cameron if he'd like to take an early lunch and come for a chat with me.'

She got up, taking her jacket from the back of his chair and shrugging it on. She flipped her hair loose from the collar. 'Do I arrest?'

'Only if you have to.'

'The threat of a scene in the office should suffice. "Woman Officer Handcuffs Respected Newbury Surveyor in Broad Daylight – Pictures Page Three".' She held up both hands, fingers splayed. 'Ten minutes.' At the door she paused and said to Harry, 'You all right, sir?'

'Yes, fine, thanks.'

'Right.' She left.

'Get your murder sorted out?' Greg asked Stratton.

'Yes, tucked up in bed.'

'Good.'

'Yeah.'

'Wish they were all that simple.'

'Yeah.'

Harry clearly had something on his mind but Greg knew from experience that he wasn't going to give it up unasked. 'So what happened?' he asked. 'Barbara said it was a pub brawl.'

'Bloke A's having a quiet drink with his girlfriend,' Stratton said, 'and accuses Bloke B of eyeing of her up. Bloke B says she's a right bow-wow and he wouldn't have her if she came gift wrapped. They've both had a lot to drink – all three of them have, in fact, the girl could scarcely stand. Bloke A says, "Step outside and say that," and, two minutes later, Bloke A's bleeding to death in the car park, his girl's screaming blue murder and Bloke B's puking up in the bushes.'

Greg made a face. 'What a pathetic waste. Whatever gets into them?'

'Alcohol. Trouble is Bloke B – that's B as in Barney. Barney Chase.'

'Fuck!' Greg sat down hard on his chair and heard it sigh.

Barney Chase had been a newly-promoted sergeant eleven years earlier, twenty-five, keen and talented, destined for great things, lately engaged to his childhood sweetheart and taking out a mortgage on their first house. A man much as Gregory Summers had been fifteen years before. Until he and Greg, then an inspector, had got a shout early one August afternoon in 1987 to go to Hungerford where something strange and terrible was happening, although no one was sure of the details. Not then. Later that day the whole country would know the name of that charming Berkshire market town.

The centre had been shut off to prevent more people walking into Ryan's murderous sights and they'd been left kicking their heels on the outskirts, waiting for the Tactical Firearms Team to show up from Kidlington. Finally, with the gunman cornered at the comprehensive school, they'd made their way across the common to South View where seven bodies had been lying for several hours. It had been a blazing hot day.

Barney had been dazed by what they'd found there. He'd wandered about among the corpses of Ryan's neighbours and his mother, of casual passers-by whose life-luck had run out that day, of their brave colleague shot dead in his panda car.

He'd stared at the foetid blood, the riddled limbs, muttering, 'No, it can't be. Human beings can't do this to each other,' until Greg had sent him home as worse than useless.

Stress counselling had been offered to the traumatised policemen, an offer which Greg had gratefully accepted, and perhaps being one of the station's representatives at PC Roger Breretons' funeral had helped too, had given him some sort of closure. But his young sergeant couldn't forget what he'd seen. Over the next year Barney had hit the bottle big time, arriving drunk on duty on more than one occasion. As usual, his colleagues had done their best to cover for him as his life disintegrated, his faith in humanity withered, but a stinking sewer couldn't be disguised with cologne, or not for long. His fiancée had called off the wedding, the house hunting ended and Barney had resigned from the force a few days ahead of the boot.

He'd not held down a proper job since then, doing odd bits of work to pay for his drink. Sometimes Greg saw him in the street, a man of thirty-six who looked fifty, and emptied the loose cash from his wallet for him, knowing that it would go on booze, hoping he didn't want to chat. And now Barney Chase was in a cell in his own station, facing a murder charge.

He fiddled with a couple of letters in evidence bags on his desk. One, on pink paper with red roses, jumped out at him, too many capitals, like German. He saw the words 'Little Baby Jesus', 'God's Unfathomable Will', and 'Reunited in Heaven.' It made him queasy and he thought he preferred the abusive one. It was anonymous and the handwriting might aptly be characterised as loopy.

'Maybe he'll dry out inside,' Harry said, 'get help. Maybe it's what he needs to get him straight.'

'Yes,' Greg said. They both knew it wasn't. If he couldn't get drink he'd turn to drugs, freely available in every nick in the country. He'd get no help with his problems. He was finished.

'So I can come back on the Abbot case, unless it's really broken.'

'We've got some sort of break by the look of things,' Greg said, 'but I don't suppose for a moment it'll be as simple as that. I'm sure I can use you.'

'Good. I like to be busy, take my mind off Barney. There but for the grace of God . . .' Greg nodded agreement. There but for the grace of God went any of them. He felt guilty and knew that Harry did too. Am I my brother officer's keeper?

Douglas Cameron looked less relaxed than he had the morning before and much paler. He'd been offered a solicitor but had refused one. Estate agents did business with law firms and didn't want to thrust their dirty washing under their noses and say, 'Smell this.'

'You told me yesterday that you didn't speak to Jordan Abbot,' Greg reminded him. 'I've spoken to a witness who says that's a lie.'

Cameron chewed his bottom lip. 'I was afraid to tell you I'd spoken to her. It was a minute, no more.'

'Want to start again? I'm listening.'

'I saw her, as I said, at ten o'clock, crossing the road and skipping along the pavement. I thought she was too young to be out by herself. I've got kids of my own, who are my whole life to me, so I pulled over to her side of the road and wound down the driver's window.'

'Was she afraid?'

'Not at all. In fact she came over and leant her arms on the window ledge and looked in at me, all smiles. She was a darling.' He intercepted the glance between the two police officers. 'Not like that! A lovely, sweet child. I said something like, "Does your mummy know you're out alone so late, sweetheart?" and she giggled and said, "It's a secret –"'

'"It's a secret." Those were her exact words?'

He nodded. 'I asked where she lived but she wouldn't tell me, shook her head and kept repeating that it was a secret, the two of them –'

'No name for the second person? If it was a man or a woman?'

'No, and then she said goodbye, nice as pie, very polite, and skipped away into the alley and I didn't know what to do. I couldn't follow her up there in my car. I could hardly get out and grab her – I really would have looked like a child molester then. So I drove on in the end.'

Greg and Barbara looked at him in silence for a moment and he burst out, 'If I'd abducted her, why would I come forward yesterday and tell you I'd seen her at all? Why wouldn't I keep my head down?'

'I was wondering that,' Greg said. 'Would it be because you knew you were seen by the occupants of a passing van?'

'No! It was because I heard what happened and I felt guilty about not doing more to help her and I truly thought my evidence might be of some use in your investigation, in pinning down where and when she was seen alive that night, in finding the motherfucker who did this.'

'You're sure about the time,' Greg said, 'ten o'clock?'

'Yes, I told you yesterday, I'd heard the pips.'

'You told me a lot of things yesterday and half of them turn out to be courtesy of the Brothers Grimm. And it was, say, half a mile from your house. So if I ask your neighbours they'll say you got home at about five past ten.' Cameron didn't answer. 'Mr Cameron? Is that what they'll tell me or will they by any chance say it was a lot later?'

'Yes,' he said reluctantly. 'The nosy bastards will tell you it was after midnight when I got home. Mrs Horobin next door complains about me slamming my car door, however careful I am.'

Greg felt excitement in his stomach. 'Long time to drive from one end of Hungerford to the other, Mr Cameron.'

'I stopped off to see a . . . friend. A special friend.'

'Oh?'

'With my wife away . . .'

196

'A lover?'

'Yes.'

'In Hungerford?'

'Yes.'

'And this woman will alibi you, needless to say?'

He thought about it. 'I don't see why the hell not.'

'Then I need her name and address.' Cameron was silent. 'Douglas, you're in big trouble, I must warn you. Is this woman married too? Is that it? You're afraid her husband will find out.'

He laughed, cutting it off abruptly, when he realised he was in no laughing matter. 'No, my lover isn't married, lives alone.'

'We shall be discreet, I promise you, but if she can account for your time between ten and midnight then I suggest you give me her name right now.'

Cameron held up his hands in surrender. 'Very well, but I'll hold you to that promise of discretion.' He gave Greg the name of his lover and the superintendent stared at him in stunned disbelief.

13. Tuesday Afternoon

'Ah, you've brought a chaperone this time. Don't trust yourself, Gregory?'

Piers was downstairs in his studio when Greg and Barbara got there, changing the bulb in a spotlight. His eyes swept over Barbara, taking her in, not hostile. He probably had women friends, Greg thought, liked them.

'Sergeant Barbara Carey.' She showed him her warrant card.

He glanced at it then back at her. 'I like your hair better as it is now, bit longer.'

'Thank you.'

'Can we go somewhere private?' Greg asked.

'With you, any time.' Piers swung the open sign on the door round to closed, clicked the Yale lock shut and led the way up to his flat.

'Do you know a Douglas Cameron?' Greg asked as soon as they reached the sitting room.

'Yes. Why?'

'Know him well?'

'Molto bene . . . Is he all right?'

Piers's chirpy, chippy manner had deserted him now and he looked worried. Greg saw beneath to the fragility of a man in love who cannot have the thing he loves. No wonder his flirtation was so unthreatening: it wasn't Greg he wanted, but another dark-haired man, not overly tall.

'When d'you see him last, Piers?' he asked kindly.

'Saturday night.'

'What time did he get here?'

'Five past ten.'

'That's precise.'

Piers managed a wistful smile. 'I've answered four questions.

Now it's your turn. You ever had an affair with a married man, Gregory?'

'No, nor with a married woman either.' He didn't count the brief encounters at training courses long ago; that wasn't what Piers meant. He was talking about the hours spent waiting for the phone to ring, the lonely Christmases and solitary holidays.

'No, well you don't know what it's like then. He said he'd try to be here by half past nine and I was looking at my watch, every couple of minutes, wondering how time could go so slowly.'

'You told me you were developing and printing your pictures of the fair that evening.'

'So I was, until Doug got here. It passed the time.'

'And how long did he stay?'

'Until midnight. I'd hoped he'd stay the night, with his wife being away, but he said the neighbours would be sure to find a way of letting her know if he'd been out all night. Now tell me why you want to know this.'

But the game wasn't played that way. 'Did he mention seeing Jordan Abbot on his way here?' Barbara asked. 'Speaking to her?'

'No.' Piers was startled. 'Why would he? We had more important things to talk about.' He looked from one to the other of them. 'Did he? Is that what you're saying? Is that why you're here?' He sat down on the sofa-bed. 'Oh!'

'Would you lie for him, Piers?' Greg asked.

'Oh, I expect so.'

'To the police?'

'If it was something trivial, or not so trivial, but not for the murder of a child.' He was thoughtful for a moment, then added slowly, 'If he was capable of that then he's not the man I love.'

'Then I'll ask you once more, Mr Hamilton. What time did Douglas Cameron get here on Saturday night and what time did he leave?'

'Five past ten and midnight.'

'And dare I ask how you spent that time?'

'We had a couple of glasses of wine. No more, as he was in his car. Then we went to bed.' His hands reached out across the counterpane, smoothing and remembering. 'I don't need to draw you a diagram.'

'All right,' Greg said. 'I shall need a statement to that effect.'

'Fine. If it's to help Doug, fine.'

'Can you come down to the station and let me have that? Today?'

'Yes. When I close at five?'

'If Barbara and I aren't there, ask for DCI Stratton.'

'Stratton. Right.'

'You understand the concept of perjury?'

'Yes, thank you.'

'Why'd he get married?' Greg asked, curious. 'Thirty years ago, maybe, when it was illegal, men married to protect themselves, but why today?'

'He's genuinely bisexual,' Piers said with a shrug. 'Loves his wife and adores his kids. I used to think men who said they were bi were kidding themselves, that they couldn't admit they were gay, until I met Doug. He's cheated on her with women too. At least when your husband's unfaithful with another man the answer to the question, "What's he got that I haven't got?" is blindingly obvious.' He preened himself, recovering some of his natural high spirits, and lisped, 'Especially in my case.'

Greg laughed, honestly amused.

'I've seen him eyeing up women when he's out with me,' Piers went on. 'He knows there isn't a single thing I can do about it.'

'Except give him his marching orders?' Greg suggested.

'You ever been in love, Gregory?'

'Yes.'

'Then try not to talk bollocks.' A shadow crossed his face. 'I'd so wanted him to stay the night, to wake up with him, just once, and this seemed the perfect opportunity, so I was horribly let down. After he'd gone I stood at that window.' He nodded to the view over the town. 'Wondering if I should do something stupid like walk down to his house and stand outside it, see if there was still a light on.' He got up and walked across to the window. 'I wanted to take a photograph of myself standing here, black and white, moody, "Beautiful Lovelorn Man".'

'Like the ones in the hallway?'

He nodded. 'I once tried to take a photo of Doug, you know, catching him unawares, naked and warm. He was furious. he ripped the camera out of my hand, opened it and exposed the film. He's so paranoid about his wife finding out. She's Catholic. Perfect bloody Verity. That means truth.'

'I know.'

'Ironic, when the truth is the last thing she wants to hear.' He smiled to himself, making fun of his own unhappiness 'Then the search party started turning out and at least I had that to take my mind off things.'

'How long have you been seeing Cameron?' Greg asked.

'"Seeing", how twee. We've been fucking for eight, nine months, since last autumn, whenever he can spare me time in his busy schedule.'

'Where did you meet him?' Greg asked.

'There's a pub this side of Marlborough, The Bag O' Bones. Big gay scene. I go there a lot, or I used to. I saw him there one night last September. He was nursing half a pint of bitter and rebuffed at least three approaches while I was watching. For a moment I thought he'd come in by mistake, a bloke wanting a beer on the way home, but in that case he'd surely have realised his mistake and left by then.'

'Well, I certainly would,' Greg said.

'Then he glanced up and saw me watching him and smiled and I went over to join him. I've always been attracted to the dour Caledonian type. I realised that the first three men weren't what he was looking for.'

'How d'you mean?' Barbara said.

'One was a biker, leathery. Butch. You know?' She nodded. 'The second very camp. The third what we call a clone – cropped hair and silly bristly moustache, white tee shirt with a waistcoat. He wanted someone like himself, someone who can pass for straight in a good light. Preferably a bloke with a wife and kids so that you're both playing by the same rules. Trouble with me. I'm not playing by the same rules. I'm gay and I don't care *who* knows it. That's why we row a lot.'

He kicked his foot against the wooden leg of the sofa-bed, a sulky child. 'Anyway, by the time he found out I was purely – or impurely – gay he was too interested to back off. Learning that I lived in Hungerford was a blow too but he was keen by then and decided to take it on the chin.'

'Did you talk much?'

'Sure, we're not animals. He told me how much he hated living in the country. He'd been in Hammersmith before, plenty of gay scene and you don't know your neighbours beyond nodding good morning to them. But his wife had gone on and on about how the local schools were full of crack dealers with switch blades and there he was, before he knew what was happening, nagged into a bijou detached house on an estate in Hungerford where the people next door take an avid interest in your private business.'

'So what were you?' Barbara asked sharply. 'A revenge fuck on his wife?'

Piers, as always, seemed unoffended. 'No, not really. There was a strong attraction, on both sides. He had an estate car, a Volvo, kiddie seats in the back, the lot. It was dark by then and we drove to a deserted farm track – a lovers' lane, I suppose – and he let down the back seat and we fucked on a blanket he kept there, no doubt for that purpose.' He paused for a nostalgic moment. 'It was good, bloody good. When he drove me back to the pub he asked to make another date and I gave him my card. I thought he wouldn't ring but he did and I've been *seeing* him ever since, once or twice a week usually. I suppose it's safer for him than going out cruising.'

'I thought you liked to play the field,' Greg said.

'Bravado, love. That and keeping it a deadly secret. We all have our secrets.' He muttered, his face close to Greg's, 'I know yours, Gregory.'

Greg didn't flinch. 'No you don't.'

'Fair enough. It usually works.'

'I hope you practise safe sex,' Barbara said.

'Oh always. He wouldn't take any risks with her or his kids.'

'Well . . .' Greg made for the door, his host trailing forlornly after him. 'We'll see ourselves out. Don't forget about that statement.' He put his hand companionably on Hamilton's arm. 'Married men don't leave their wives, you know.'

'Oh, thank you, Marjorie Proops!' Piers stood in the doorway as they went out. 'Nice meeting you, Miss Carey. It is Miss?'

'Why? Thinking of making me an offer?'

'Will his wife have to know?' he asked. 'About me? About him being here that night? About what we were doing?'

'As things stand, I see no reason she should.'

And Piers said, 'Pity!'

'Been there,' Barbara said as they descended the stairs, 'done that.'

'Got the scars?'

'Suppurating sores. And if married men never leave home, how come the world is full of deserted wives?' Greg didn't answer. 'You know Cameron will probably dump him now?'

'Why should he?'

'Because he's tainted, associated with us, the police, with something our Douglas would prefer to forget, with the day his wife might have found out. And *he* knows that.'

Poor Piers, Greg thought. He'd take it hard. But he'd get over it.

'Do you still think he's a child pornographer?' Barbara asked.

'I never actually *thought* that,' he protested and she smiled. 'Catholic tastes our Mr Cameron,' he went on. 'Men, women. Small girls?'

'Jordan wasn't sexually assaulted,' she reminded him.

'He panicked? Found she was dead and dumped her quickly? Maybe his catholic tastes don't run to necrophilia.'

'But there wasn't time, not if Hamilton is telling the truth.'

'*If.* A big if.'

'I think he was,' Barbara said. 'He's very open. See how he answered your questions first time, even the ones that weren't strictly relevant, like about how they met.' She glanced sideways at him.

'Just interested,' he said. 'Being nosy.'

'I liked him.'

'And you're a wonderful judge of character?'

'Quite so. There's a straightness about him – no pun intended.'

'None taken.'

Greg went to the offices of the *Newbury Weekly News* in Faraday Road and asked to have a look at the archives. It didn't take him long to find what he was looking for – the high summer of 1973, a damp, drizzly summer from the days before anyone had heard of global warming.

'Triple Slaying' read the headline. 'Mother and Daughters Murdered While They Slept'. Another headline boasted, 'Immediate Arrest'.

He skimmed the text quickly but it told him nothing new. There was a photograph of Smith leaving the magistrates court the following morning after remand. Handsome. No, he corrected himself, Smith had been beautiful, looking much younger than thirty whereas now he looked every day of his age. His hair was as thick and black as an animal's pelt, falling in curls over his wounded eyes. His skin was darker then without the prison pallor but Greg thought that, even through the grainy newsprint, he could see bruising. Smith wasn't hanging his head in the picture, but stared into the camera with brave defiance.

There were no pictures of the dead wife and children. Almost certainly none had existed, except postmortem.

The other photograph on the page was of the officer in charge, Detective Superintendent Joseph Snow. Joey Snowy, they called him, but only behind his back. Snowy, not because of his name but because of the dusting of dandruff that was always visible on his dark collar. Greg had never worked directly for him as he'd been in uniform at the time but knew that his men had been terrified of his sarcastic and obscene tongue.

It had been Snow's last big murder case. He'd retired a few months later with his thirty years under his belt, one of the ones who couldn't wait to get out, and been dead before sixty.

The newspaper showed Snowy leaving the court, a look of avid satisfaction on his face, a young man behind him, doubt-less a DC. Greg looked more closely at the blurred features and realised that it was Bob Holman, who'd spent less than two years in CID before volunteering a move back to the comparative order of uniform.

Josie didn't want to let Barbara in, that was clear. She was wearing a Walkman, the headphones dropped around her neck in order to answer the door, a repetitive beat just audible as if a party was going on next door. 'I'm busy,' she said.

'Yes?' Barbara was armoured only with conjecture and bluff; and one hard piece of evidence that she couldn't use. Unless she had to.

She waited for enlightenment. Her nerve was stronger than Josie's and finally the older woman said, 'Sorting through *her* things, bagging them up, so I won't have to look at them any more.'

'I can help with that.'

'I prefer to do it myself.'

'If I help,' Barbara persisted, 'then you'll have plenty of time to tell me about a blonde girl called Chrissie Prior who stayed with you and Peter for several months in Inkpen six or seven years ago. To tell me how she fits into the truth about Jordan.'

Josie looked pale, but unsurprised. She stood back from the door without further demur and Barbara went into the bungalow. Josie wrenched the Walkman off and clicked the music quiet. 'The Spice Girls,' she said hopelessly. 'Jordan's favourite. It shuts the world out, for a while.'

'Chrissie Prior,' Barbara said again when they were seated in the living room. 'Worked for one of the stables in Lambourn but left under something of a cloud seven years ago when she stole some money from her employer.'

'She wanted the money to have an abortion,' Josie said flatly, 'and she didn't steal it. She took a bribe from a bookie to nobble a horse, which is much worse than stealing in the racing world.'

'Was it Peter's child?'

'God, no!' Josie was shocked. 'Why should you think that?'

'I suppose because she looked like him.'

'Only generally, blonde hair and blue eyes. Chrissie had blonde hair and blue eyes. I don't think she was sure who the father was.'

'So how did she end up with you?'

'I was driving back from Newbury one morning after some serious shopping and she was hitching a lift on the A4, near the turn-off to Lambourn. I stopped for her – I don't usually but she was so young and her suitcase looked heavy and I was worried she might get into trouble if some man picked her up. She didn't seem to know where she wanted to go. She struck me as not being very bright, although I was later to revise that opinion. I took her home and fed her and she told me her woes . . . She was barely seventeen.'

'And you bought her baby from her?'

'It was Pete's idea. I thought he was mad. But we'd tried IVF three times, without success. We'd used up six thousand pounds on it. The success rate is horribly low but you keep convincing yourself that this time you'll be one of the lucky few. We'd got another four grand saved for a fourth and fifth try, but Pete said why not give Chrissie the money in exchange for her baby, much more certain.'

'I don't get this,' Barbara said, 'surely you two would have had no trouble adopting. Stable family, own home, still young.'

'Have you any idea what that's like? The red tape you have to untie. The prying, the assessments, the endless questions that no natural parent is subjected to. They turn every aspect of your life inside out for anything up to a year. And then, if they're finally satisfied, they put you on a waiting list and you might get a baby in two or three years time, if you're lucky, if you don't get dropped from the list because you've gone past the age limit while you were waiting. This way it would be quick, we'd know who the mother was, and it would be nobody's business but ours.'

She concluded quietly, 'Chrissie was having a baby she didn't want and we wanted it. More than anything in the world.'

'You know that what you did is illegal?'

'Yes,' Josie said, 'I know. But it wasn't illegal when I was a girl. Private adoptions were normal then. Some teenager got into trouble, her parents screamed at her a lot, then a childless couple in the same village took the baby. Everybody knew but nobody spoke of it and the girl got to see her kid from time to time. What was wrong with that? Why do they have to interfere in people's lives this way?'

'Were you planning to tell Jordan the truth when she was old enough to understand?'

'No. What would be the point? It would only have made her restless, dissatisfied. I've seen it – perfectly normal, happy kids driven to neurotic messes by trying to track down their birth mother, a woman who probably doesn't want to know them.'

Barbara didn't argue. It was academic now. 'How did you swing it?'

'We paid for Chrissie to be seen privately, by a doctor in Marlborough. I drove her there each time. Meanwhile she stayed with us, at our expense, and seldom left the house. We gave her everything she asked for to keep her happy. She couldn't have been better looked after.'

'But you must have had to pretend –'

'I wore a harness thing to make me look increasingly pregnant. I'd used something similar in a play we did at the Amdram society Peter and I used to belong to when we were courting, and we went up to London to a theatrical costumier to get one. I complained about wind and piles and having to pee a lot, the way pregnant women do. It was fun, in its way.'

'Then the baby was born?'

She nodded. 'In the private hospital in Marlborough, without complications. I was there. We said I was her elder sister, her closest relative, and they let me stay. I saw Jordan come into the world, bloody and wrinkled, and I loved her at once. As far as the neighbours were concerned I was the one who was in hospital giving birth. I brought the baby home with me a couple of days later and that was that.'

'Registered to you and Pete?' She inclined her head. 'That's perjury.'

'I know. I was desperate. *We* were desperate.'

Barbara tried to imagine this desperation and failed.

'And Chrissie?' she asked.

'Was supposed to leave the district with two thousand pounds in her pocket . . . except she didn't.'

'Ah!'

'She hung around like Banquo's ghost and every so often she'd ring up and ask for money.'

'Blackmail?'

'Nothing so explicit. Never any threats. She didn't need to threaten. She was an old friend who needed a loan, a loan that was never repaid.'

'Did she want her child back?'

Josie shook her head. 'Oh, no. She showed no interest in her, in her development. Never asked after her.'

It was as if a light bulb had come on over Barbara's head. 'Was that who Pete was with the night he was killed?'

'Yes,' she sighed, 'although he wouldn't admit that was where he was going. She'd said a while before that she was getting married and we worked out that she didn't want her fiancé to know about Jordan and we hoped that she'd leave us alone at last. But she rang up that evening, asking for money again. She said she was short for Christmas. He went to meet her. He must have been het up, driving back. I daresay they'd quarrelled. I blame her for the accident. I blame her for his death.'

'You must have been so angry with her.'

'And with him, for giving in to her again, and for trying to keep it from me. I was sitting here, tight-lipped, angry with him as he lay dying in the road. She killed my husband and now I've killed her baby.'

'What!'

'I mean that I didn't take good enough care of her. What did you think I meant?' She read Barbara's face. 'Oh, no. Not that. That wasn't what I meant.'

'What did the girl do then?'

'Backed off. I think Pete's death knocked the wind out of her and she must have known the well had dried, that I was a penniless widow. I haven't heard from her since. If I had I don't know if I could have been responsible for my actions. I've no idea what's become of her or if she went ahead with her wedding, or if she's still in the area.'

'Lucky she didn't know about the trust fund,' Barbara said. Josie laughed hollowly. 'That's irony for you. The fuss the Abbots made, and she wasn't their granddaughter at all.' She ran her hand through her hair. 'I'm glad it's come out. It's one thing lying in private – it becomes a way of life and often you forget it is a lie – but in public, on a platform in the Town Hall, in front of the media of half the country. I felt like someone taking a lie detector test and failing, as if I had liar branded across my forehead.'

'No wonder she said she wasn't meant to have her,' Greg said. 'We're going to have to find this Prior girl, and quick.'

'Tall order, sir, since no one knows where she went when she left the district after Abbot's death. I've checked the PNC but she's not on there, not under that name.'

'She probably married as she said she was going to and changed her name.'

'It would make life so much easier if women didn't do that.'

'Marry?'

'Change their names.'

'She could be in the area again,' Greg said. 'She might have tried to snatch her kid back. Perhaps she's been brooding about it. Perhaps she and her husband have been having difficulty conceiving and she got obsessed with getting her first child back, then found it going horribly wrong. Do you remember what Cameron claimed Jordan said to him?'

'That it was a secret – "between us two".'

'Exactly! What two? Her and her biological mother?'

'Why not go to social services and claim the child back? DNA testing would prove her the mother and Josie wouldn't have a leg to stand on.'

Like the *Caucasian Chalk Circle*, Greg thought. 'I'm not so sure. The courts are supposed to put the child's interest above everything these days and Josie was clearly the better mother. Besides, she might have thought *she'd* done something illegal.'

'She had: blackmail.'

'True, although proving it in court might be tricky.'

'"Lying becomes a way of life." That's what Mrs Abbot said to me. "And often you forget that it *is* a lie."'

He sighed. 'You've done well, Babs. What put you on to this, of all things?'

She shrugged. 'A hunch. Call it women's intuition.'

'Indeed! Well, I shall reward you by giving you a tedious job, which you can delegate to some other poor soul, but worth doing. Check the local papers for the last eighteen months to see if you can find either an engagement or marriage announcement for Chrissie Prior. She may have married out of the area or they may not have seen the point of announcing it, but it's worth a try.'

'I'll do it myself as soon as I've got time,' she said.

'You need to learn to delegate, Babs. It's one of the hallmarks of a good leader, a future superintendent, which you may well be.' She flushed. 'I know that nobody can do the job half as well as you can, but you've got to let them do it anyway, and make a hash of it if they must.'

'Right,' she said, 'and I'll check with the Register Office too. At least, somebody will.'

Greg hung on until Bob Holman came on duty at ten – he had plenty of paperwork to keep him occupied till then. He gave the inspector time to brief his men for their relief then sought him out in his office.

'Haven't you got a home to go to, Sunshine?' Holman asked, glancing up. 'Or do you live here?'

'Seems like that at times,' Greg said, since he knew it was expected of him. 'Bob, you didn't mention you'd met Smith. That you worked on his case.'

'Did I?'

'Don't you remember?'

Holman stopped what he was doing and thought about it. 'Matter of hours,' he said finally. 'Snowy had the case sewn up by closing time.'

'He had no doubts?'

'None, and nor did anyone. The jury were out less than an hour. The gippo tried to do a runner at first but he must have realised it was hopeless and came back.'

Not hopelessness, Greg thought, or not that sort. Smith had proved that he could disappear if he wanted to. 'So you never considered any other explanations?' he asked.

'There *was* no other explanation. Look, Greg.' Holman got up and made a few alterations to his wall chart. 'I've nothing against Smith. Okay, if it'd been up to me he'd have hanged for what he did but it wasn't up to me and he's done his time and that wipes the slate clean as far as I'm concerned. If I have to protect him then I will, but don't go getting daft ideas about Snowy cocking up. It was an open and shut case. You didn't see Smith that night and I did. *He* was sobbing and wailing about how it was his fault.'

Was Holman one of the men who'd beaten him to a pulp in the cells that night? Greg thought him capable of it. 'His fault?' he said. 'Because he'd left his wife and children alone and vulnerable that night, perhaps.'

'Come to that every man who's got a job leaves his wife and kids alone and vulnerable,' Holman said reasonably. 'I know I do.'

He'd divorced his wife five years earlier and married a woman twenty years his junior, proceeding to start a second family with what seemed indecent alacrity. He'd been the object of canteen ribaldry and derision, not least from Greg.

'Is that all, sir?' Holman asked, clearly wanting him gone.

'That's all, thank you, inspector.'

14. A Midsummer Day's Nightmare

It was the morning of Wednesday, the 24th of June. Jordan Abbot had been dead three days and a few hours and if they didn't find her killer soon the trail would begin to go cold. Greg still had all the uniformed men that could be spared working on the case, dozens of them, knocking at doors, stopping people in the streets of Hungerford with her photograph, taking statements, none of which had yet led him to a solution.

At 11.30 his office door opened and Barbara came in. He could see by the look on her face that he wasn't going to like what he was about to hear.

'I'll take the bad news first,' he said.

'Only sort there is. Douglas Cameron killed himself half an hour ago. DCI Stratton was out that way and took the shout. You'll find him there.'

'Where?'

'On the industrial estate, next door to the Savemore supermarket.'

'What a mess,' Greg said.

The remains of a car and the remains of a man, barely separable, both twisted almost beyond recognition. Cameron had driven to the industrial estate three miles outside Newbury, found a disused unit, perhaps a hundred yards from the Savemore supermarket, and driven a hatchback into a solid brick wall at what must have been breakneck speed, since it had broken his neck.

On TV the car would have exploded into a fireball but in real life that didn't often happen. Even so the fire engine was there as well as an ambulance and two squad cars, the full expensive fanfare of emergency.

The car was a cheerful yellow, not lemon, nor yet banana, a second car, a wife's car. There was a lot of blood caused by the shattered windscreen cutting his face, but Cameron had died on impact as his neck snapped, as quickly and cleanly as Jordan Abbot's had.

Poetic justice, Greg wondered? Why would he do anything so drastic, except as an admission of guilt? 'Considerate of him to use his wife's car and not the company Volvo,' he remarked.

Harry Stratton said dully, 'Volvos are marketed on their safety at impact. It would also have had a driver's airbag. He knew what he was doing.'

Greg shivered: how could anyone think so clearly at such a time? Or did desperation offer a terrible lucidity? There were a lot of people standing around, as at any disaster, watching, excited, avid for detail to relate to their families that night. One man had a camcorder and was filming the scene. 'Any of this lot eyewitnesses?' Greg asked with distaste.

'Several.' Harry gestured round the car park. 'He got a good run at it, must have got up to seventy, eighty miles an hour. Half a dozen people in neighbouring buildings or in the road heard the roar of his acceleration and the skidding of tyres and looked to see what was happening. The noise of the crash naturally brought dozens more running. No one else was involved. No mystery here.'

'Except why he did it. You've got the names and addresses of the witnesses, of course?' Stratton nodded. 'Then can you get these gawpers cleared away before I chuck up my elevenses over them?'

Harry spoke to a number of uniformed officers and soon Greg heard the familiar shouts of, 'Come on, nothing to see, please clear the area, ladies and gentlemen,' and the slow and reluctant departure of the last stragglers.

What went through a man's mind, he wondered, as he saw a brick wall rushing towards him of his own volition, knew that he was seconds from death? What sort of despair or guilt could push you to that?

The doctor pronounced death and the paramedics began to extricate the remains of Cameron from the wreckage. His handsome face was cut and slashed, ripped apart by flying glass that he could never had felt. A jagged piece of torn metal, apparently from the disintegrated bonnet, was embedded in one cheek. 'You never met him, did you?' Greg asked.

Harry shook his head. 'I read his two contradictory statements when I was catching up last night.'

'We'll have to go to his house,' Greg said, 'break the news to his wife.'

It was a detached house in a road of ten identical houses on the far side of the canal from Hungerford proper, built too near together for Greg's taste, small gardens running down to the river Dun. You'd have to be careful of that with young children. They had elaborate porticoes like a Greek temple, white stucco, double doors in a variety of colours. An estate agent – perhaps Cameron himself – would have called them executive houses.

A solid house built on the sand of the big lie.

If he hadn't had Cameron's address, Greg would have identified the dark red Volvo estate in the drive, its hatch open, a number of suitcases stacked in it. Those big Volvos had always looked like hearses to him.

'Looks like she's going away,' Harry said.

'No, she's coming back from a trip to her mother's.' Except that then, he realised, the suitcases would not be in her husband's car since she must have come back by train.

The front door was closed and he rang the bell. He'd brought a WPC with him, always desirable when breaking news like this. He had to ring twice before he was aware of a twitching curtain, of a face peering out of the front window.

He held up his warrant card for her to see and, a moment later, the door opened.

Verity Cameron was a woman of about thirty who must normally have been pretty but who looked haggard and ill today. She was not much over five foot, dainty, feminine, and he wondered at the vagaries of male taste which made Cameron desire her and Piers, perhaps on the same day, when all they had in common was age. He might have identified her as one of Barbara's fluffy bunnies if she hadn't had such a hard mouth. It was difficult to imagine it melting beneath a kiss, he thought oddly.

'I thought you were him,' she said as if this was an explanation, 'but he has his key. I'm going mad. I suppose you want to come in. I didn't think it was illegal any more. More's the pity.'

He was having trouble making sense of her words but followed her in before she changed her mind. There were more suitcases in the hall, a trio of stuffed animals perched precariously on top, a panda, a teddy and a giraffe. Greg propelled her before him into the sitting room with the momentum of his awkwardness. The room was stuffy because the windows were closed and he thought for a moment that he wasn't going to be able to breathe in there. 'I think you should sit down, Mrs Cameron,' he said. 'I'm afraid I have some very bad news.'

To his embarrassment, she began to laugh, a faint note of hysteria. 'Bad news? What sort of news do you think you can tell me that's worse than the news I've already had this morning?'

Greg and Harry glanced at each other. Was it possible that she'd found out? How? 'It's your husband,' Greg said.

She said bleakly, 'Yes. It's him.'

'Won't you sit down?'

She stared at him for a moment, then slumped onto a pure white sofa. It took a strong nerve to have a sofa like that with small children in the house. She was tougher than she looked. 'Is that better?' she said acidly. 'Can you talk now?'

'I'm very much afraid, very sorry, but he's dead.'

Her head jerked back. 'What! What are you talking about?'

He explained as succinctly as he could. The WPC said inevitably that she would make some tea.

'He said he would,' Verity Cameron said, dry-eyed. 'He said he'd kill himself if I left him and took his children away. I didn't believe him. I didn't think he had the guts.'

Greg sat down on the sofa next to her. She was trembling. 'Why did you threaten to leave him, Mrs Cameron?'

'Because of the letter, of course.'

'Letter?'

She jumped up, as if on springs. There was a desk in the alcove next to the fireplace, its folding lid closed. She opened it, took out an envelope and handed it to Greg. He paused to take a handkerchief from his pocket and used that to cover his fingers as he took it from her. It was a white oblong, a first class stamp with a Newbury postmark, the address printed by a word processor. It had been slit open with a paper knife, not ripped apart anyhow like his own post.

He glanced up at her. She nodded and he drew out the single sheet of white A4 paper inside and unfolded it. Also printed, with neither salutation nor valediction. 'Your husband sleeps with other men,' he read. 'For the last few months he's been sleeping with Piers Hamilton, the photographer who lives in the High Street.'

Short and to the point, despite the childishness of its euphemism. He was dimly aware of Harry behind him, reading over his shoulder. 'When did this come?' he asked.

'By the nine o'clock post.'

'And what did you do?'

'I didn't do anything for a while,' she said. 'I was numbed. I walked up and down the house, in every room, looking at things, at the things we'd bought together to make a home for us and the children, seeing it for the hideous lie that it was.'

'You never doubted the truth of this letter?'

'Why should I? What sort of maniac would *invent* something so evil?'

What sort of maniac, Greg wondered, would break the truth to her with such brutality? 'What did you do then?' he asked gently.

'I rang his office, told him he had to come home at once, that it was an emergency.'

'And he did?'

'He didn't want to. He wanted me to tell him what the trouble was, but I wouldn't, I couldn't, not on the phone. I felt terribly calm, as if the worse thing in the world had happened to me and I could never suffer anything any more. I just kept saying that he had to come home and finally he said he would.'

'What time did he get here?'

'It must have been about ten. I showed him the letter. He stood there utterly horrified. He didn't try to deny it. He could see that it would do no good. I told him that I was leaving him, that I was taking the children, that he would never see them again. I called him – I don't know – everything imaginable, words I didn't know I knew, a filthy pervert, a sick scumbag who didn't deserve to be among decent people and he said he'd kill himself if I left him and I said, "Good!"'

She paused for a moment, running her hand up over her narrow face and through her pale brown hair. 'I hadn't finished unpacking from the visit to my mother's. I went to fetch the suitcases down again. I heard him bang out of the front door and I heard my car start up. I thought for a moment he'd taken it to try to stop me leaving but that was stupid because I had a key to the Volvo.'

'He . . . needed a car without an airbag,' Greg said.

'Yes. I see. Of course.'

'This was at ten o'clock you say?' Harry said.

'Yes.'

'The accident was at about eleven,' Harry muttered to Greg. 'What did he do with the intervening hour?'

'Drove around?' Greg suggested. 'Screwed himself to the sticking point?'

The WPC brought in a tray of tea at that moment. 'The children are playing in the back garden,' she remarked. 'Let's leave them for the moment, eh?' There would be time enough to tell them that their daddy was never coming home.

Greg could see them through the window. About four and two, he guessed. One with her father's face and dark colouring, his stocky build, the younger, the boy, fairer, daintier, like his mother. They were playing some chasing game, in dumb show, their childish squeals cut off by the double-glazed panes of the closed french windows.

'Is there someone we can get for you?' he asked. 'Your mother? Sister?'

She was still calm, but recognised the need. 'My mother isn't well; she mustn't hear of this yet. She adored Doug. My sister lives in Oxford, in Headington. Nothing surprises her. Her number's on the pad by the phone in the kitchen. Grace Crane.' As the constable went to telephone, she added, 'She lectures at Brookes university. Term has just finished. Isn't that lucky?'

'Yes,' Greg said. 'She'll be able to stay with you for a while.'

He noticed that she wore a silver crucifix on a chain round her neck and remembered that Piers had said she was a Catholic. She pulled it out as he watched and put it childishly in her mouth for a moment. It seemed to give her comfort. 'She was the brainy one, you see, my big sister. I was the pretty one, the one with the perfect husband, the beautiful children, the nice house in the country, the whole stinking, fucking lie.'

When Greg was young only men had said 'fuck' in public and only rough men at that. His first arrest in 1969 had been of a man in a pub who'd punched another man for saying it in front of his wife. The magistrates – all white and well-spoken in those days, men with pipes and women in tweeds – had thrown the case out, thinking the man within his rights, and reprimanded the dismayed young PC for not exercising better judgment.

'Magistrates is a law unto theirselves,' Sergeant Dickie Barnes had told him, sympathetic for once.

Now well-brought-up young women punctuated their speech with the word and its variations audibly in the street and he'd long given up wincing at the sound of it, but he knew, somehow, that it was a novelty on Verity Cameron's lips, that the daintiness of her life had disappeared the moment she'd opened her post that morning.

'Suicide is a mortal sin,' she remarked clinically, 'and he is damned for eternity.' The thought did not seem to give her pain. She looked at the tray of tea sitting on the tiled coffee table. 'I think I'll have something stronger.' She got up, opened a cupboard, took out a bottle of whisky, poured half a glassful and tossed it down like milk. 'That's better.' She waved the bottle at him. 'Don't suppose I can tempt you?'

'Thank you, no.'

'Not on duty,' she said, and sat. She looked at Greg. 'It is true, isn't it?'

'What?'

'All the stuff in the letter.' He hesitated. 'I have to know. Tell me.'

'Yes, it's true.'

'I knew it was. He didn't deny it but I had to be certain. Piers Hamilton. I don't know him. What sort of a man can he be?'

'He's –' What could he say? She saw Piers with two horns and a tail, the devil who'd corrupted her husband. 'He's just a man.'

She looked round the room with its velvet curtains and its expensive carpet, the array of built-in shelves and cupboards in limed oak. 'I'm glad he's dead because now I don't have to

220

leave my home. There'll be insurance, pensions. He would have wanted to see the children too, and the courts might have let him.'

'Undoubtedly.'

'But he would have corrupted them – a man like him. And I shall be a widow and not a divorcée, not excommunicate. Not that I shall want to marry again, to take that risk again.'

He could think of no reply and was glad that the constable came back into the room at that moment. 'Dr Crane will be here within the hour,' she reported.

'Constable Foster will stay with you till your sister arrives,' Greg said. He put the anonymous letter in an evidence bag. 'I'm going to take this, if I may.'

'I hardly want it as a souvenir.'

'No. We shall need you to identify the body some time later today, when you feel up to it. Is that all right?'

'Yes,' she said faintly.

'I'll send someone for you when we're ready.' He hoped to God they'd manage to tidy the corpse up before she saw it.

'Yes.' She got up. 'He didn't kill Jordan Abbot, you know. He wasn't capable of . . .' She was suddenly angry with herself. 'What the hell am I talking about! I didn't know that man, Douglas Cameron. He was a complete stranger. I have no idea what he was capable of. Ask Piers Fucking Hamilton.'

He felt inadequate, as always in this situation. 'I am so very, very sorry,' he said, and meant it.

'Will it have to come out at the inquest?' she asked. 'About *him* I mean? What he was.'

Greg didn't know what to say. 'If the Coroner is satisfied it's suicide, and there seems little doubt about that . . . I don't know. It depends who it is. He might want you to give evidence, to explain your husband's state of mind when he left the house for the last time this morning. You'll be on oath, like in a regular court. It would be perjury to –'

'Surely,' Harry put in quickly, 'it will be enough for Mrs Cameron to say that she'd told her husband the marriage was over, that she and the children were leaving. She won't need to go into detail.'

Greg looked at him gratefully. At the door Verity offered her hand to them both. Greg shook it briefly. Harry, however, took her hand in both his and pressed it until she winced.

'I'm sorry,' he said. 'So very, very sorry.'

They walked into Collins and Mather twenty minutes later. It was a genteel, upmarket estate agents with a specialist and lucrative niche in waterside property. The door opened directly into a large room which was open plan, with two private offices at the back, both doors closed. There were four desks out front, one empty, two where the occupants were busy with clients in the booming housing market.

The man at the fourth desk gave them a big smile and said, 'How can I help you, gentlemen?' He was a handsome black man, late twenties, in a loose-fitting brown suit, a cream shirt and a tie over which Pink Panthers danced. His name plate said that he was David Pilgrim. Greg showed him his warrant card. 'Oh!' he said.

'Is Mr Collins in?' Greg asked. 'Or Mr Mather?'

'There isn't a Mr Collins these days,' Pilgrim said. 'Mr Mather has someone with him.' He glanced at one of the closed office doors and lowered his voice. 'If it's important . . .'

'It's about Douglas Cameron.'

'He's nipped out, I'm afraid. I don't suppose he'll be long.'

'I'm afraid he will,' Greg said. 'I'm sorry to have to tell you that Mr Cameron was killed in a . . . car accident about an hour ago.'

'Oh my God!' The young man put his hand over his mouth as if he might be sick. He was as pale as a man of his race could be. 'No, I don't believe it. He was here, not much more than an hour ago.'

The other two employees glanced up, sensing agitation, wondering. Greg gave them a reassuring smile.

'He was called out in a hurry about twenty to ten,' Pilgrim went on slowly, 'then he came back about half past ten, twenty to eleven. I noticed he had his wife's car that time and I called out, "Volvo playing up, Doug?" as he went through but he didn't answer me. He was in his office maybe ten minutes then he came out again, still not speaking to anyone, his face . . .'

'His face?' Greg said.

'Like he'd made an important decision.'

'Is that his office at the back?' Harry asked.

'Yes.'

'I don't think we need disturb Mr Mather for the moment then,' Greg said. 'We'll take a look in the office.'

Pilgrim got up and followed them, apparently on automatic pilot. 'Does Verity know?' he asked in an urgent whisper.

'We've come from there.'

'She's such a lovely lady, and those beautiful children. It isn't right.'

The offices had opaque glass along the top half of the partition wall and the door had a matching panel. It wasn't locked and Greg opened it and walked in. To his dismay he heard himself humming the Pink Panther theme tune. Dum, der dum, der dum, der dum, der dum. He made himself stop.

'He's cleared his desk,' Harry said.

'No, it's always like this,' Pilgrim said. 'It's an office joke that he's so orderly. We call him the housemaid because he clears up after the rest of us mortals. Oh!' He put his hand over his mouth once more, remembering that the nickname would never be heard in this office again.

'Why don't you get yourself a glass of water?' Greg said kindly. 'You look as if you could do with one.' Pilgrim nodded dumbly and left the room.

A neat man, Mr Cameron, Greg thought. A tidy man with an untidy personal life. On the otherwise empty desk was a white envelope, A5 size, exactly centred. Greg went behind the desk and examined it without touching it. The address was hand written in ink, one line, also neat.

Superintendent Gregory Summers

Well, no one could say he hadn't the right to read it. He picked it up and slit it open without further ado. It contained a second, smaller envelope addressed to the coroner – the ultimate tidiness – and a single sheet of white A4 paper folded once. He glanced at Harry who shrugged, then unfolded the paper and read.

Dear Mr Summers,

You promised me discretion and I believed you. Clearly I'm a bigger fool than I thought. No doubt the whole of Newbury police station has been having a good laugh over my personal problems. No matter. I am finishing it now. I've been juggling the different aspects of my life for so long and now I've lost control of the situation and can think of only one way out.

I didn't kill Jordan Abbot, by the way. What I told you – the second time, anyway – was literally true: I spoke to her, asked her if her mummy knew she was out and watched her skip away to her death a minute later. If I had grabbed her into my car and driven her home or to the nearest police station she would be alive now. If I hadn't come forward like the public-spirited citizen I am to tell you I'd seen her, I would be alive now. They say that no good deed goes unpunished but I like to think this is my punishment for passing by on the other side. I do not think that I am a bad man, although I have sometimes done bad things.

Goodbye, Mr Summers, I used to be afraid of death, but now I see it as a great unburdening. I feel light-headed, like a schoolboy with the long vacation stretching before him.

Yours sincerely,

Douglas Cameron.

P.S. Please make sure that Piers is all right.

Greg handed it silently to Harry who read it.

'The press is going to love this,' the DCI said.

'It may not have to be read out at the inquest. It depends what he's said in the other letter.'

'A letter to you and one to the court but none to his wife.'

'I imagine he wanted to make her suffer.'

'And I think she's suffered enough. The innocent party here.'

'Can I help you?' A thin, fussy-looking man of about fifty had appeared in the doorway, accompanied by Pilgrim. 'Mr Pilgrim tells me that you're from the police. Something about Douglas.'

'It's bad news, I'm afraid,' Greg said, and explained it again, but in more detail this time.

'Suicide!' Mather exclaimed.

'There can be no doubt of that. He's left a note. Two notes.'

Mather made as if to take the envelopes from him but Greg held them back with a courteous smile. 'Evidence in a case of sudden death, I'm afraid.'

'Of course. I wasn't thinking.'

'It isn't anything to do with the murder of that little girl, is it?' Pilgrim burst out. 'Only I remember how upset he seemed when he saw the headline and the picture in my paper on Monday morning. He more or less snatched it out of my hand. Then he rushed out of the office a minute later. He lives in Hungerford so I thought maybe he knew her.' He looked pleadingly at Greg. 'It wasn't that, was it?'

'No,' Greg said, 'it wasn't that.'

'And a woman came here yesterday. A young woman, brunette, attractive. It was about midday, and he went out to lunch with her which was odd because we'd arranged to lunch together. I thought, maybe . . .'

''She was one of my officers,' Greg said, 'and they didn't go to lunch.'

'Oh! Thank goodness. I was afraid . . . Verity is such a lovely lady.'

'Yes.'

'I . . . I . . . shall close the office for the afternoon as a mark of respect,' was all that Mather could apparently think of to say.

'I'm sure he would have appreciated the gesture,' Greg said.

Outside, he handed the evidence bag with the anonymous note in it to Harry Stratton. 'Can you get that to Forensic? And get the other envelope over to the coroner's office.'

'It isn't a crime to send an anonymous letter,' Harry pointed out.

'No, not even when it drives a man to take his life, but I'd still like it checked over.'

'Some might say she had the right to know,' Harry said. He held the coroner's envelope up to the daylight but it was thick and opaque. It was also well sealed down. 'Could take a kettle to it,' he suggested.

Greg looked at him sharply. 'Just . . . get it to the coroner.'

Harry turned away in the direction of the roundabout, then stopped and said, 'Isn't that young Angie?'

'Where?'

Harry pointed towards the pub on the corner, perhaps forty yards away, The Rising Sun. Greg followed the line of his finger. A thin girl of medium height, a dishwater blonde, was walking into the saloon bar with a man. He was about thirty, Greg thought and, spitefully, wearing a cheap blue suit and polyester tie. He held the door open for her and she laughed up at him as she ducked under his arm into the darkness within.

'Nothing like her,' he said, turning away. 'You want to see an optician.'

'My mistake. Where will you be, sir?'

'I'm going back to Hungerford to break the news to another interested party.'

226

'What does he mean about seeing if Piers is all right?' Stratton asked.

'Piers Hamilton. I thought you took his statement yesterday evening.'

'I did, and very unsavoury reading it made.' Harry was clearly impervious to Piers's easy charm. 'But what did Cameron mean?'

'That's what I'm going to find out.'

15. Wednesday Afternoon

The door to Piers' studio was locked, the closed sign up. Greg rang the bell and got no answer. He pressed his ear to the door but could hear no sound. He rang again with the same result. The door had two locks, a Yale lock and a mortice but he could see that the mortice wasn't set. It was market day and the High Street was bustling. Glancing up and down to be sure that he wasn't observed, he picked the Yale lock and let himself in.

Dum, der dum, der dum, der dum, der dum.

Bugger!

He yelled, 'Piers!'

No reply. He might have gone out for an early lunch or to take some photographs, in which case Greg would have some explaining to do, but the final words of Cameron's letter still spun through his brain. A man who was about to die by his own hand need fear no reckoning with the law. With a horrible sense of foreboding he climbed the stairs and threw open the door to the bedsitting room. It was in darkness, the curtains drawn. He could make out a figure recumbent and motionless on the bed.

'Oh, Jesus, God!' he moaned. Was this what Orlenda had seen in this sweet young man's hand? *Perhaps I haven't got a future!*

He used his handkerchief to flick on the light switch so as not to contaminate the crime scene. The perpetrator of this crime was all too obvious and beyond punishment, lying in the morgue awaiting the pathologist's knife, but rules were rules.

The room was more chaotic than usual and he found himself thinking that a neat man like Doug could never have lived in harmony with a slattern like Piers, only with Verity who opened her anonymous letters with a paper knife. He could no longer put off going over to the figure on the bed, which he now saw was face down. There were no overt signs of violence, no blood, no broken skull beneath the skin.

He stepped gingerly forward and touched the younger man's neck. It was warm. He realised that the room smelt like a distillery and his foot banged against a half bottle that had once contained brandy, lying empty on its side on the floor.

Then Piers stirred, rolled over on his back, opened his eyes, groaned, closed them again and said, 'Come to give me the kiss of life, Gregory?' His voice was thick and groggy.

'Oh, fuck!' Greg sat down heavily on the bed, weak with relief. 'I thought you were dead.'

'That's the difference between us, darling, because I *wish* I were dead.'

Greg got up and drew the curtains and the younger man complained as the sun penetrated the room, placing his hands over his eyes. He threw open the windows to let out the stale smell of alcohol. He fetched a glass of water from the kitchen and a plastic bucket. He forced Piers to drink the water, much against his will, and held the bucket ready in case he wanted to throw up. He went back and forth with water five times until Piers had drunk about two pints and was begging for mercy.

'Florence Nightingale,' he said, gagging, 'as well as Marjorie Proops.'

Greg foraged in the kitchen, pouring orange juice into a glass, spooning in some dubiously ancient honey from the cupboard and a couple of soluble Paracetamol. 'This will help,' he said and Piers drank it obediently. He was gradually becoming aware that his friend had taken a terrible beating. Raw, new-minted bruises marred his pretty face, one eye, both cheeks, his chin. And it wasn't just the face, he suspected, since he winced every time he moved.

'How hideous do I look? the photographer asked, aware of his scrutiny.

'I should fetch a doctor,' Greg said.

'It's not as bad as that. There's nothing broken. I've had worse than this falling off a bicycle when I was ten.' He ran his finger over his teeth to check that none of them was missing.

'I don't need to ask who did this,' Greg said. 'And it was no bicycle accident.'

'I won't press charges.'

'Contrary to popular opinion it isn't up to the victim to "press charges". The Crown Prosecution Service has highly-trained lawyers to decide if someone is to be prosecuted for grievous bodily harm or not.'

'I won't give evidence against him in court then. Not even if you get the thumbscrews out.'

'No,' Greg said quietly. 'There won't be any charges. It's too late for that. Want to tell me exactly what happened?'

With difficulty, Piers sat up and Greg plumped a pillow up behind him. 'He came in about ten past ten, maybe quarter past, and I was so glad to see him. I had a customer and said, "Won't keep you a moment, sir," and he smiled and winked like he does if I'm not alone. I sensed nothing different about him. When the bloke had gone, I said, "Playing truant, darling?" and he said could I close for a bit so of course I did, thinking he meant . . .' He gestured wearily at the bed.

'I led the way upstairs and as we got in this room I turned to say something to him, I suppose to kiss him, and he punched me straight in the face. I was flabbergasted. I think I fell backward onto the bed. But he dragged me off by my hair and hit me again and when I fell to the floor he began kicking me in the ribs and stomach. I had no idea he had that . . . that *violence* inside him.'

'No, it's strange what we turn out to have inside us.'

'I was begging him to stop, begging him to tell me what the matter was and he kept saying, "You told my wife, you fucking little poof. I'm going to kill you".'

'And did you tell his wife?'

'No! Oh, I'd threatened to right enough, more than once, in the middle of a lovers' tiff but I would never have done it and he must have known that.'

'Didn't you fight back?'

'No. Partly because I was too stunned. Partly because I could never hurt him. I love him too much.'

'How long did this go on?'

'It seemed a long time but I suppose it was only a couple of minutes. I was crying by then, with the pain, and . . . it's not pretty, you get *snot* running out of your nose when you're snivelling that badly . . . Well, he could see that I'd had enough and he pulled the curtains across and walked away. I must have passed out at that moment but I'm sure I heard him say, "Goodbye, Piers. I'm sorry."'

'Then what?'

'I don't know how long I was out – a minute or two, I expect. I fetched the brandy, hauled myself onto the bed and drank the lot, straight from the bottle. Funny how it dulls the pain. Temporarily.' He reached out and grabbed Greg's hand with surprising strength. 'And now you're going to tell me what you meant about it being too late.'

Greg was silent for a moment, then he said, 'Well, *someone* told his wife.'

'Who?'

'I wish I knew.'

'Nobody else knew about us.'

'You're living in a fantasy world, Piers. Someone always knows. She got an anonymous letter this morning.'

'What . . . what did it say?'

Greg told him, remembering the exact words easily. Twenty-five words that had killed Douglas Cameron and destroyed the lives of his wife and children. Not Piers's life though, he thought. Piers was a survivor.

'Poor Doug,' Piers whispered. 'He sets so much store by being a good family man, upright, a model citizen.'

'Yes.' Greg was going to have to find a way to tell Piers the rest of it, and soon. 'I want you to be brave,' he said.

'Oh, no, Gregory! My father was a doctor and that was what he used to say before he stuck a particularly painful needle in my arm.'

Greg held his hand tightly. 'Verity Cameron confronted her husband with the letter and told him she was leaving him. He came here and beat you up because he thought you were responsible. He went back to his office and wrote a letter to me which he left on his desk, along with one to the coroner. Then he got in his wife's car and drove it at eighty miles an hour into a brick wall on an industrial estate in Newbury.'

Piers whimpered, 'Dead? Doug?'

'In a second. He'd have felt no pain.'

'Did . . . did he say anything about me in his letter?'

'He asked me to make sure you were all right. That's why I'm here. Look, are you sure you didn't send his wife that letter? Piers, because if you did it would be better if you told me now. You haven't committed a crime, however disastrous the consequences and –'

'I swear on my immortal soul it wasn't me.'

'You've got a computer, I suppose, a printer.'

'No.'

'How do you run a business without one?'

'The same way people ran businesses ten years ago. I've got an electric typewriter and a set of double-entry account books which I methodically keep up to date myself, amazingly enough. Why won't you believe me?'

'I do. Look, can I send for someone to sit with you? Your parents – ?'

'They haven't spoken to me since I picked a family party on my eighteenth birthday as a suitable time and place to tell everyone I was gay. I'm your original party pooper, me. My mother had gone to a lot of trouble. That was the last thing she ever said to me: "After the trouble I went to with my volau-vents".' He began to laugh but it pained his bruised ribs too much and he stopped abruptly. Then he began to cry.

'It hurts,' he said as the tears burnt into the wounded flesh of his face, stinging as they fell. Wiping them made it worse. 'Why am I so upset? We were through, anyway. When a man comes round and beats the shit out of you like that, he doesn't come back the next day to propose.'

'I wouldn't be so sure about that.' Barbara had told him lurid tales of her time in the Domestic Violence Unit. She hadn't wanted to go there and had been asked to leave after four months as she kept telling the women not to be so bloody feeble.

'I won't get invited to the funeral,' Piers said. 'Funerals are for wives, not mistresses.'

'Look, let me get you a friend. Someone you trust. There must be one.'

'Yes.'

'Who?'

'You, Gregory. I trust you.'

He sighed. 'I'll stay an hour or two but I have work to do.'

'Thank you.'

'It's all right,' Greg said. He put his arms round Piers. 'It's all right.' Piers laid his head on Greg's shoulder and began to sob anew. 'It's all right.'

'Have you ever lost anyone close?' Piers asked after a while, when Greg's shoulder was soaking wet. 'Yes, you have. I remember. You said so but you didn't tell me who.'

'My son, to leukaemia, a year ago. I suppose we had time to get used to the idea.'

Piers was wide-eyed. 'A child?'

'He was 22.'

'Why didn't you tell me before, Gregory?'

'I didn't know you well enough.' Which was absurd because he felt as if he'd known Piers Hamilton all his life. He hesitated, then plunged in, as if in the confessional. 'And I think

I'm losing the woman I love and there isn't a single thing I can do about it.'

'She's leaving you?'

'Getting ready to, I think.'

'Why?'

'Why do I think so?'

Why did he? An unexplained train ride, an innocuous phone call, perhaps a hidden letter. It didn't add up to much, except a lot of secrets. And then today at the pub in Newbury. That was harder to explain away. The man in the cheap blue suit had been ordinary-looking, he thought, commonplace, couldn't compare to Fred, wasn't good enough for her.

'Why is she leaving you?' Piers asked patiently.

'Because she needed me for a while and now she doesn't, I suppose. Or because my son asked her to look after me and she has for a whole year and she's had enough. Or perhaps because I needed her and now she thinks I no longer do.'

'And do you?'

'None of us *needs* another person. Not really. We want to have them.'

They sat for about half an hour without saying much. From time to time Piers would lapse into tears, never apologising for his emotion as most people did, as Greg would have felt compelled to do.

He made them both some coffee. The cupboard was bare and he went to Somerfield and bought eggs, cheese and tomatoes and made an omelette which fell to pieces on its way out of the pan, the way his omelettes invariably did. It made no difference to the taste, as he always maintained, and he forced Piers to eat two-thirds of it. He opened a tin of peaches he found in the cupboard and they ate them with their fingers. They were orange and slithered down their throats like wriggly goldfish. They licked their fingers clean when they'd finished.

He'd fetched some arnica from the chemist and anointed the swelling bruises. 'A few days as the Phantom of the Opera,' Piers said, 'and I shall be as beautiful as ever.'

At four o'clock Greg said, 'I must go. I'll look in this evening.'

'Take the spare key at the top of the stairs. Let yourself in.'

'Right.'

'How did you get in, anyway? I assumed Doug had slammed the latch shut behind him on his way out.'

'Old coppers' trick.'

'Oh.'

'Get some rest. Think about a visit to your GP.'

'I'll be all right now. Catchy tune, that.'

'Eh?'

'The Pink Panther.'

When he got back to his office, Susan Habib told him that John Smith had been asking for him for the past hour and a half.

Smith! Thank goodness he was all right. 'Where is he?' he asked.

'He said he'd come back. He's been back twice, at half hourly intervals. I offered to try your car phone if it was urgent but he said he'd go for a walk by the river until you got here.' She flushed. 'An odd man, Mr Summers.'

'Mmm.' Did she know, he wondered? Had she heard what Josie had said about him on TV and seen not a man but a monster? The telephone rang at that moment and he answered it himself. 'Tell him I'll be right down.'

Smith offered him his strong handshake and followed him into an unused interview room. 'Lashlo,' he said, at once, no waster of words. 'Rufus says he couldn't get in to see you when he came either yesterday or this morning. He's getting desperate.'

'I've been frantically busy. Honestly.'

'So I said I'd try.'

'He seemed perfectly happy when I rang this morning to check on him.' Lashlo was staying at a secure unit for juveniles.

'Hardly *happy*,' Smith said. 'He's coping surprisingly well, in fact, but when Rufus and I went to see him this afternoon he was asking to come home. Rufus is still there with him. He doesn't understand why he can't take his son home and, I must say, nor can I.'

'Are you satisfied that he'll be safe at the camp?'

Smith thought about it, stroking his chin as if he had a beard to caress. Greg noticed the gashes, the thin streaks of blood dried black on his cheeks and below his strong mouth. 'Cut yourself shaving?' he asked.

'Something like that.' Not very like, Greg thought. He knew the marks of human nails when he saw them. It was not his business. 'Look,' Smith said after a moment. 'Rufus is talking about moving on tomorrow, Friday at the latest. They're due in Salisbury by the end of the month. I think we can keep Lashlo safe until then. I think the heat's gone out of that would-be mob.'

'Yes. I suppose.' He'd passed Templeton in the street that morning and the hefty builder had blushed and looked away. 'I shall get uniform to keep an eye on the place at night. Like Monday night.'

'So. You haven't charged Lashlo with anything. He isn't under arrest. Do you want me to apply for a writ of *Habeus Corpus*?'

'Will you believe me, John, if I tell you I've honestly been trying to act in his best interests?'

'I believe you.'

'But I agree that we can't keep him any longer.' Greg held the door open for his visitor. 'If you're prepared to take responsibility for him, why don't we both go round there and sign him out into your and Rufus's safe keeping?'

'Thank you.'

'I was worried about you,' Greg said, as they crossed the roundabout, Smith automatically leading him through the quiet underpasses, a man who'd had enough excitement in his life.

'I can take care of myself. These days.'

'I'm sorry about Mrs Abbot. She's turned into a loose cannon.'

'It was my fault, not yours. I told her about my past, not you. Don't try to take the ills of the whole world on your shoulders, Mr Summers.' His face had a wintry look. 'I trusted her. She was desperate and I wanted to help her, if I could.'

'You won't make that mistake again in a hurry,' Greg said.

'Oh, I daresay I will.'

'How did you get off the common without the two policemen seeing you?'

'Gypsies can make themselves invisible.'

'I'm serious.'

'So am I, in a way. We're often invisible because people don't want to see us, in the same way they don't want to see beggars in the streets.'

'But –'

'I will keep my secrets, if it's all the same to you.'

'Fair enough. Where are you camped now?'

'At hand.'

It was half past four and the worst of the heat had gone from the day as they strolled through the streets into the suburbs of Newbury. Greg liked this time best, when the shadows lengthened across the rivers Kennet and Lambourn. On a fine summer's evening you longed to take a turn out on the downs, maybe watch the horses on their evening exercise, nestle down until eleven at a pub with a garden and drink warm English beer.

After a while Smith said, 'Rufus is still exercised about his granddaughters. Do you know where they are?'

'Not the exact address although I know they're both together with a nice foster family a few miles out of town.'

'Rufus and Orlenda would like to see them, at least.'

'I explained to him that he had to talk to social services about that. I understand that grandparents have certain rights of access these days.'

'I'll chase it up. Thanks.'

'Didn't Romy go to see them on Monday?'

Smith looked startled. 'No.'

'Oh. It's just that I saw her get on a train heading for Hungerford and I assumed she would pay them a visit.'

'From what I know of little Romy she'd have business of her own.'

It was odd, though, Greg thought, as if she wasn't close to her grandparents, although she'd travelled with them all her life. 'Did you know their father?' he asked. 'Huwie?'

'He was a child when I went away,' Smith said. 'Four? Five? Ordinary enough kid, bit wilful, but Rufus took a strap to him if he got out of hand.'

'Rufus did?'

'He had the bringing up of him with his parents being dead and he believes in old-fashioned discipline, does Rufus.' His voice was sour and it dawned on Greg that Smith hated Rufus Lee as much as Lee hated him, he was just better at hiding it. 'Huwie grew into a man with a hell of a temper,' he said. And they said a boy to whom violence was done grew into a violent man. 'All the Lees have filthy tempers. All that branch of the family, except for Lashlo, who literally wouldn't crush an insect under his foot.' He smiled faintly. 'Annie, my wife, she could dish it out with the best of them.'

'Yeah?'

'That was one of the things I loved about her, her spirit. She gave as good as she got.' His face clouded. 'That was one of the reasons I was so quickly pinpointed as the murderer, why they didn't consider other possibilities. We'd had a blazing row in the Down Gate pub the night before, two dozen witnesses to say we were fit to kill each other. But we were like that all the time, rowing and kissing, kissing and rowing.'

'There must have been some evidence against you for the jury to find you guilty.'

He shrugged. 'Circumstantial. No alibi. No one else with an obvious motive. Those were more innocent times, anyway – before the Guildford Four or the Birmingham Six – and juries thought that if the police had collared you and put you in the dock then you must be guilty and their role was a formality.'

Greg remembered those days well. Easy days for the police, before the West Midlands serious crime squad had spoiled things for the rest of them, before Operation Countryman had shattered public faith in their guardians.

'I was too shocked and damaged to defend myself,' the gypsy went on. 'My barrister didn't put me in the witness box. He said it would do no good.'

'A mistake, perhaps. Juries think men who won't speak up for themselves have something to hide.'

Smith said, 'In fact, it was a happy marriage.'

'I'm sorry. Or do I mean that I'm glad?'

'Don't you fight with your woman?'

'No.'

'Never?'

'Not really.' They were too careful of each other.

'Horses for courses. It was so long ago and now I can't remember her face.'

'But you can remember the faces of the policemen who beat you up?'

'I have reason to remember those, but I've not been looking. You might say that I avert my gaze every time I come to the station.'

'Those men will mostly be retired, or moved on to other stations by now. Or dead.'

'I know.'

239

'Rufus seems mild enough,' Greg commented, 'for a Lee. I'd call him a placid man.'

'Rufus used to drink and he used to fight until Annie died, and the babes, then the stuffing was knocked out of him and he was dried up and angered out. They say anger pushes out fear, but suffering can push out anger too.' Greg remembered that flash of fury he'd seen on first meeting Rufus, when he told him his grandchildren had been taken into care, and the primitive fear it had aroused in him.

'He didn't want Annie to marry me,' Smith said.

'Because you're not a Lee?'

'That's right. How did you know?'

'Something Huwie said.'

'We had to elope.'

'How romantic.'

'No, it's commonplace among my people.'

Greg remembered his own wedding. He'd hated every minute of it. It wasn't that he hadn't wanted to marry Diane, he had, but she'd insisted on the full panoply of big white dress and bridesmaids, with champagne, prawn cocktails and rubber chicken for sixty. His best man, Mike Trewin – whatever had become of him? – had told embarrassing and inaccurate stories about him and he'd found the whole thing horribly vulgar.

Fred and Angie's wedding had been simple and dignified and Diane had pronounced it 'Hole in the corner.'

'Hole and corner,' he'd corrected her but she hadn't appreciated it.

'What's the matter with Lashlo anyway?' he said. 'Is it genetic?'

'No, he was damaged at birth. You see how big he is and you've seen how tiny his mother is. She was in labour for two days, making little progress, and by the time the baby was born, his brain had been starved of oxygen.'

'Why didn't somebody send for an ambulance, get her to hospital, for goodness sake?'

'Because that isn't how things are done among my people, as Rufus will be the first to tell you.'

'You mean he wouldn't get help for her?'

'Oh, she shares his traditional views. She'd have despised him if he had.'

Greg found to his surprise that they were at their destination. Rufus was pacing up and down outside the concrete building, his arms folded.

'About bloody time,' he growled.

'I was going to bleep you,' Barbara said. 'I tried your car phone but it rang and rang and Mrs Habib had gone home and DCI Stratton didn't know where you'd got to.'

He decided not to apologise. His two errands of mercy had been important. 'What's so urgent?'

'Forensic on the letters.' She followed him into his office. Two transparent evidence bags lay on his desk. The anonymous letter with its attendant envelope, now stripped of its stamp; the suicide note with its envelope. Every time he came in his office now there seemed to be an anonymous letter in a bag. If the government privatised the Post Office he should buy shares. 'There are no prints on anon,' Barbara said, 'predictably, except Cameron and Mrs Cameron. Also no saliva.'

Greg started. Everyone knew about fingerprints, but saliva?

'It's a self-seal envelope,' Barbara went on, 'and the stamp was moistened with tap water. It was printed on an inkjet printer in Times New Roman, 14 point, bold for emphasis, in case Mrs Cameron didn't get it otherwise. It was posted at the central sorting office in Newbury yesterday evening in time for the midnight collection.'

And delivered in Hungerford nine hours later. You could rely on the GPO to be efficient when you didn't want them to be.

Greg picked up the bag and read the message through again, although the words were engraved on his heart. He had one of those silly executive toys on his desk, with silver balls that clicked back and forth. He wouldn't have kept it but it was one of the last things Fred had given him, describing it as a stress-buster, a joke birthday present. He pushed the balls at one end and set them going.

'Who knew?' he said over the irritating rhythm. 'Who knew that Douglas Cameron was bisexual and, more importantly, that he was having an affair with Piers Hamilton? Piers insists it was a deadly secret. Me, you, Piers himself, anyone on our team who had access to the case files, especially to the statements made by Cameron and Hamilton yesterday afternoon . . .'

'Gregory,' she said gently, 'let's stop lying to ourselves. We both know who sent this letter.'

Harry Stratton himself answered the door of a neat semi in the suburb of Newbury where he lived with his wife and daughter. He'd changed out of his invariable office suit and looked wrong in jeans and a black tee shirt which betrayed the beginnings of a beer belly. A grubby tea towel was slung over his shoulder. It was just after seven and Greg could hear the theme music to *The Archers* coming from a tinny radio in the kitchen.

'Well,' Harry said. 'I wasn't expecting a visit. Not that I'm not pleased to see you –'

'I've got a warrant,' Greg said. 'I wanted to do this by the book.' He handed his junior the papers. 'May we come in?'

Harry moved to one side to admit them, not looking at the warrant. 'I can't imagine what this is about,' he said with an attempt at a smile. 'I haven't been fiddling my expenses, have I? You know what a duffer I am at arithmetic.' He plucked the tea towel from its perch and fiddled with it.

'May we see your home computer, sir?' Barbara asked.

'Ruthie's using it to do her homework project at the moment.'

'No I'm not, Dad. I've finished.' A puppyish girl of fourteen but looking younger pushed past them without greeting. She had straggly, greasy-looking hair and unflattering spectacles. A short skirt betrayed fat legs. If she had a boyfriend, Greg thought, it proved that love was blind. 'Just going out for an hour. Okay?'

'No, wait a minute,' Harry called after her, but she was gone. He stared after her for a moment with a look of hopeless distress on his face, then shrugged. 'Kids. Who'd have them? It's in here.'

He took them into the sitting room, long and narrow with a three piece suite at one end and a dining table at the other. On the table was an Olivetti computer and inkjet printer. Barbara sat down at it and switched it on. It took a minute to load.

'You had so better be right about this, Babs,' Greg muttered into her ear.

'Trust me.'

Harry clicked off the radio on the kitchen hatch and draped his tea towel over it. 'She's doing a project on *Romeo and Juliet*,' he said. 'She has to pretend she's Juliet and write up her diary, about how she met Romeo and . . . whatever it is that happens after that.' They let him ramble on. 'I ask you. Wasn't like that in our day, was it? We had to *learn* things.'

When nobody answered he continued, 'We don't seem to use the dining table any more. Never sit down to eat as a family these days. Not even Sunday lunch. It's grab a burger standing up in the kitchen. No wonder we have indigestion. No wonder family life is breaking up.'

'Is Prue in?' Greg asked gently.

'No, you missed her. It's her aerobics class Wednesdays.'

Barbara went into the word-processing software and scanned a group called Letters. They had names like School2 and Taxman.

'I hardly use the thing,' Harry said. 'You know me. Just about mastered the video when we got this.'

A whiskered face peered round from behind the list of files and the computer made a mewing noise.

'What's that!' Greg yelped.

'A virtual cat,' Barbara replied serenely, 'or kitten, by the look of it.'

'His name's Liam,' Harry offered. 'As in Gallagher.'

'Dear God,' Greg said.

With a frown of dissatisfaction Barbara exited to DOS, apparently killing off Liam in the process. She accessed the letters group and typed in UNDELETE. The software offered her a file called ?ARRY1.WPS, deleted the previous day at 21.32 hours. It was in good condition.

Did she want it undeleted?

Yes, she did.

Please supply missing first letter.

H.

'File HARRY1.WPS successfully undeleted,' the machine announced triumphantly less than a second later.

Greg looked at Harry who was pale and still. 'Not much of a one for computers, Harry, as you said. Bet you didn't know it could do that. Bet you thought deleted was deleted.'

As if he, Greg, might have known better.

'You should have created it, printed it and not saved it,' Barbara told him, for future reference. She went back into the word-processing software and called the file up on the screen. Those same twenty-five deadly words, Times New Roman, 14 point, bold for emphasis. On the second page, the name and address of Mrs Douglas Cameron.

Liam reappeared and looked at the pages dolefully, then pawed the cursor.

'Oh, Harry,' Greg said, in sorrow, not anger. 'What have you done? A man is dead, a man you'd never met. You saw him, crushed and bleeding, and you're morally if not legally

244

responsible for that. Is that what you wanted? Did Douglas Cameron deserve *that*?'

'She had the right to know,' Harry said stubbornly. 'It's men like him who spread disease, who pass Aids into the heterosexual population, who give it to normal people. I'm glad he's dead and I'm not afraid of the responsibility.'

'He *always* practised safe sex,' Babs murmured, 'and how many of us can say that?'

'Most of us don't need to, you slag.'

Greg winced, although Barbara seemed unperturbed. He said, 'Even if he deserved punishment, according to your warped ideas, did his family deserve it? You saw his wife, his children. Did two pre-school kiddies deserve to lose their father?'

'I did what I thought was right. What sort of father would he have been?'

Greg got up. 'You've committed an offence under the 1985 Regulations, as I'm sure you know. I shall talk to Mr Barkiss tomorrow but you can consider yourself suspended from this moment.' He held out his hand. 'Please give me your warrant card.'

As Harry went to fetch the card from his suit, Barbara took a floppy disk out of her bag and made a copy of the file.

'He's been under a lot of strain,' Greg said as they drove away, leaving Harry to pick up the pieces of his dyspeptic family.

There but for the grace of God . . .

'We're all under strain, all the time. I've thought often enough that he was a ticking bomb.'

He was angry with her and her efficient certainties. He spoke sharply. 'If you think a fellow officer is unable to do his work satisfactorily, Sergeant, then you have a duty to report it to me. It's no good sitting round after the event, Miss Clever Clogs, saying, "I told you so!"'

She glanced at him in astonishment. 'Sorry, sir.'

He subsided, conciliatory. 'Do you think we should have left him alone like that?'

'Oh, he's not going to kill himself. He doesn't think he deserves to die. Do you think he sent other letters? Any of the ones to Josie, for example?'

'I don't think so. They were written by hand or on a type-writer. They came from other . . . lost souls.'

You can't try to justify what he did, sir.'

'I'm not, but not everyone is as strong as you are, Babs. He's another casualty, another walking wounded, another Barney Chase.'

And she said, 'Who?'

16. A Midsummer Night's Dream

'I've got something to tell you,' Angelica said when Greg got home half an hour later. She'd been waiting for him in the hall, perhaps for some time. She was either nervous or excited, he couldn't tell which. Perhaps both. His fluency in body language had deserted him and he felt like a man abandoned in a strange city where he understands nothing and no one and has no map.

He went into the sitting room without answering and sat on the sofa. All his working life he'd been telling people to sit down so he could break terrible news to them. It was good advice, even if you were prepared for it.

She'd come in after him. She was standing. That was right. The person *breaking* the terrible news was always standing; it was an unwritten law. The first thing he heard her say was, 'I'm leaving,' and he felt blood rush through his brain, deafening him. He was going to have a stroke. That unhealthily red face on the TV had not been a trick of the lighting after all. Good. He was glad he was dying. When he'd come out the other side and could hear again she was saying, 'Well, aren't you pleased for me?'

'What?'

'Gregory, have you heard a word I said?'

'Sorry. I felt a little faint.'

'I said I'm leaving Savemore. I gave in my notice today. I'm working out a month. Well, until the end of July, in fact. There's no mad rush.'

He stared at her. 'Why?' he asked stupidly.

'Because . . .' She paused for dramatic effect. 'I'm going to university in the autumn, as a mature student.' She giggled. 'Seems twenty-three is mature.'

'University!'

She frowned. 'You're acting dumb this evening.'

'Sorry. I probably am "dumb".'

'You think it's a bad idea?'

'I think it's a wonderful idea. I always said you were too bright to waste your life behind a shop till. What are you going to study?'

'Psychology. I thought I might like to be a counsellor one day. Maybe a bereavement counsellor.'

'And you've been accepted, you say?'

'It seems my eight GCSEs and my "life experience" will get me in. Seven years in a bloody shop and they call that *living*. I've got to do a prelim year, sort of fast-track A-level, get me back into the habit of studying. And I've got a pile of reading to do through August and September.'

'What, no more bruised fruit?' he said.

'You'll have to buy your own.'

'So you're going away, in the autumn?'

'Going away?'

'Wherever.'

Bemused, she said, 'It's at Reading, Greg, not Ulan Bator – wherever that is.'

'Ah.' Waves of relief crashed over him and he murmured, 'Hence the London train on Monday – calling at Thatcham, Theale, Reading and all stations to Paddington.'

'What! How did you know about that?'

'I have my methods, Watson.'

'Been spying on me, Gregory?'

'I happened to see you get on the train by the purest coincidence.'

'You didn't say anything.'

'Well, nor did you.' He thought about it. 'Still not that easy to get to every day, Reading. It's not as if the university is in the centre of town.'

She was going to say that she'd stay there during the week, that she'd be home with him at weekends, a sop, a gradual withdrawal, desertion in easy and painless instalments.

'I've booked in for one of those intensive driving courses in August,' she said instead. She picked up a pamphlet from the sideboard and he saw that it was that perennial best-seller, the *Highway Code*. 'Morning and afternoon sessions every day for two weeks then test on the second Friday, and every Friday after that until they can't bear it any more and think they might as well give me a licence. Then I can get a car, nothing flash.'

'You'll make a good driver. I'm glad you didn't ask me to teach you, all the same.'

'Are you kidding? The thought never entered my head.'

'Very wise.'

'I'm really happy,' she said.

He could see now that she was. He was no longer in need of an interpreter. 'I'm happy for you, Angie.'

She would be surrounded by boys her own age, younger, laid-back in a way no one of his generation could hope to be, especially when it came to sex. Soon there would be a boyfriend with the body of a young god, instead of the body of an old dog.

Or a lecherous lecturer who had read Jung.

'What do your mates at the supermarket think about this?' he asked.

'Its no big deal these days, not like when you were young. Almost everyone goes now. You can hardly get a decent job without a degree. Half of them have got brothers and sisters at college. They think I'm a lucky cow not to have to take out a student loan. I've got the money in the bank and I can do weekends at Savemore if I run short. I sorted that out with the manager today, quick lunchtime drink, bit of smarm, laughed at his jokes – which are worse than yours, incidentally.'

'At the Rising Sun by the roundabout,' he murmured.

'Christ! You *have* been spying on me.'

'It's a small town, Newbury. It's not the place to choose if you want to keep a secret. You don't need to do weekends at that dump. You know I can afford to support a harem.'

'Oh, no you don't, Gregory Summers!' she laughed. 'The minute my back's turned.'

'I wish you'd told me. I've been imagining . . .'

'What?'

'All sorts of stupid things.'

'I didn't tell you because I'd have felt embarrassed and humiliated if they didn't take me.'

'Can't you trust me with your failure?'

'Sorry?'

'Nothing. No, not nothing! I thought you might be able to trust me of all people not to mock you if you didn't make it.'

'Well, I don't know. It felt personal. Don't make a drama out of it.'

There was a tension growing between them, the sort of thing they'd both backed away from over the past year. For once he wasn't going to retreat. He got up. He could hear himself. He was shouting. He could imagine himself slapping her, the way a father slaps a child who's narrowly missed being run over by a speeding lorry and frightened him half to death.

'That's not good enough! Who am I? Some nobody you share the house with? Your landlord, perhaps?'

'Gregory!'

'No, shut up! *I'm* talking. I've had the most horrible couple of days because I thought you were preparing yourself to leave me and all the time it was that you didn't trust me with such a simple, plain thing.'

'There's no one I trust the way I trust you.'

'Oh, it looks like it, doesn't it? I love you like a madman and I'm terrified of losing you and sometimes I think you're jollying me along, tolerating me until something better comes along, somebody your age who can share your execrable taste in music.'

'Now you do sound like a father. And no, I won't shut up. I'm your partner, your *equal*, and you can't tell me what to do.'

250

She flung herself at him, her fists beating against his chest. He was surprised at how much it hurt. He seized her wrists and she kicked him hard on the shin and began to cry as he winced with the pain and hopped a few paces back across the room. 'I bloody love you, you stupid sod.'

'Angie. Darling.' He put his arms round her, crushing her still-clenched fists safely into her sides, burying his nose in her hair. 'Why could you never say that before? It was all I wanted to hear.'

She snuffled into his shirt front. 'Pig.'

He began to laugh. Then she did. The anger was gone and the air was clear like after a thunderstorm. He lifted up her head and wiped her cheeks with his thumbs and kissed her. He sighed. 'Angel, when you're forty I shall be sixty-five, a pensioner, white haired – if not bald – and probably impotent.'

'Forty?' she echoed incredulously. 'I'm never going to be *forty.*'

'Of course not. My mistake.'

'Gregory, I don't want to hide any more. I want us to tell people we're a couple and let them make what they like of it. We're not doing anything *illegal* and I won't be ashamed any more.'

'I'll put an announcement in *The Times* tomorrow.'

'College doesn't start until the end of September. Tell them Greg and Angie are going away on holiday together, same room, same bed.'

'And where are Greg and Angie going?'

'Venice is nice, I hear, for lovers, in September.'

He tried to imagine what Diane would say.

Sod her. *Honi soit qui mal y pense.*

'Say what, Professor?'

'I didn't realise I'd said it out loud.' He grinned and pulled her to him and kissed her again. 'Loosely translated it means: If they don't like it they can stick it up their arse.'

'Come on,' she said, wriggling out of his grasp. 'I'm taking you out to dinner to celebrate.'

She ran up the stairs to change and he could hear her singing. It was so long since he'd heard her sing. He felt faint. It hadn't been much of a row but it was a start. The eggshells were broken and would soon be pulverised. He slumped down on the sofa and bowed his head between his knees. Then he took his shoes off and lay stretched out on it for a while. He closed his eyes but all he could see was Douglas Cameron's shattered body, then Verity's bewildered and angry face, Piers's delicate tears and, above all, Harry's tortured expression when he realised he'd been found out; so he opened them again.

All he wanted after the trials of the day was to have a hot bath and a night in front of the telly with a takeaway, but she was shouting to him to come upstairs and get that bloody office suit off.

He got slowly up. He realised he was trembling.

They found a pub near the canal where the food was edible and they could sit outside, although the weather was beginning to cloud over now, turning muggy. The water was still tonight and a heron stood watching their arrival from the far bank like a miniature pterodactyl, then flew awkwardly away with a cumbersome flapping of its too large wings.

'Looks like we might have some thunder tonight,' he remarked as they took their seats.

'Good, clear the air.'

'In a gothic novel the storm would have arrived while we were shouting at each other half an hour ago.'

She smiled at him. 'Nature has no sense of drama.'

A handful of gnats flocked to her head and admired her fair skin but she made no effort to brush them away. On the canal a tourist narrowboat went past, towed at excruciatingly slow speed by a patient horse the size of a small mammoth.

Elderly faces were static, bored behind the glass like a crowd scene on TV.

'Have you been to Fred's grave lately?' she asked him, out of the blue.

'I go every weekend, tidy up, water the rose bush if necessary.'

'I'll come with you this week.'

'That will be lovely.'

Greg wasn't an adventurous eater but this time he decided to take some risks, as if he was starting a new life. He ordered couscous, which he'd never tasted, but found he liked, with aromatic fish in a hot sauce, and a salad of mixed lettuce leaves. He drank chilled, low-alcohol lager instead of warm bitter. He undid another button on his shirt and felt daring.

Angelica wore a scarlet dress, sleeveless, tight in the bodice but with a full skirt. It was like the fashions of the fifties that he dimly remembered, proving that there was nothing new under the sun. Her lipstick matched the dress, as did her sandals, and the colour suited her, endowing her fairness with a vibrancy that it usually lacked. She'd brought a black velvet stole in case she was cold later and it lay on the bench beside her like a short-haired dog. Next to it lay a black suede bag since the meal was her treat. He'd learnt that he had to let her pay for things sometimes or anger her.

She drank white wine and ate pasta, bilious with basil and flushed with sundried tomatoes.

'What are you thinking?' she asked.

Truthfully, he replied, 'I was thinking that when you've passed your test I won't have to be the designated driver all the time and I can drink proper beer.' She snorted and he apologised for the banality of his thought.

Usually they were reserved in public but tonight their hands often touched and held across the slatted wooden table, not caring who might see them. As his fingers twined with hers he noticed with a slight shock that she was no longer wearing her rings.

She did the talking, bubbling about her psychology course, and he was content to listen. He realised that he envied her her opportunity, that he'd regretted not passing the necessary exams to get him into university, that it was too late now. 'It will open up a new world to you,' he said wistfully.

'I certainly hope so.' She glanced across the garden and made a face. 'Guess who's come in. Is he following you?'

Greg looked round and his face hardened. 'He'd better not be.'

'It's Superintendent Summers, isn't it?' Adam Chaucer stopped by their table. He wore white silk trousers and a black silk shirt, a jacket hooked casually by one thumb over his shoulder. He appeared to be alone.

'You know bloody well it is,' Greg growled. 'You've seen enough of me in the past few days. Are you following me?'

'Paranoia, Mr Summers?' Chaucer made a deprecating motion with his free hand. 'I heard the food was tolerable here and stopped for some supper.' He glanced at the red and green swirls left on Angie's plate. 'I may have been misinformed.'

He looked Angie over the way, Greg thought, a man like him looks a woman over – pondering whether he fancies her or, alternatively, if she can be useful to him. Greg found himself unable to tell if Chaucer fancied Angie or not. Nor did he know whether he would be outraged if he did or offended if he didn't. Or vice versa. If he recognised her from the supermarket he gave no sign of it. Shop assistants to him would not be individuals but a cohort of robots in striped overalls with a logo on the breast pocket. She stared back at him, managing to convey with the smallest movements of her eyes and mouth that she didn't think much of him.

'Won't you introduce me to your daughter?' he asked finally.

'This is *Mrs* Summers,' Greg said, 'and she knows who you are.'

He raised his eyebrows, his hazel eyes flickering from one to the other, a scornful look on his face, studying anew the gap of years between them, thinking no doubt that there was no fool like an old fool. 'Look, I'm sorry about the other night, Summers, but you should have agreed to be interviewed.'

'I might have done if you'd asked me.'

Chaucer laughed and didn't deny it. 'Getting close to an arrest? Or is poor Mrs Abbot still your only suspect?'

Greg wished he'd ordered soup. He could visualise it glooping down that dry-clean-only white silk. Minestrone would be best.

'And is it true,' Chaucer went on, 'that a man has been driven to suicide following harassment by your people, and that a senior officer has been suspended from the case?'

Where did he get his information?

Greg got up. He and Chaucer were about the same height and weight and he could give the younger man ten years, but he knew from experience that there are few things more intimidating than an angry policeman.

The cocky newsman duly took a step back. 'I'm just doing my job.'

'And I'm just trying to have a quiet meal with my . . . I'm trying to have a quiet meal,' Greg said in a deceptively soft voice, 'so why don't you fuck off?'

'Can I quote you on that?'

'Gregory,' Angelica said warningly.

'Is there a problem?' The owner of the pub, a giant of a man with a face both red and grim, had appeared, soft on his feet for such a big man. 'I've got my licence to think about and I'm warning you both that I won't hesitate to call the police.'

'That won't be necessary,' Greg said. 'This gentleman is leaving.'

The reporter turned away and Greg heard him say, 'Looks like we'll have to try somewhere else, Josie. They don't have a table for us here.'

He spun round and looked into the cold eyes of Josie Abbot standing a few feet away from them in the shade of a willow tree, watching the scene, seeing him play the heavy. She didn't acknowledge his existence and he thought how badly he had failed there.

'A Pyrrhic victory, I fear.' Greg resumed his seat, the land-lord still hovering. 'Thanks for ruining my quiet meal, Chaucer,' he murmured. Journalists had more contact with violent death than anyone, except policemen. Sometimes it made them hard, sometimes tender. Usually hard.

'He still thinks there's a story there,' Angie said as the couple walked briskly away, Chaucer's free arm in the small of Josie's back, half protective, half propulsive. 'He still thinks he can get something useful out of her, maybe something that'll get him out of local news and into the dizzy heights of ITN.'

'He's left it too late,' Greg said cruelly. 'If he was gonna make it, he'd have done it by now. It's get up or get out.'

'Are you two nearly finished?' the landlord asked aggressively.

Greg folded his arms, fed up with being the bad guy. 'No. We want some pudding.' Although a moment before he'd decided against it. He picked up the menu in its plastic folder. 'I'd like some raspberry pavlova.' Something he wouldn't normally dream of eating. 'What about you, darling?'

The man began, 'I think it would be better –' Greg took out his warrant card and showed it to him. 'Oh! Sorry. I didn't realise. I don't want any trouble, that's all.'

'It's all right,' Greg said, 'the trouble has left.'

'Glass of pudding wine, perhaps, officer? We have a lovely Muscat. On the house, of course.'

'Thank you,' Greg said, 'but I don't take bribes.'

The man bridled and left and Angie said mildly, 'Uncalled for.'

'I know. Sorry. It was Chaucer asking me if I was anywhere near an arrest. To which the plain answer is no.'

She was dismissive. 'You'll solve the case. You always do. His sort know how to get under someone's skin.' She shivered theatrically. 'He's all smarm on the surface and rotten fish underneath.'

A line of verse came floating to him across thirty years and he quoted, '"The smiler with the knife under the cloak."'

'Sounds ancient,' she said. 'Shakespeare?'

He shook his head. 'Our Adam's great-great-whatever-grandfather, Geoffrey. Who must be turning in his grave.'

They ate their pavlovas with extra cream. They ordered Muscat and paid for it.

'I wonder,' Greg said after a while.

'If Geoffrey Chaucer's turning in his grave?'

'No, if Adam's sticking round for the story. We took it for granted that he and Josie Abbot met for the first time over the murder of her daughter, but what evidence have we for that? They live in the same area. How do we know they weren't friends – more than that – before?'

'She's not his type, that's how. He goes for actresses, fashion models, girls with no tits and legs a yard long, not plump widows with nuisance kids in the way.'

Nuisance kids. Quite.

'So you say,' he said, 'but we don't know his tastes. Josie's attractive –'

She raised her eyebrows. 'Aye, aye?'

'No. I don't mean . . . I wasn't . . . I would never . . . Oh, bollocks!'

'I know. I was teasing. Seriously, she's not *important* enough for him, or she wasn't until this happened. Trust me.'

'I expect you're right. I thought . . . We've found no evidence that Josie had a man in her life but if she did, he'd have to join our list of suspects.'

'Which is how long?'

'Plain white paper. Oh, well. I expect you're right. I suppose women understand these things better than men.' He would ask Barbara. He remembered that Josie would now have a comfortable lump sum from her daughter's trust fund. There was a world of difference between a poor widow and a rich one.

They drove home and walked up the drive entwined in the darkness, beating the thunder by ten minutes. 'I remember another bit,' he said as he drew the curtains to make his castle fast. From those far-off days of A levels.

'"And what is better than wisdom? Woman.

'"And what is better than a good woman? Nothing."'

17. Thursday, 25th June

Chief Superintendent Barkiss tried to find a way to stick up for Harry Stratton and failed. 'He's admitted it then?' he said finally.

'It didn't seem to occur to him to deny it.'

Odd for a policeman, since they were notoriously hard to convict, knowing the immovable power of saying nothing, even without the right to silence. It might have been interesting to hear a tougher man explain away the deleted computer file.

'Twenty years in the force,' Barkiss said with a sad shake of his head, 'thrown away in a moment of stupidity. Discreditable conduct, improper disclosure . . .'

'He's been under a lot of strain.'

'Yes. And a man is dead.'

'I thought if he could be persuaded to see a doctor. If he's been depressed, say –'

'Has he?'

'I ought to know. Yes, he has.'

'You're his superior officer, not his nursemaid. Family problems?'

'Nothing out of the way. I think he finds life hard, the ordinary bits of it, the husband and father and mortgage bits. He has rigid ideas of what's right and wrong and finds it difficult to adapt. God knows, bringing up teenagers is hard.'

'Tell me about it,' Barkiss said. 'So you think if the doctor could be persuaded to find him ill, he could be invalided out ahead of an enquiry?'

'It sort of crossed my mind.'

The Chief shook his head. 'A couple of years ago, a year ago with a bit of luck and a tail wind, but they're cracking down on that sort of thing now. Too many people have slipped out from under a charge by that door, even a criminal charge. Still, a trip to his GP can't hurt. We don't want another suicide on our hands.'

Barkiss confirmed the suspension and put the events in motion that would lead to an internal enquiry by the Complaints and Discipline Department into Harry Stratton's misdemeanours. At best it would mean a reduction in rank; at worst, ignominious dismissal.

'I suspect he'll jump rather than wait to be pushed,' Barkiss said. 'I know I would. There's always work for an ex-policeman, a plausible explanation to be offered as to why he left – unsocial hours, stress of the job. Security consultant. Nine till five. You have almost to envy him.'

Neither of them believed it.

'This will leave me short handed in CID –' Greg began.

'Sorry, Gregory, you should have thought of that before you started suspending your own officers.'

As he was leaving Barkiss called after him, 'How's young Angie going on these days?'

'Fine, thanks. We're . . .' He couldn't say it.

'You're what?'

'Nothing.'

He went quietly back to his office and told Barbara, 'Barkiss is willing.'

Susan Habib came in mid morning, looking bemused. 'There's a young lady asking for you, Mr Summers,' she said, 'insistently.'

'Lucky old me.'

She smiled. 'A very young lady, about ten I should say.'

'Ah.'

'A "Miss Romana Lee" was how she instructed me to announce her. She won't talk to anybody else. Said she wanted to see the trainer and not the stable boys.' He laughed. 'She's waiting at the front desk.'

260

'Fine,' he said, 'I'll go down.'

Romy was sitting on the duty sergeant's desk engaging him in conversation about horse racing, one of his passions. Greg hoped she was giving him better tips than he usually got. She jumped down when she saw him and took his proffered hand with perfect trust.

'Let's go and find somewhere quiet to talk,' he said.

The grouchy sergeant watched her go with a reverent look on his face. What it was to have charm, Greg thought, the conman's greatest weapon.

He took her to McDonalds. He had coffee. She ate a Big Mac, a cheeseburger, two helpings of fries, two milk shakes – one chocolate and one strawberry – and a portion of apple pie. He glanced at his watch. It was eleven o'clock. 'Didn't you have any breakfast?'

She nodded and said through pastry, 'Muesli with semi-skimmed milk.'

That said it all.

'Now.' She finally finished eating, pushed her debris away and folded her arms on the table. Time to talk business. 'I want to see my dado. I got rights. I read about it in the library and there's children's rights now.'

Her mother had spoken sense: teach them to read real good and they'll have all the knowledge in the world at their fingertips. She wouldn't have got that information at school, only the dates of the Kings and Queens of England and the chemical formula for potassium. He knew nothing about children's rights. It was an idea whose time had come only recently, long after he'd had to swot up on the law for his exams.

He envisaged her in a prison visiting room, accompanied by some aggressively cheerful minder, probably the woman with the purple hair who was presumably Jude. He'd been in many such places and found them hard to take. Huwie would be there, cowed, broken, perhaps with the marks of a beating from a fellow inmate, in his heavy blue cotton shirt, his drill trousers. She was strong but he hated to think of her there. His best bet was to treat her like an adult and convince her rationally that it was a bad idea.

'I know you love your dad, Romy.' She nodded. 'Because children do love their parents, and I hope everything will work out –'

'We have no word for "hope" in Romany,' she interrupted him. 'Only for real things like "eat" and "drink".'

'Really?' He decided not to go down this side road: a language without hope.

'We have the same word for life and death,' she went on, 'and for yesterday and tomorrow.'

No wonder poor Lashlo found time a difficult concept.

He tried again. 'About your dad. You're going to have to come to terms sooner or later to being without him. I know he's the only father you've ever had but, as he used to hit you and –'

'Hit me?' She looked astonished. 'My dad never laid a finger on me.'

'But . . . you and your mother –'

'He used to hit *her*,' she agreed, as if it was an understandable evil, a promise made in the marriage vows, regrettable perhaps but unavoidable, 'but not me or Bonnie. Never.'

'I don't understand,' he said. Was she in denial? 'Those bruises on your arms and legs that night in the boarding house. You said something to me about what a temper he had. I remember.'

'Oh!' She laughed, catching on. 'I was talking about grandado.'

'Rufus?'

She nodded. 'All us Lees got tempers.' She was proud of the fact. 'But grandado Rufus, he's got the worse of the lot. Oh, but he's fearsome in a rage. Can I have a banana milkshake now?'

He opened his mouth to answer in the negative but his bleeper went off. He read the display, which said simply 999. He jumped to his feet, thrust a five pound note at the little girl and said, 'I've got to go, Romy. Order what you like.'

Barbara was in the car park in the driving seat of a powerful saloon. As she saw him she started the car, drove towards him, slewed to a halt and thrust open the passenger door. He jumped in and she roared away before he could fasten his seat belt, accelerating and changing gear rapidly as they shot out of Newbury, heading west towards the A4, their siren wailing.

'What?' he said.

'There's been a three-nines shout, a death on Hungerford Common. It's vague at the moment but it sounds horribly like Lashlo Lee.'

'Shit!' Greg banged the dashboard. 'Shit! Shit! Shit!'

Three caravans remained: Smith's, returned as quietly as it had vanished, Rufus and Orlenda's, and Huwie's which was now Lashlo's. He saw that Smith's van had been moved closer to the others since its return, as if the ghost had been accepted once more into the land of the living. Otherwise there were a few bare patches where van wheels had rested and some burnt areas where fire had been kindled and food cooked.

Along with an ambulance and two patrol cars, a Rover and a Metro, four uniformed constables in shirt sleeves. His eyes flickered over them: Whittaker and Clements, Tom Reilly and Sharon Moore. They stood uncertainly by their cars, suspecting a hoax.

No sign of a lynch mob. Please God, let it be a hoax.

'Where did the emergency call come from?' he asked his sergeant. 'They picked up the number, I take it.'

'Mobile, so they didn't get the number. No name left. The person gave the alarm and hung up. We don't even know if it was a man or a woman. Just a message – "The gypsy boy is paying the blood price".'

A merciless message, he thought, like an executioner's song.

Barbara jerked the car to a halt next to the Rover and the constables, recognising the new arrival, automatically straightened their backs and Clements, who'd taken his cap off, hastily put it back on. Greg was out of the car before it stopped, Barbara not three seconds behind him. 'What's happened?' he demanded.

They looked at each other and Whittaker said, 'It's a bit of a muddle at the moment, sir. We were patrolling out Ramsbury way and got a shout of a fatality here. No, an "imminent fatality".'

'That was the weird thing,' Sharon Moore said, 'imminent fatality.'

'Lashlo?'

'Is that the gypsy boy who's queer in the head?' Clements asked. Greg frowned and the young man corrected himself. 'Sorry, sir.'

'Well, where is he? What's happened? Is he dead? Who killed him?'

'That's what's a bit of a muddle,' Whittaker said after a pause. 'Only when we got here we found the place deserted, no body, no one in sight.'

'Well, have you tried any of the caravans?'

'We were only a minute ahead of you, sir, there's been no time, but we've seen no sign of life.'

Greg marched up the steps of Rufus's caravan and hammered on the door. The gypsy's great horse neighed at him and the mongrel dog raised its head from its front paws and watched him without interest from its station tethered to the front wheel of its master's home. It clearly didn't see guarding the place as one of its duties, since it let the stranger open the unlocked door of the van without comment.

'I guess they left in a hurry since they didn't lock up,' Greg said to Barbara who'd joined him.

'All shipshape,' she said, glancing round. 'No blood shed here. A hoax?'

He shook his head slowly. 'I can't think so somehow.'

He went back out into the air, stood on the top step and surveyed the surrounding area. Immediately, the downs were more or less flat, the odd undulation which wouldn't qualify as a hillock. The ditch ran east-west for perhaps fifty yards, then a gentle slope down to the railway line. A small copse stood a hundred yards away to the east, thickly overgrown, with gaps giving walkers admittance at the four points of the compass. He listened. The silence had a coldness about it.

Then a fighter plane flew overhead, making the earth shake.

'Jesus!' He put his hands over his ears. Bloody RAF Welford. 'Jesus!' He turned and almost fell down the steps as he found himself face to face with a short, middle-aged woman who'd appeared out of nowhere. It took him a moment to recognise her as Orlenda Lee, since she wasn't wearing her fortune-teller's costume.

'Where in hell did you spring from?' he demanded.

She didn't answer, but said, 'Come with me.'

He followed her without question, recognising the voice of command, across the common towards the copse. She was going at a fair pace and Greg panted to keep up with her. She was wearing jeans and a black tee shirt today, her iron grey hair in a bun at the back of her head, greying plimsolls on her feet. Barbara trailed them a few yards behind but Orlenda didn't acknowledge her presence. The uniformed officers stayed uncertainly where they were, awaiting instructions that were not forthcoming.

'I bore him in terrible pain,' she said over her shoulder, 'for two days and nights.'

'I'm sorry?'

'My only son. He tore me open and I was never rightly comfortable again. You might think it would make me hate him . . .'

'You should have seen a doctor,' he said lamely.

'But it didn't. Nor Rufus, though I was no more use to him as a woman. We loved him the more because he was damaged, because we all were.'

'Mrs Lee . . . Orlenda –'

'Hush.'

They'd reached the copse and she passed easily through a gap in the summer foliage. He fought his way in more ponderously. He could hear a noise now, what he'd once heard described as keening, mourning for the dead. He stopped, looking down into a sharp dip in the ground. In a clearing full of nettles in the centre of the copse, Rufus Lee stood with his son held in his arms, splayed out, his arms and legs hanging loose, along with his head. There could be few men on earth powerful enough to lift that great and ungainly body, to make that Pietà. As he watched, Rufus threw his head back and howled with grief and rage. For a moment Greg thought of Lear and Cordelia. 'Why should a horse, a dog, a rat have life and thou no breath at all?' There was no obvious mark of violence on the boy but, even at that distance, Greg knew when one is dead and when one lives.

Opposite Lee, covering him with a shotgun, stood John Smith. The barrel was pointed straight at Rufus's head, the man's finger white on the trigger.

Greg froze.

'Smith!' His voice sounded croaky in his ears. 'Put the gun down, Smith.'

The gypsy turned towards him, his face unfathomable, the gun swinging round and up automatically to point at the newcomers. Greg heard Barbara behind him take a sharp breath and duck into the undergrowth, while Orlenda stood watching the scene with an unnerving calm.

'No!' Barbara's voice hissed behind him. 'Sir. No.'

Greg, hardly knowing what he was doing, began to make his way awkwardly down the slope towards the clearing. In this sheltered place the ground was damp and slippery: roots lunged at his feet and branches tugged at his head as he slithered to the bottom. He was lucky not to do the last few yards on his arse.

Smith was waiting for him in the dell, the gun pointed safely skywards now and handed it over. His face was white and his hands were shaking. His expression was misery and terror.

'I swear I didn't know,' he said. 'I had no idea why Rufus was so anxious to have Lashlo home.' He began to cry, splaying his fingers across his face as if his hands must be huge to contain his tears. 'This is what he would have done to me twenty-five years ago, if he'd had the chance.'

'Why didn't you stop him?' Greg waved the gun angrily, dangerously. 'Why didn't you use this? Pull yourself together, man.'

'I tried, but he said the only way I'd stop him was to blow his head off and I couldn't do it, not even to save Lashlo. I stood there and I pointed the gun at him and, God help me, I couldn't bring myself to pull the trigger. I was afraid of what *they* would do to me.'

'Who?'

'The Home Office, the prison service, the parole board. *Look*, they'd say, *you let this man out on licence and he's killed*. I would never have seen daylight again. So I let Lashlo die because I was afraid for my own skin.'

'Was it you who called the emergency services?' Greg asked.

'I called them,' Orlenda said from behind his left shoulder. He spun round in surprise, not having heard her come down, moving like a squirrel in this wasteland. She tapped the mobile phone strapped to her belt. 'Same as I did the day the lynch mob came. I didn't know then. If I had I'd have left them to it. The kindest way.'

Rufus fell to his knees as they watched and laid Lashlo's body on the ground, arranging the limbs carefully, reverently. What did that remind him of? The way Jordan had lain on the towpath. Greg moved gingerly forward. He had the shotgun but it didn't occur to him to use it as a threat, even to check if it was loaded. It hung uselessly in his hand.

'Rufus. What have you done?' He stood over him, unsure if the gypsy could hear him. At these close quarters he could see that Lashlo had been strangled, manually, and he didn't have far to look for the hands that had done it. Rufus spread them out as if for inspection by a fussy nanny, palm up, then palm down. The backs were hairy, the knuckles prominent; the fronts were pinkish-brown and streaked with dirt.

Greg, too, knelt and felt for a pulse in the striated neck, finding none. He put the gun on the ground to free his hands, tilted the boy's head back, gripped his nose firmly with his left hand, opened his mouth with his right, felt for any obstruction of the airway and, finding none, exhaled the biggest breath he could manage into the boy's quiet lungs.

'You're too late,' Rufus growled.

He knew it, but he tried for five minutes, alternating with heart massage. No one was to say that he hadn't tried. Finally he gave up and sat back on his heels. 'Why?' he asked quietly, although he knew the answer.

'Why?' Rufus looked up. 'Because he killed the little girl and I won't let him spend his life locked up in a *gorgio* prison. That would be worse than death. He understood that, among all the things that he didn't understand, and he made no resistance.'

Greg let out a long, deep sigh. 'How long have you known? he asked.

'Always.'

'Always?'

'She was not yet cold when I took her body from him and hid it under the camper van until it was full dark, not yet stiff when I took her and laid her out by the canal. I was careful with her. I closed her eyes. I was polite.'

Greg stood, picking up the gun again. He offered his hand and raised Rufus to his feet. The gypsy towered over him but Greg wasn't afraid of him, not at that moment. 'What happened?' he said. 'I need to understand exactly what happened.' Nothing else seemed to matter, not justice, not his own safety, only to know.

The man said heavily, enunciating each word, 'The little girl wanted to run away with the gypsies.'

'Like half the girls we meet,' Orlenda said, behind Greg once more, making him jump again. He'd never known a woman so light on her feet.

'Yes,' Rufus agreed, 'but Lashlo couldn't understand that. She was so pretty and sweet and he thought he could have her – oh, not for any sinister or sordid purpose that you're thinking, he knew nothing of *that* – but as a pet, a doll. He told her to come that night, as it grew dark, a children's secret, and promised that she could go away with him in his van.'

'I don't suppose it would have occurred to him if he hadn't suddenly acquired his own van,' Orlenda said, 'Huwie's van.'

'You knew about this . . . arrangement?' Greg asked Rufus.

'Of course not. What sort of a man do you take me for?'

Greg looked wordlessly down at the body at his feet. What sort of a man was Rufus? A murderer, clearly. Or an executioner?

'How could he let such a little thing come all the way to the common by herself in the dark?' he wondered aloud.

'He didn't think like that,' Orlenda said. 'She was a child his own age, not in need of protection, as well able to care for herself as he was, better.'

Out of the corner of his eye, Greg saw Barbara tiptoeing away, going to fetch help, and the paramedics, who were too late.

'What time did Jordan get to the camp?' he asked Rufus.

'I don't know. I didn't see her. I knew nothing of it. He hid her in his van. I don't know for certain what happened next. I can only guess. She played happily in the van for a while, maybe as much as an hour, playing at being a Romany girl; then maybe she tired of the game, began wanting her mother, thinking of her comfortable bed and she said she wanted to go, that it had been a good game but now it was over. No doubt Lashlo tried to stop her, he probably became distressed –'

'He often got distressed,' the boy's mother said, 'by things that are unfathomable to you and me.'

Rufus went on. 'He tried to stop her. I expect he took her by the arms and put his hand over her mouth. He strangled her or stifled her. It was an accident. He has no conception of his own strength. He probably thought it was a game, at first, that she was playing dead. Then he came running to me, distraught that his little friend wouldn't wake up. I could make no sense of what he was saying, but I followed him back to Huwie's van and found the child with the rabbit's face. Her neck was broken. There was nothing to be done for her or I would have done it, whatever the cost. My one thought was to protect my son from the consequences of his terrible mistake.'

'So you hid the body.'

'There were still a number of people about on the common, dog walkers, cars passing through, people coming home from the pub. I put her body under the camper van, the one belonging to the stringy man.'

What a perfect description, Greg thought, of Clive Peel, except that string was useful.

'They wouldn't have heard me,' Rufus said sourly, 'the way the whole bloody van was rocking back and forth, they wouldn't have heard an earthquake, just thought the earth was moving. I left the body there until after midnight, then, when I was sure there was no one about, I carried her across the railway tracks to the towpath, to the place where I left her, near the town so she'd be found easily.'

Greg could see Rufus in his mind's eye, not seeking a way round as he and Piers had had to do, but walking over the hedges and fences, across the tracks, as if they didn't exist.

'I left her tidy,' the gypsy said. He added again, like a refrain, 'I was polite.'

'Yes,' Greg said. 'You were.'

'I warned Lashlo to say nothing, to deny ever having seen her again after the fair, and he understood that well enough and I thought we'd be okay but that mob came the next day for him, and then you showed me those photographs and I realised that everyone knew that it was Lashlo that had done it and that it was only a matter of time before they could prove it.'

'I doubt we'd ever have proved it,' Greg said. 'To be honest I didn't suspect him. I'd have let you both go. I'd have had nothing to hold him on. He'd probably have got away with it.'

'And who would you have fitted up instead?' Smith asked. 'Josie Abbot? Me, the convicted child-murderer?'

Greg whirled round, wanting to protest at this, to say that the case would have remained open for as long as it took, like that of a boy called Derek Fielding in Northampton, but Rufus was speaking again. 'Then I knew there was only one thing I could do, that I couldn't let them lock him up in prison or a mental home, only you took him away and it's taken me forever to get him back and then I hesitated, because to kill him was to kill part of myself.'

Greg ran his hand down his face in anguish. He'd wanted to keep Lashlo locked up for his own safety. He'd misidentified the threat. He stifled a sob in his throat. 'He'd have got off with manslaughter,' he said weakly, 'diminished responsibility. Whatever happened, he didn't deserve to die.'

'Manslaughter,' Rufus echoed. 'It would still have meant prison, locking up for years.'

'Don't you know what they do to boys like Lashlo in prison?' Smith said. 'Especially child killers.'

'And our ancient creeds demand a life for a life,' Orlenda added.

Greg was afraid. There was himself, the dead boy, and the three gypsies, three aliens, three foreigners whose values he could hardly guess at. He looked wildly round. Where the hell was Barbara?

Thank goodness. He could make out her dark cap of hair coming through the undergrowth above them. Following her were Whittaker and Clements and two ambulancemen with a stretcher.

He felt rather than saw movement. Then Rufus was on him and trying to wrest the shotgun from him. Greg clung to it as if it was his beloved, with a strength he hadn't known he possessed, and the gypsy, giving up, broke away from the small group and was then scrabbling back up the slope towards the exit.

'Stop him,' Greg yelled, setting off in pursuit.

A lesser man than Rufus would have headed for a different exit, but Rufus had been born to do things the hard way and he was running directly at the five police and ambulancemen.

Barbara Carey, first in the line, knew her limitations. She wasn't a coward but to try to stop Rufus would be like throwing herself in the path of a speeding lorry. She pressed herself into the trunk of a tree as he ran past her, moving with surprising speed for a man of his build. It was as if he left a wind in his wake.

Whittaker and Clements looked at each other with an air of resignation and hurled themselves into the fray, but Rufus upended Whittaker onto his back in a pile of last year's dead leaves and brushed Clements aside with a slap in the chest like a man swatting a fly, sending him slithering helplessly down the slope, cannoning into Greg, the two of them rolling close as lovers into the dell. They hit the ground with a curse, scrambled up, glared at each other and set off upwards again. The ambulancemen had taken their cue from Barbara and stepped aside, and Rufus was out of the copse and running full pelt back towards the vans and horses.

'For God's sake!' Greg snapped, reaching the top of the slope at last, slightly ahead of Clements and Smith. 'There were five of you.'

'Sorry, sir,' they muttered.

He gestured back behind him to the ambulancemen. 'There's a body down there, nothing to be done about it. Leave it until scene-of-crime get here. Barbara, you stay with them. Summon some backup. You two, come with me.'

Rufus had a hundred yards on them now and Greg gestured to Reilly and Moore to head him off. He, Whittaker, Clements and Smith spread out, moving into a horseshoe shape, hoping, with the help of the other two constables, to enclose the fleeing man and take him that way. Orlenda came after them, observing not pursuing, moving as fast as any of the men, silent and watchful.

Seeing the two officers approaching from the triangle of vans, Rufus veered away towards the stone circle. He tripped and fell headlong with a force that seemed to shake the earth, but was up again in an instant. Limping visibly, he ran on, and hurled himself against the first sarsen stone, then rounded it, putting it between him and his pursuers, pressing his body against its cool height, stopping to take his breath, his thought.

Then he was heading for the railway tracks, slowed by the foot he had wrenched in falling, but bruising across ditches and hedges and wire fences. This side of the common was well protected: not merely the trains but the canal separated it from the outside world, but they were no perceived obstacle to Rufus who would limp through fire and flood if he must to make his escape.

He burst through briars onto the rails, blood streaking his cheeks a darker red, streaming from his defensive arms. He stopped for a moment, looking back to see how close his pursuers were, how much these unimpeded runners had gained on him.

They were close, and closing.

A sharp hooting noise pierced the warm air, once, twice. The third time it was shriller and more desperate.

'Lee!' Greg shouted in disbelief, hearing his voice break up over the distance, the syllables flying in all directions. He went on trying. 'Lee! It's the express. Get out of the way.' There must surely be time, he thought, for Rufus to save himself if he wanted to, but perhaps not; perhaps it was a temporal illusion, as if the thing were happening in slow motion.

As the hooting of the train gave way to a relentless grinding of the brakes, a shower of sparks glittered over the grass verges. Rufus stood unmoving, like one of the stones, in the very centre of the track, facing the oncoming train, his eyes wide open to his chosen fate.

He was laughing.

At the last moment he held out his arms to embrace the tons of hurtling metal, to embrace his death. The train struck him full on. He let out one cry, although not of pain or fear – 'Orlenda!' – and was silent.

'Jan!' she screamed and buried herself in Smith's arms, her eyes tight closed against his chest. He stroked her hair.

Orlenda stood watching from a high grassy bank as what remained of her husband was taken away from the railway line half an hour later. There was no expression on her face, although the sight would have turned a more delicate stomach.

A few hundred yards down the track the Exeter express was making an unscheduled stop in Hungerford and shocked passengers were being helped from the carriages, seated on the normally quiet station until arrangements could be made for them to continue their journey west. Some of them sat in silent contemplation while others asked again and again what had happened.

The driver sat weeping in his engine as if superglued to his seat, refusing all offers of help, all suggestions that he should come down and have a nice hot cup of tea.

In the copse, Lashlo's body was being photographed and removed. His mother had about her an air, Greg thought. Not resigned – that wasn't the right word. *Fatalistic.* As if she'd known all along exactly what would happen. Had she? She saw him looking and came over to him.

'Did you know?' he asked in a low voice. 'Did you foresee it?'

'The *duckering*?' She almost laughed. 'It's an act, a fairground piece to take money from the credulous. I thought you knew that.'

'Well, yes,' he said, shamefaced.

'And yet,' she went on, 'you can work out what the future's going to be. I knew the characters and the circumstances of the people involved and could project their actions. Then you can follow a line forward in time to the inevitable outcome. You could do it yourself if you put your mind to it. But that's science, not clairvoyance.'

Except in its literal sense, he thought: clear-sightedness. 'So you let your husband kill your son,' he said.

'Rather than let him rot in prison, yes.'

'Then why call the emergency services?'

'Because I knew you would be too late to stop it, and because that had to be the end of it. There could be no more deaths, not after all these years.' She went on, 'I knew you would find the truth.'

'You saw it in my hand?'

'I saw nothing in your hand, fool, since there's nothing there to see. I saw it in your eyes and in your heart – that you're a man who wouldn't rest until he had the truth.'

'I don't think I can claim any credit for uncovering the truth,' Greg said.

'Tell me something,' Greg said.

He'd driven Smith and Orlenda back to the camp himself after they'd made their statements and was sitting in Smith's van, his back against the thin wooden wall, a window by his head. It was late afternoon and the shadows of the caravans were lengthening over the brown grass.

'If I can,' his host said.

'I asked you once about Lashlo's condition, whether it was genetic, and you said he'd been brain-damaged at birth.'

'That's right.' Smith produced a pipe from somewhere about his person and began to fill it with tobacco from a pouch.

'You seemed to know about it, but Lashlo was seventeen and you've been in prison for the past twenty-five years. How could you know?'

'From the person most nearly concerned.'

'Orlenda?'

Smith nodded, struck a match and lit his pipe. He puffed at it until he was satisfied it was alight, marking time. 'She wrote to me,' he said finally, 'every week. I used to write back too, although sometimes it would take the letters weeks to reach her, because I had to send them post restante ahead of her and it was important that Rufus shouldn't know.'

Greg leant across and opened the window beside him. The door was ajar and a cross breeze curled the pipe smoke out of the window in a thin line. It smelt too sweet for plain tobacco. Marijuana, he thought. He didn't care. 'Later,' Smith went on, 'she got that mobile phone and I used to ring her sometimes, always at the same time of day. If Rufus was there she'd switch off the phone.'

'Still got the letters?' Greg asked.

'No.'

Greg raised his eyebrows. 'I know how welcome letters are in prison.'

'Oh, then, yes. I kept them and read them over and over, more than a thousand of them in the end, but one of the first things I did when I got out was to burn them. I didn't need them any more, you see, and I burnt them to put an end to my old life and acknowledge my rebirth.'

Just as Orlenda had wanted to burn Reyna's things, Greg thought, that her spirit might rest in peace. Or perhaps Romany spirits didn't rest, but travelled for eternity. 'Want to tell me about it?' he said.

'Why not? We grew up together – me, Rufus, Orlenda and Annie. Rufus and I both loved Orlenda but she loved *me*.'

'But – let me guess – she was a Lee.'

'You're good at this.' Smith poked the illegal tobacco down with his brown finger and sucked on it again. 'Yes, her parents and Rufus's intended them to marry, from a young age.'

'Couldn't you have run away together, as you did with your eventual wife?'

'I would have, but she wouldn't. Because it mattered to her, the family thing, the *Lee* thing. Tradition. She was fond of Rufus and she accepted what was meant to be – her destiny, if you like – and gave me up and married him when we were twenty.' He sighed. 'I heard her weeping on her wedding night, sobbing with the pain.'

'You mean . . . ?'

'He hurt her. You've seen him. And her. How could he not?'

'That must have been horrible for you.'

'We can't always have what we want, can't always possess the person we love. You *gorgios* don't understand that, or you've forgotten it in the last few decades, but we Romanies know it.'

Greg was beginning to feel light-headed, a secondary smoker of the dope. 'And your wife?'

'I married Annie a couple of years later, as a second best.'

'And you and Orlenda carried on seeing each other in secret? Were lovers, perhaps?'

He shook his head. 'Now you're getting cold. Annie and I were well suited and, by the time our first daughter was born,

277

I realised that it was her I loved, that my feelings for Orlenda had faded into a sort of . . . nostalgia. We did use to meet in secret sometimes, for old times' sake, to walk and talk, not to betray our spouses, and I could never bring myself to tell her that my feelings had changed.'

'So she went on believing that you loved her?'

'I suppose so. I know so. Perhaps she still does. And Rufus went on believing it too and knew that she loved me, and the jealousy grew in him and gnawed at him until he couldn't bear it any more. As I told you once, in those days he couldn't control his temper. I don't think he tried. I don't know for sure how Annie died. I can't prove anything . . .'

Greg was shocked. 'Are you saying what I think you're saying?'

'That Rufus killed my wife? Yes. I think it more than possible.'

'His own sister?'

'Positively Jacobean, isn't it? But it would have been in a moment of madness, maybe a moment of drunkenness, certainly a moment of terrible, terrible rage.'

'His own sister,' Greg repeated stupidly, 'and the tiny, innocent children.' No wonder Lee had borne the mark of Cain: like Cain, he was the author of his own suffering.

'I've tried hard to think what happened, to envisage it. I was out that night. I can only imagine that Rufus went to see Annie and told her I was carrying on with Orlenda, bringing shame on both our households. She would have told him she didn't believe it, probably shouted at him, maybe attacked him since she had a temper to match his. He would have lost his rag and killed her, throttled her with those great hands of his in an instant.'

'And the children?'

'The girls were asleep when I went out. I expect they woke up in the commotion, dangerous witnesses, so he killed them too. Or perhaps they were asleep when he choked the life out of them, doing it because he knew it would be the worst blow of all to me.'

'That's monstrous!'

'And then he let me fry for it, so he succeeded in destroying me but in the process he killed part of himself.'

'Where were you that night?'

'Out walking on the common. With Orlenda. She was my alibi which is why I never gave one. And I was hers which is how I know it wasn't her.'

'Orlenda?'

'She'd have been capable of it. Maybe. She was jealous of Annie. At least I've had the comfort of knowing that it wasn't her.'

'Let me get this straight: you could have told the police that Orlenda was your alibi but you didn't.'

'She had to go on living with Rufus and if he'd known we'd met that night it would have been impossible, intolerable. She had Reyna to think of.'

And now Reyna too was dead, as almost everyone who came into contact with Rufus seemed to be. 'And she didn't come forward,' Greg said, 'didn't volunteer? I thought you said she loved you.'

'She did and she knew that I didn't want her exposed to that.'

His pipe had gone out and he banged it impatiently into a tin lid, dissatisfied with the effect that day. 'So I came back after twenty-five years to see if I could find out the truth, and I stood there with the gun trained on him, and I could have killed him, I had a *reason* to kill him, to save Lashlo, and I couldn't do it. I couldn't kill another human being, no matter what he'd done. Could you?'

'Kill a man I hated? To save an innocent life?' How could he know until he was tested? 'I don't know.'

'And I realised too that it didn't matter any more if it was Rufus or if it was me – as the authorities continue to insist – or if it was some passing madman. That Annie and my children are dead and that no amount of revenge can change that.'

'Will you apply for your case to be reopened?'

'What's the point? I have no fresh evidence to offer and I'm free now.'

'On licence. They can dog your footsteps wherever you go. You could be recalled to prison at any time, almost on a whim.'

'They'll have to find me first.'

'What now?' Greg asked after a long silence. 'Will you and Orlenda be together now?'

'We shall leave here together, travel together for a while, at least. No one knows the future.' He laughed. 'Least of all her.'

'Do you think Rufus was right?' Greg said. 'That death was preferable to prison, for both of them?'

'No. While there's life there's hope.'

'I thought there was no word for hope in the Romany language.'

Smith said, 'There is in my vocabulary.'

18. Monday, 29th June

Greg sat in his office, with only minor matters demanding his attention. Rufus and Lashlo had been formally identified, autopsied and reported to the coroner's office for inquest. The Jordan Abbot case was closed, the investigation ended, the men stood down. CS Barkiss had congratulated him in person on a speedy conclusion to a high-profile case and the DCC had telephoned.

With his desk temporarily clear, he and Angelica had spent Saturday night in London and gone to the National Theatre and to an exhibition on Sunday. He felt refreshed. Three men and a girl had died in the last ten days and left those behind who would grieve for them, but for everyone else life went on, as it must, and things drifted gradually back to normal.

If he took the burden of other people's troubles on himself then he would know no peace.

Josie Abbot had been informed of the outcome of the investigation and had turned coat again, appearing pathetically grateful to her old friends in the police force. Since there would be no trial she was free to bury Jordan at once and had invited him and Barbara to the funeral that afternoon, which invitation they had accepted. He was happy to forget any previous acrimony if she was. He doubted that Adam Chaucer would be there, the story cold.

He'd read a notice in the local paper to the effect that Douglas Cameron was to be cremated privately on Tuesday. Tomorrow. No flowers, the notice said, no letters. Verity hadn't invited him and he wouldn't gate-crash. He suspected it would be a low-key affair.

The coroner had opened the inquest that morning without a jury, delivered a verdict of suicide after reading out Cameron's brief and businesslike letter – very different to the one he'd left for Greg, which had not had to be admitted to evidence – and released the body for burial. He hadn't asked Verity to account for her husband's despair but had merely conveyed the formal sympathies of the court to the ungrieving widow.

Greg was reminded of the old-fashioned formula 'While the balance of the mind was disturbed', still commonly used in his early days, dating from the time when *felo de se* was illegal and a suicide's property forfeit. It had always struck Greg as insulting: if a man had the guts to kill himself, at least do him the courtesy of allowing that he knew what he was about.

He'd been wrong: Adam Chaucer was there.

He stood with his arm round Josie's shoulders. Still got your eye on that trust fund? Greg wondered.

As he stood in his best dark suit at two o'clock that afternoon while Jordan's heart-breakingly tiny coffin was confided to the earth in the same grave as her official father in St Saviour's cemetary on Folly Hill, he tried to ignore the reporter. There were so many wreaths that the coffin was invisible beneath them. He hadn't sent a wreath himself, but cut flowers, all white – jasmine, carnations and roses – for her dead innocence.

Hungerford County Primary school had closed for the day as a mark of respect and the streets of the town were thick with tearful infants.

Barbara stood beside him with bowed head and he saw her lips move silently and realised, with a shock, that she was praying.

Josie had let it be know that the funeral was private and most of the townspeople had respected that. Those who were there kept their distance and Greg locked eyes with George Templeton across the graveyard and Templeton's said, *I told you so*, while his own said, *That doesn't make what you did right*.

At least he hoped they did.

The service ended and he and Barbara joined the queue to throw a handful of earth into the grave.

Whittaker and Clements were there, both on nights this week, keeping their polite distance. He also recognised Whittaker's wife, Tina, a pretty blonde in her mid twenties, dressed in a smart black suit and unsuitable shoes. She was crying her eyes out.

'Stupid woman!' Barbara exclaimed.

Greg was shocked. 'She's showing a little emotion. It's not a crime.'

'Not her. Me. I went to their wedding.'

'Did you?'

'I like weddings, so long as they're not my own.'

'I wasn't invited,' he said, hurt.

'I expect they thought you'd put a damper on the proceedings.'

'Thanks very much.'

'Someone of your seniority, I mean.'

'Oh.'

She quoted. '"You are invited to the wedding of Andrew Glenn Whittaker and Christina May Prior".'

'My God!' Greg stared at the young woman with new eyes.

'So Chrissie Prior turns into Tina Whittaker and becomes invisible.'

'I thought you were checking the local papers, the Register Office.' She went red. 'Let me guess, you wouldn't delegate it and you didn't have time to do it yourself.'

'I'm sorry.'

'Remember what I said?'

'Only too vividly. It won't happen again. I'm sorry.'

'I'm relieved to discover you're not infallible.'

She added defiantly, 'They got married in church, anyway.'

'Do you think he knows?' Greg asked, as his young colleague put a protective arm round his weeping wife.

'I very much doubt it. Men are naive. They think a pretty face means a snow-white soul.'

'Look at her crying. She wanted to abort the baby seven years ago.'

'It's not the same as having a live child die on you, one with your blood in it, your genes, even if you never paid it any mind while it was alive.'

'What are we going to do, Babs?'

'What should we do? The child is dead, and now buried. Josie insists that it wasn't blackmail, only a kid in trouble asking friends for money occasionally. Are we going to charge her with perjury after what she's been through? Do you want to ruin an honest copper's career and his life?'

No, he didn't want to do any of that, although he couldn't face working with Whittaker in CID, knowing what he knew. The young man was doomed to remain in uniform and to wonder why.

They shook hands with Josie as the ceremony ended and refused an offer to come back to the bungalow in Fox Close for sherry and cake.

'Must get back to the office,' Greg said lamely. Barbara embraced the older woman warmly and said, 'You'll be all right, Josie.'

'I'll be all right,' she agreed doubtfully.

Greg turned and saw Mrs Whittaker's black back departing, her husband's arm still affectionately around her shoulders. He looked at Josie but her face was turned resolutely the other way. If she'd seen Chrissie, then no one would ever know it. She *was* a good actress, he thought, and lying *did* become a way of life.

Chaucer caught them up as they walked back to their car. He looked like a fashion plate in a black silk suit and Greg was glad to see mud on the trouser legs. 'I've been making a few enquiries,' he said without preamble, 'about you and "Mrs Summers".'

'Oh, yes?' Greg used his remote control to unlock the car from ten feet away, wanting a quick getaway. Chaucer's car stood next to his. It was as Angie had imagined it: a red, shiny monstrosity with leather upholstery.

'It's not my field, of course. I'm a news reporter. But human interest stories are always popular and I thought you might like to give me an interview. If I don't want to use it myself, I can pass the material on to someone who'll be grateful for it.'

He stuck his bland face close to Greg's and Greg wanted to punch it hard and watch him reel into the dirt, muddying the rest of his poncy suit. Then he might kick him in the ribs for a bit, break a few. What pleasure. But he wasn't going down that road, the path taken by the likes of Barney Chase and Harry Stratton. He had too much to lose.

There are a lot of things you don't know about, Adam, Greg thought, and a pile of things you won't understand if you live to be a hundred, and one of them is love. That's my consolation. That's why I pity you instead of hating you. He saw Josie coming up behind Chaucer, unseen by him, her feet silent on the grass. He said calmly, 'I don't think so. I'm sure it's of no interest to anyone but the two people most nearly concerned.'

Chaucer's expression hardened and his voice grew louder as he dropped any pretence of goodwill. 'You'd be better off speaking to me, Summers, old man. If you don't I shall have to talk to your neighbours, your colleagues, perhaps your ex-wife. If I get it straight from the horse's mouth then you'll know I've got it right, that you're giving me your side of the story.'

The old trap, Greg thought: you damn yourself or be damned by somebody else. He got into the driving seat without answering and started the engine as Barbara climbed in beside him. He clicked the switch to lock the doors and drove away, leaving Chaucer standing there with his hands in his pockets, grinning. He saw the look of contempt on Josie's face as she watched him and understood who and what he was, this man who had seemed to offer her his friendship.

Barbara said, 'Well done, sir. You called his bluff.'

'Is he bluffing?'

'Like he said, he's a news reporter. He wanted to watch you squirm and you didn't.'

'I wish I knew somebody I could pay to have him beaten to a pulp,' Greg mused. 'Clearly I don't move in the right circles.'

Later that afternoon Susan Habib told him that a Ms Jude Carlyle from social services was downstairs, kicking up a fuss about two children gone missing from a foster home. 'Miss Carey seems to think you might be interested,' Susan said with doubt in her voice, 'although it sounds like a job for uniform to me.'

'I think I might, though.'

Jude Carlyle was in her late twenties and had the harassed look endemic to social workers. He recognised her as the woman who'd taken the children after the siege, although her hair was now not so much purple as magenta. As they spoke together in his office she chain-smoked, not asking permission, using his empty coffee mug as an ashtray.

'They left for school this morning as usual,' she explained.

'I doubt that.'

'Sorry?'

'I doubt if they usually went. Certainly not Romana.'

She looked puzzled but let it go. 'But they never arrived. We didn't know they were missing until they failed to return from school this afternoon and by that time they'd been gone seven hours. Given the extreme youth of the children, ten and six, we are naturally concerned.'

Greg wouldn't normally have dealt with such a minor matter but he assured Ms Carlyle that she could leave it in his hands and drove out alone to see the foster parents.

The ugliest village in the neighbourhood, Thatcham sprawled out a good two miles along the Great West Road in a mish-mash of houses and bungalows, mostly inter-war, some 1960s, a few Edwardian. The Cluxman house was a small, 60s semi about half way along – a former council house, he suspected, the sort of thing the modernists were designing in the '30s, which had somehow transmogrified itself into this brick and glass prison. Some scrappy vegetables grew in the front garden where most people had roses and he wondered if they fostered for the money since the allowance wasn't bad.

He remembered what Huwie had said to him at the beginning, that Romany children couldn't live in houses, that it killed their spirit. This house would kill any spirit.

He decided that it wasn't a question of money, though, as the door was opened by a capable if fussy woman in her early thirties, younger than he'd expected from Romy's description of her. Her husband, she informed him, was still at work and she'd seen no point in summoning him home. She peered past him into the garden as she let him in.

'Sorry,' she explained, 'it's just that the cat's gone missing too.'

'Oh dear,' he said.

'I hope they're all right,' she told him as she made him a cup of tea that he didn't want. 'Of course I do. But, well, the truth is that I'm not sorry to see them go. Bonnie was a nice enough little thing, but I could never get that Romy to listen to a word I said, let alone do a thing I asked. And she refused point blank to come to chapel with us on Sunday and phoned Miss Carlyle about it – without asking if she could use the phone – and she backed her up, as if an hour's prayer could do her any harm. I had to stay home so she wouldn't be left alone. I'm not saying she's a bad child, Mr Summers, but she's been too long on the road and they're not like us, are they?'

'No,' Greg agreed. 'They're not like us.'

'I mean what sort of life is that for a child?'

An exciting one, he thought. 'They'll be fine.'

Which was almost certainly more than could be said for the cat.

As she showed him out he noticed a desk in the alcove under the stairs, a pad of paper with a half-written letter on it, pink paper with red flowers at the top. No doubt Woolworth's sold them by the van load. He looked away.

He wasn't surprised to find the last three caravans gone from the stone circle, barely a trace that they'd ever been there. He put out a call to neighbouring police forces and his own to watch out for Smith and Orlenda and search their vans for the missing children but he knew they would never be found. Smith had made himself invisible again.

One day he'd get a phone call from a frantic policeman searching the PNC for unsolved child murders and missing children and he'd tell him he was morally certain the Lee girls were back where they belonged.

Smith had got his two daughters back from the dead after a quarter of a century and Greg believed he would take good care of them this time.

He would look out for them in Hungerford at next year's summer fair, but he knew that he'd be wasting his time, that they wouldn't be there, that he would never see any of them again.